ICE CASTLE

Elizabeth Wolfe

LEISURE BOOKS   **NEW YORK CITY**

A LEISURE BOOK

Published by

Dorchester Publishing Co., Inc.
6 East 39th Street
New York, NY 10016

Printed in the United States of America

One

The train burst from the tunnel mouth at Wildhaus, the plumes of steam from the locomotive curlicuing into the high, cornflower-blue Swiss sky. The twin steel rails wound down through the high passes toward the border at Liechtenstein far below across the silver-blue ribbon of the Rhine. The high, cold mountain peaks towered above all. Impassive, timeless, they flushed slightly in the fading light of late afternoon.

"You will have your passports ready," the conductor said in a monotonous voice as he moved slowly through the swaying cars. "Please be certain you have your passports ready for the border guards."

A stolid, mustached man of forty years, the conductor let his eyes linger for a moment on the young girl in 23 A. A beautiful thing, he decided. Not much over twenty. Chestnut hair framing an intelligent face, distant blue eyes, dressed simply but attractively in green velvet.

"We will soon be into Liechtenstein, miss," he told her.

Sarah nodded faintly, smiled, and checked her handbag, assuring herself that her passport was at hand. Traveling in these times was not as uncomplicated as it had been even a few short years ago. In the fall of 1913, the tensions in Europe were again at the breaking point, the Balkan states a cauldron of intrigue and threat. With the Russians supporting the efforts of Serbia to obtain a port on the Adriatic Sea and the Kaiser equally solid behind the Austro-Hungarian throne, the outlook, which had been bleak, inexorably grew grave.

The conductor walked on, continuing to call. Sarah Chamliss turned back to the window and let her thoughts unravel as the long hills flashed by, rife with fiery poppies and blue harebells among the silver-turning grass.

She watched the craggy, broken slopes of the jutting white peaks, imagining that Robert had seen them with the same feeling of intensity, with an eye to the deep shadowy clefts, the crumbling, snow-scoured ridges.

Robert Chamliss had the artist's eye, despite his shy disclaimers. Her brother could have been a fine painter. Perhaps the necessity of working to pay for her own education had muffled that ambition in his own heart. He would never have admitted that, even were it so. Instead he raved about his career as an archeologist, claiming— perhaps truthfully—that he had seen more art in his travels to Egypt, to Babylon, and India than one could see in a lifetime of gallery visits.

"It is there that art lives, Sarah," he had insisted. "In these places where men touched the roots of our own beginnings, where our seed was planted, where art sprung up naturally, primitively without benefit of codified rules and textbooks.

"Their hearts, hopes, prayers, were carved into stone or ivory, man's secret longings, his tendencies toward the immortal."

She still did not know what had beckoned him to Austria, although Robert was usually talkative where his projects for the university were concerned; she only knew that he had never returned.

At the border they detrained. Sarah was grateful for the chance to stretch her travel-knotted legs. The air was biting at this late hour, the border town dark, squat, and dirty.

With the other passengers she went through the yellow customs office, the gray-clad officers perfunctorily, politely, opening luggage, asking brief questions.

A few peasants, a seedy looking man with a red mustache, and several young French students lounged around the building on the wooden benches. Near the door an impeccably dressed man in tweed puffing a drooping pipe watched her with interest. When she looked again, however, he was gone.

"Mademoiselle?"

"Yes. I'm sorry."

"If you please," the customs officer said, nodding his long face, "your passport."

Sarah gave it to him. He studied it momentarily, cap tipped back on his head.

"American?" His face was vaguely perplexed.

"Yes."

"And you are traveling . . .?"

"To Feldkirch. In the Tyrol."

"Yes." He hesitated, his eyes flickering toward the office door at the far end of the building. Then he shrugged, smiled, and handed the black passport book back.

"Thank you, mademoiselle."

The night was clear, the stars cold, shimmering in the deep sky. The locomotive at the water tower shuddered and gasped tiny puffs of steam.

Sarah stood alone on the platform, awaiting the conductor's call. She hardly heard the man step up beside her.

"I overheard you speaking," he said. It was the man in tweed. "British, aren't you?"

"No. My mother was British. My father American," she responded.

The man nodded as if it were of no importance and again touched a match to his pipe, illuminating his features. Sharp nose, wide, thoughtful mouth, large dark mustache, he was obviously English himself.

"Rather chilly," he remarked.

"Yes." Sarah found herself leaning away from the man, hoping the train would soon be called.

"You'll find it quite chilly in Feldkirch," he persisted, waving out his match.

Then he turned and wandered up the platform, becoming lost in the crowd, his collar turned up. Sarah was left to wonder about the brief conversation.

For a complete stranger he had known quite a bit about her business. But then the depot had been crowded; he may have been right next to her at some time or another as she explained to the customs men. More likely, he had merely heard her speaking English—travelers naturally seek out their own. Still, there was something unsettling in his manner, his interest.

He had never even mentioned his own name, she recalled.

"*Einsteigen!* All aboard, please!" the conductor called, moving past with a slowly swinging lantern. "Aboard, please!"

The train lurched forward with a spasm of steam, a grating clank, and a whistle blast. Sarah unpinned her hat and leaned her head back, watching the land, deep in shadows, flicker past, her own reflection superimposed upon it.

The night train lunged on through the countryside. The stars, one by one, had punctured the deep velvet of the night with brilliant pinpricks of light. A gaudy, orange half moon had risen, splashing the snow-daubed mountain peaks with color.

In less than an hour they had traversed tiny Liechtenstein. Then again the train sagged to a halt for border customs at the Austrian line.

The Austrian guards, in peaked caps, were more

thorough in their work, brusque, cool and—Sarah couldn't help noticing—they were armed.

"Where will you go, miss?"

"Feldkirch," Sarah replied to the pink-faced guard.

"There is no train to Feldkirch," the man said dubiously.

"Then I'll hire a car."

"It may be difficult to find a car. And there are no facilities there for travelers," he added crisply.

"Is it permitted to travel to Feldkirch, or is it not?"

Sarah felt the weariness of the miles. Her feet seemed to have turned to stone hours before, her clothing felt stiff, dry. Her voice had more of an edge to it than she intended.

The guard puckered his mouth, shrugged, and stamped her passport, handing it back with a stiff, short salute. "Of course, miss."

"Thank you," Sarah sighed, managing a smile. The guard nudged his partner as Sarah turned to walk away, saying something she didn't get. Then the two of them laughed until Sarah felt the tips of her ears burning.

The wind had risen off the western mountains. Chill, gusting, it creaked in the walnut trees. Already the station was nearly empty, the train vanishing into the far reaching cold night, only a thin, distant stream of white smoke against the blackness to mark its passage. Soon even that was gone after one last, long, mournful whistle.

The depot was deserted, dark except for the wireless window. The guards had gone off to their barracks, the homecoming Austrians to their waiting families and farms. She stood alone on the low platform, her two leather bags beside her, the wind lifting her tresses, toying with the fabric of her dress.

"Robert," she whispered to the utter darkness, "please be out there."

The wind took her whisper and twisted and flattened it, overcoming it with its cold, constant force. *Please.*

9

It is a long way from the Sorbonne, she thought. From Dr. Lacroix's lecture hall, from her tiny apartment over Madame LaFortune's bakery shop with the constant fragrances of chocolate, powdered sugar, and butter mingling with the odors of her oil paints, turpentine, and wood in a comforting, somehow cheerful blend.

How far away Paris seemed, with the extravagance of light and sound, the rambling, sometimes strident, always intense conversations with Philippe and Susi in the coffee shop on the rue aux Ours.

She felt suddenly frail, ill-equipped as she surveyed the bleak countryside. Yet what else could she have done?

Dr. Flandin, that serious, thin man who was Robert's superior, had shed no light at all on the purpose of the excursion to Feldkirch. Neither did he seem particularly concerned over the fact that Robert Chamliss had been six weeks overdue.

"Undoubtedly an interesting dig," Flandin had remarked casually.

"He hasn't written in a month, Doctor. He has never done that before. We were to holiday together at Bordeaux."

Finally, exasperated, she had gone to the American consul. Nothing, she was informed, could be done.

"It's probably as the professor says," the consul conjectured, "an interesting dig in an isolated area. Your brother has simply forgotten himself."

"I would think it will become increasingly difficult to work with snow on the ground," Sarah had commented, but the sarcasm eluded the counsul.

No—something had gone wrong. She knew it in her heart as one knows so many things in life. She had waited another week, then feeling concern more strongly with each passing hour, she had packed her bags and come.

"Are you in trouble, Fraulein?"

The voice snapped Sarah's reverie, causing her head to

come around sharply. Turning, she found a stout, amiable-looking gentleman with white sidewhiskers.

"No. No trouble, thank you."

"The sergeant," he said, hooking a thumb toward the barracks, "told me a pretty girl was needing a ride to Feldkirch."

"You're going there?"

The old man nodded affirmatively, thrusting his hands deep into his pockets against the wind.

"*Ja.* And I would like nothing more than a young lady's company. But please, I would like to go before the night is later. It will be bitter cold, this night, Fraulein . . ."

"Chamliss," she said with a quick smile. "Sarah Chamliss."

Just for an instant it seemed that the old man's eyebrows arched slightly at that, but it was difficult to tell in the poor light.

"Fraulein Chamliss. I am Hans Huchting," he said, doffing his green cap with a short bow. "Now please. My wife is waiting my dinner for me. Liver dumplings," he said with obvious relish, "my favorite."

The trail was a long and winding one through deep forest and foggy vales. Sarah sat uncomfortably on the badly sprung wooden seat of the cart as Herr Huchting urged on his white pony with frequent touches of the light coach whip and constant mutterings.

She drew her coat more tightly around her and watched the frosted orange moon flicker through the ghostly treetops. The horse steamed from the flanks, the little bells on its red harness tinkling reassuringly. Hans's lips were oddly tight, his hands constantly snapping the reins as the forest grew deeper, colder still until the moon was blotted out by the forest, the grass frozen underfoot.

They crossed a tiny, cold stream and climbed a gradual slope beyond. Cresting a knoll Sarah suddenly caught sight of it. She felt her throat constrict, and involuntarily

11

she put a hand to her breast.

"Steinbock," Hans said, catching her wonder from the corner of his eye. He halted the pony for a moment.

The castle, situated on a craggy mountain slope, a mile distant, was bathed in the strange orange glow of the moon. Shadows bled out across the mountainside, the turrets seeming to waver and change before her eyes in the eerie light.

"Steinbock, you say?" Sarah asked. It was like nothing she had ever seen before. A strange castle, like a fairy castle diabolically transformed. Of course it was only the light, the weariness which crept into her just now, the suddenness of the apparition.

"Steinbock Castle," Hans said thoughtfully, "has a way of startling strangers. They do not expect such a hideous, baroque collection of battlements and spires in this out of the way place . . . we have grown used to it. Gradually." His voice faded off and he snapped the reins once more, the pony moving reluctantly forward down the long, tree-lined dell.

Steinbock sunk into the rising landscape until the last, wavering spire had vanished. The darkness, the cold of the forest returned, but this time they seemed comforting allies.

Sarah's head lolled from side to side, her eyes drooping shut as the cart worked through the forested glades, along the corridor of a trail where the underbrush from the pines rubbed the cart wheels.

When they came, they came like night beasts, shadows, stalking silent cats from the forest depths. A hand took the bridle of the pony, another snatched at the reins, and two clambered into the wagon, front and rear, their eyes moon-bright, riveted on the young woman.

Sarah's heart pounded wildly against her ribcage, a scream growing in her throat, but a hand was clasped over her lips before she could make a sound.

12

Sarah felt a powerful arm around her shoulder and another under her legs and she was plucked from the cart, the coldness of the forest suddenly closing around her, the trees moaning with a rising wind as they swayed in unison, rubbing bough against bough in a primitive chorus.

And beyond it all, through the long ranks of black trees she saw, just for a second, the ghastly spectre of the moon-bathed Steinbock Castle.

Two

They stood in a circle in the forest clearing. Four men, two of them with pistols thrust into their belts. Hans was on his knees, his cap nearby where it had tumbled during the brief fray.

Their leader was a tall man in gray trousers and black shirt, a cap tilted back on his head, allowing dark curls to escape across his forehead.

He stepped nearer and held a lantern up.

"*Che bella. Che carina!*"

The lantern lingered a moment longer, then slowly the tall man lowered it, smiling amiably, but with a certain discordant grimness.

"We have nothing," Hans said firmly. He had not moved from where he had fallen.

"Of course you have something. The lady here," the bandit said, moving around her in a slow circle, "how finely she is dressed. These hands," he said abruptly, taking Sarah's hands and turning them palm up. "Are these a peasant woman's hands?"

"They are traveling toward Steinbock," a second man put in. A dark-eyed man with a heavy beard, he seemed angry.

"It was late," Hans said. "I wanted to get home as quickly as possible. We are going to Feldkirch. The girl is a traveler, nothing more."

"A wealthy traveler, I assume," the bandit leader said.

"You may take what you wish," Sarah said. Now she was indignant. These men, appearing out of the night to rob them—what right had they to terrorize, amusing themselves with her?

"We will."

Sarah's hair had come unpinned and it fell across her shoulders. Her eyes sparked in the flickering lantern light, her cheeks flushed with the glow and the displeasure she felt toward this stranger and his crew.

"You may take it all," she repeated. "My mirror and brush, my pins, my shoes and petticoats. Perhaps they will become you."

At that one of the bandits grunted with amusement.

"She spits fire."

"What right have you to what is mine?" she demanded, her eyes going to those cool, dark eyes of their leader. He had crouched down, surveying her closely with a thin smile on those annoyingly indulgent lips.

"What right have you to it?" the bearded man put in. "Stolen from the purses of the poor."

"I have little of value," she told him, her hands going to her hips. "But whatever I do have is mine. If I were rich, you would still have no right to it.

"Many a rich man has worked harder for what he has than you seem to realize. What do you know of the people you waylay?"

"That they're rich," someone cracked.

"Perhaps that wealth represents a lifetime of honest toil, long years of suffering, scrimping, doing without. Because you are thieves yourselves, you assume the worst of others."

"Open her bags," the bearded man said. A hulking man with tiny eyes, he was single-minded and undoubtedly unused to being rebuffed.

"Do what you will—I have nothing!" Sarah said, turning away in disgust.

"All you gentry are the same," the bearded man said gruffly. "You never have anything until the pockets are turned out. Then, of course, it is all you have left in the world . . . or it belongs to your grandmother, poor old thing."

He moved to the cart and began unbuckling the larger suitcase.

"Miss Chamliss has no fortune," Hans said, coming finally, unsteadily to his feet. "She's not from the Steinbock, nor does she know anyone there. Her people are not nobility."

The big man turned around with a growl, a surly, tight expression knotting his heavy features. It seemed for a moment that he would strike Hans. He stood there trembling, his massive fists clenched tightly.

Another hand stretched out and took his above the wrist.

"No, Ferrara," the bandit chief said softly, "we go."

"Go . . . !" the bearded man's jaw muscles twitched violently for a second, his thick eyebrows rising with bitter bewilderment. Then his face slackened, he shrugged and nodded. "Surely."

In mere seconds they were gone, the woods swallowing them up. They left hardly a trace of their passage, there was no sound in the underbrush. Only a quick wave of the hand, a curt bow, a brief mysterious moment when the tall dark man stepped close and studied her face deeply before smiling somewhat wickedly and vanishing like a will-o'-the wisp.

It was a long moment before Sarah could compose herself. She noticed her knees trembling—with the cold, she told herself. But she knew it was partly the aftermath of fear, partly something else. It was that something which puzzled and vexed her.

"Devils," Hans muttered, stepping up beside Sarah. The old Austrian dusted the dirt from his knees and yanked his cap on. He stood for a moment glaring toward the wall of forest.

"I apologize, Fraulein. I should never have taken the forest road at night. Not with you. These bandits infest the mountains. Only it was late. I was in a hurry."

"It's all right, Herr Huchting," Sarah said, hoisting her skirt as the Austrian helped her into the cart. "But who were they? They hardly seemed Austrian?"

"*Nein! Gott sei Dank!* Thank God, they are not. They are Italians. Their leader," he went on, starting the pony forward once more, "is the young vandal, Carlo Bramante. The one with the black eyes."

They came out of the forest on a long grassy succession of rolling hills stretching toward the hamlet of Feldkirch in the shadow of the colossal bulk of the Alps

The moon had gone a pale silver, creating deep shadows in the depressions, turning the grass to running quicksilver.

The pony moved eagerly, recognizing the landfalls, wishing for a dry barn, oats, and a rub. The bells on the harness tinkled merrily, the cold wind nipped at their noses and ears. Below, in the village, lights flickered in the thatched-roof homes of Feldkirch. A long line of migrating geese showed as silhouettes against the deep purple sky.

As they entered the cobblestone boulevard, Sarah heard somewhere an accordion echo, a child restlessly crying. The pleasant, cheery fragrance of freshly baked bread filled their nostrils, causing Sarah's stomach to respond and Hans to encourage the pony more quickly on toward the small farm which lay just on the outskirts of the village behind a windscreen of mature alder.

Hans put the pony away, leaving Sarah to her thoughts. When he returned he found her standing quietly, looking to the north.

"You can't see it from here . . . Steinbock Castle," he explained in response to her puzzled glance.

"I wasn't looking for that," she said quietly.

Her mind was still on the bandits. The dark-eyed young man, Carlo Bramante. So intent on robbing them, searching her luggage—what had stopped him? Some primitive chivalry? Certainly not fear. It was only after Hans had mentioned her name . . . could Robert have known this brigand!

It seemed unthinkable, yet . . . it must have been coincidental.

"Hans," Sarah asked, turning suddenly to face the man who was making haste toward the house and his dumplings, "did it seem to you that the mood of Bramante changed when you told him my name was Chamliss?"

"I did not notice," Hans said hesitantly. He rolled his eyes beseechingly toward the house. "Come, let us eat."

"Hans. Herr Huchting. Did you know my brother?"

"I believe it was mentioned in Feldkirch that an American was around the area." Perhaps he would have said more, but the door to the house suddenly swung open, painting the garden with a wedge of yellow light. A stout, matronly woman, her hair in thick braids coiled on top of her head stood outlined in the doorway.

"Well," she snapped, "shall I give your dumplings to the dogs, *du Gans!* Where have you been all evening?" She leaned forward slightly. "And who is that with you!"

"A guest, Renate. We are coming. We are coming."

"A guest," Renate grumped, "you told me nothing. Now do I serve cold food to a guest? What is the matter with you!"

Renate turned and went into the house, still muttering as she worked in the kitchen, banging utensils and dishes around.

"Come, please," Hans said.

"But you never met my brother?" Sarah asked insistently.

"Please, Fraulein. Renate is angry. Our food is growing colder. It is chilly out here." Reluctantly Sarah let go of his arm, following Hans into the comfortable, clean house.

Their dinner was set on a plank table. Renate, bustling about, served a pewter mug of warm cider to each of them.

"So," she said, wiping her hands on her flowered apron. She surveyed Sarah's unpinned hair, the dirt on Hans's trousers, and made a small clucking sound with her mouth. "Eat, Fraulein."

"It was Bramante," Hans explained from around a mouthful of his longed for dumplings. "From out of nowhere," he said, making a vigorous motion with his hand. "Fortunately, they respected me. We were detained, but not robbed."

"And what would they rob you of, Hans?" Renate demanded. "You don't have the money to repair the barn roof."

Renate refilled Sarah's cup, looking expectantly at the younger woman.

"I will be happy to pay for my meal, Frau Huchting," Sarah said. "And for lodging if you have the room."

Renate broke into a pleasant smile. "Yes, of course we have the room. Stay as long as you like."

Hans started to interrupt, but Renate silenced him. "Five marks a week, perhaps. If that is not too much."

"Renate . . ."

"It would be fine," Sarah assured her. "I know a household can't run on nothing."

"Yes. You see, Hans, she is a woman of common sense. Not like you. Fine. Five marks then."

"Oh, yes," Sarah said, digging into her purse as she realized that Renate was waiting for an advance.

"*Danke, Fraulein.* Stay as long as you wish. Please."

Sarah nodded. The long hours and the suddenly warm

room had made her drowsy. That and the cinnamon spiced cider which warmed her and filled her with a lazy, good humor.

Frau Huchting showed her to the neat, dry room above the kitchen. A cozy loft with a hand-hewn bed and a thick, goosedown comforter. She undressed and brushed out her hair, standing at the open window.

When her arm was weary she reached out to close the shutters, and her breath caught.

Across the road, in the shadows of the linden trees she saw—or thought she saw—the hulking shadow of a man.

Surely she was wrong. For when she rubbed her eyes and looked more closely, she could discern nothing but the trunks of the trees, the gracefully swaying boughs, the lingering whitish moon.

But just for a second there . . . it had looked like that bearded bandit, Ferrara.

On the bare outcropping of granite called the Emperor's Nose, Rovato, the thin man from Naples, kept watch, his Enfield carbine across his knees.

A low whistle, and then two more echoed up the long canyon. He answered with a whistle of his own.

Ferrara—he thought—back from Feldkirch.

The lumbering Ferrara found the camp circle and squatted near the fire, taking coffee from the scorched pot.

There were four men around the fire, three more sleeping away from it. Bramante, cupping his coffee in his palms, waited until Ferrara had warmed a bit.

"Well?" the young bandit chief inquired.

"She went to Huchting's," Ferrara said, still slightly out of breath. He ran his fingers through his thick, black beard, combing the bread fragments from it.

"She is staying there?"

"It looks that way, Carlo. She has the loft over the

kitchen."

"Bad," Carlo Bramante said, rising. He stood for a moment, studying the distant lights of Feldkirch. "Why did she have to come?"

"Do you think she could know anything?" Ferrara asked. Bramante's mouth turned down in an undecided frown.

"Who knows. Let us hope not—for her sake." Carlo turned back toward the fire, the flickering shadows catching the thin, firm lines of his face. "If she does know, something will have to be done about it."

"She must know," Ferrara guessed, throwing the dregs of his coffee onto the fire to hiss and steam. "Otherwise why would a girl like that come so far. A Parisian, an artist, a *lady*." Ferrara made a sound of disgust with his rubbery lips.

"It could be she is not what we believe. It could be that this Sarah Chamliss is much more than meets the eye." Carlo worriedly unrolled his blanket, still deep in thought.

"We shall have to be attentive to her movements," the young man said. "Most attentive. Until we are quite sure."

"I am quite sure," Ferrara muttered before rolling over in his blanket, gazing at the deep skies with fierce, hooded eyes. "Quite sure," he repeated under his breath.

Three

The early days of October were brisk, with hardly a cloud to crease the crystal, piercing sky. The Alps loomed above the valleys, cold and staid in their quiet vigil. The trees, ash and maple, shed their colored leaves silently, gradually turning to gray skeleton figures along the long, rambling roads.

The stubbled fields, golden in the morning brightness, checkered the rolling hillsides. Fruit still hung heavily on the apple and pear trees in the village orchard, and the cider press was being renovated, oiled and painted in anticipation of the pressing festival.

There was frost in the early mornings on the rooftops of the neat white houses along the main avenue of Feldkirch; and a thick, nearly milky fog steamed off the deep forest where the river wound through the stands of spruce.

By midmorning, however, the days invariably assumed a yellow lightness, a warming aspect as if nature had chosen to display her last dazzling artifices before the looming winter enveloped the high valleys.

Despite the early hour and her weariness, Sarah Chamliss rose early, a restless eagerness entering her mind as soon as the first golden rays of light struck through the shutters of her loft room.

Robert.

It was the first thought in her mind as she awakened, a demanding calling from some deep-rooted anxiety. Not a day had passed that the certainty that Robert needed her had not increased.

Even as she dressed, straightened the bed, and rinsed off her face in the icy water bowl Frau Huchting had placed on the bureau, the idea gnawed at her heart.

He was here. She knew that without any fragment of doubt. Or he had been here. How she knew it, she could not say. As she gazed from the window into the morning brightness, across the brown and deep yellow fields toward the bluish forests beyond, she felt the confidence rising in her once again. Strange vibrations, slender threads of knowledge that pass between people who are truly close, perhaps. But it was no longer an uncertain proposition.

What was perplexing was the attitude of those she had so far met. Hans seemed to know something, yet that cheerful, white-haired Austrian grew suddenly evasive at the mention of Robert's name, puckering his lips, wagging his head slightly at the question.

The bandit, Bramante seemed also to know something. But what?

And there was the Englishman back at the border, the one in tweed with the drooping mustache who warned her that "it is chilly in Feldkirch." Was it only the weather he had meant?

"Fraulein Chamliss," Renate called up the staircase, "will you be joining us for breakfast?"

"Yes. In a moment, please."

"*Sehr gut.* I will make coffee."

"*Danke,* Frau Huchting."

Sarah pinned her hair up quickly, patting the chestnut curls into place with practiced hands before going down.

She wore her leather, ankle-length skirt, a plain white, high-necked blouse, and a leather jacket. Hans had already gone out, it seemed, although his plate had been served with ham and sweet potatoes, biscuits and honey.

"Frau Huchting," Sarah said, pausing halfway through her breakfast, "I am making inquiries concerning my brother, Robert."

"I do not know about him," Renate said, shaking her head as she fussed around the iron stove.

"It would seem that an American visitor would be noticed in a small town."

"I do not know about him," Frau Huchting repeated, turning to face Sarah. "More biscuits?"

When she had done with breakfast and helped the tight-lipped Renate with the dishes, Sarah went out, wrapping a pale blue scarf around her head.

The day was perfectly clear; she could see fifty miles to the Brenner Pass in the high Alps. The crows in the stubble field took wing, cawing, at her approach. She walked the country lane, through the hedges of blackthorn, along the weir by the barley mill, enjoying the long striding gait she had fallen into. She was glad to be about, walking in the open air after the cramped days of sitting.

She stopped for a moment near the weir, watching the thin, silver gush of water over the yellow brick wall, racing downstream over the cobbled riverbed as it escaped the miller's dam. When she looked up a boy was watching back.

"Hello," Sarah said with an easy smile.

"*Guten Tag, Fraulein.*"

He was fourteen or fifteen with flaxen hair, open blue eyes, and a rather impish tilt to his mouth. He twisted his cap in his hands.

"A beautiful day," Sarah ventured.

The boy nodded, some idea working in his head. He wore lederhosen and a white linen shirt, sturdy boots and a green cap with a jaunty feather which he now slapped back onto his head, leaping from the wall where he had

24

been sitting, his blue eyes eagerly lighted.

"You are English," he said with a deep accent. "*Ja? Nicht wahr?*"

"*Nein,*" Sarah replied, "*Ich bin* American."

"*Amerikanerin?*" The boy appeared crestfallen at first, and then merely puzzled as another thought formed behind those clear blue eyes.

"In America," he asked falteringly, "do one speak English, *oder* American?"

"English, after a fashion," Sarah laughed.

"*Schon gut!*" the boy said, breaking into a relieved grin. "I am Rudi Uhlmann. I have English so good from the school. I am happy to practice it."

"I'm happy to have you practice it too," Sarah said. "I'm afraid my German is not so good."

"Then you have no need to worry," Rudi said proudly, tapping his chest. "I am the better translator and guide for tourists."

"Perhaps you can help me," Sarah said thoughtfully as they walked slowly toward Feldkirch. "I am looking for a man—my brother, also an American. Perhaps you have seen such a man."

"No," Rudi responded, scratching his head. "No one like this. But I have just returned from Innsbruck from my aunt."

"Is there someone who might know?" she asked. In all towns there are gossips, especially in small towns. People who pass the time by accumulating news and by transmitting it. Surely a stranger could not have gone completely unnoticed.

"I know this person. A man who knows everything," Rudi said eagerly. "You will come with me, and I will take you, okay?"

"Okay," Sarah replied with a laugh. "Take me to this man."

The church was small, modest. Mostly of frame, there

were numerous signs of more ancient buildings, an abandoned, obviously burned-out wooden structure set among the pear trees behind the rectory, a crumbling stone wall which surrounded the neglected rose garden, and farther back, low hummocks where structures once might have been, where now there were only mounds of earth covered with dry brown grass.

Father Bruno lifted his head from his breviary, his glasses perched on the tip of his longish nose. A good-humored man with sparse, unmanageable red hair and a ruddy complexion, he was surprised by nothing after his sixty years of life and nearly forty of ministering to souls. But he was curious immediately.

That impish son of Klaus Uhlmann, out of school as usual, was standing in the rectory door with a tall, unusually attractive woman, apparently a foreigner.

"Yes, Rudi?" he said, closing the breviary after marking the page with a tasseled golden ribbon. "Do you need me?"

"It's the lady, Father Bruno," Rudi said, nodding toward the blue-eyed woman as if believing the priest did not see her. Nervously Rudi rubbed first his leg and then his arm. "I brought her," he added superfluously.

"Yes," Father Bruno said with a warm smile and a nod of his head. "Please come in, won't you. I'm Father Bruno."

"Sarah Chamliss," she said, taking the priest's extended, freckled hand.

"Chamliss . . . Robert's sister? Or his wife?"

"Sister," Sarah said, barely able to get the word out in her excitement. "Then you know my brother?"

"Umm, not exactly, Miss Chamliss. But we met, had tea and conversation on several occasions. Yes, I suppose I know him, if slightly.

"But, Rudi," the priest said with a remonstrating shake of the head, "has the schoolhouse burned down?" He looked at the large, oak cabineted clock on the wall opposite and then once again at Rudi.

"No, Father . . . I was helping a stranger. I was being a good Samaritan . . . but now," he stammered, "I will be late."

Rudi hesitated a moment longer before turning to shuffle off through the garden path.

"He's taken with you," Father Bruno laughed. "Will you have some tea with me, Miss Chamliss?"

"Call me Sarah, please. No tea, thank you."

She waited with ill-concealed impatience as the priest meticulously built a fire in his tiny stove and put the battered brass pot on to simmer.

"You have come about your brother then?" Father Bruno asked, turning to face Sarah. "Sit down," he encouraged her, "please. What I know of your brother's business is little . . . am I to assume there is trouble?"

"He is missing, Father. No one seems to know his whereabouts." Briefly Sarah explained about Robert's absence, her reasons for believing him lost or hurt, and about the townspeople's reluctance to help.

Father Bruno sipped gingerly at his tea, his eyebrows lifting slightly as Sarah talked. He peered over his wire-rimmed glasses, now and then screwing up the corners of his mouth. When she had finished, the priest stood and walked to the window.

"He is a fine man," Father Bruno said finally. "Gentle, but with a great deal of inner fortitude, one could see that. He carried himself with a degree of humility, yet with great confidence. He impressed me in that way."

Sarah sat rigidly in the stiff wooden chair. It touched her deeply to hear Robert described, and in much the same terms she herself might have used. She wished to interrupt, to blurt out questions, but she allowed the priest to continue in his random manner.

"Yes, surely I recall him," Father Bruno said, retaking

his seat behind the desk. He placed his hands flat on the dark desk top, spreading his fingers wide. The sunlight caught the reddish hairs below the cleric's knuckles.

"Tall, broad shoulders but not excessively bulky, straight dark hair and aquiline nose . . . but I ramble. One becomes used to our leisurely pace. I apologize."

"When did you see him, Father? And where did he go? Where was he staying?"

"It was nearly two months ago," the priest said, closing his eyes in recollection. "He came to examine one of the old buildings. Your brother was an archeologist?"

"Yes."

"Yes, he wished to see the old fort. He came two consecutive mornings and took tracings of the inscriptions. He believed them to be Avarian from the eighth century."

"Avarian?" Sarah said distantly. In her mind she worked over the simple puzzle—if Robert had traveled halfway across Europe to study these inscriptions, why had he spent a mere two days here?

"Very interesting," Father Bruno said, interrupting her chain of thought. "The Avars, as you may not know, were originally a Mongolian people, driven south in the sixth century or so.

"There was intense warfare between these new arrivals and their cousins, the Bavarians, along the Danube valley for several centuries. Then, as always in human struggle, a new conqueror appeared, the Emperor Charlemagne who devastated the Avar kingdom, pushing them south and east into the high reaches, the last stronghold in the Tyrol. Somewhere near here, it is speculated.

"It is quite a thrilling tale," Father Bruno said, rising once more. "A king, Avaradt, a princess stolen from the Franks, a vast treasure and a final bloody struggle. I know all of this only second hand. I am not the scholar your brother is."

28

"It is fascinating," Sarah admitted. "Especially when, as Robert, one can read the texts scratched into stone, reconstruct buildings from the clues of a few stones, or a life-style from shards of pottery."

"But you, of course, are more concerned with finding Robert. I apologize again, Sarah. I find I talk more as I grow older, perhaps to less purpose. As to where Robert is now, or even to where he was staying during his visit to Feldkirch, I am sorry to say I know nothing whatsoever that could be of the slightest help."

At these last words Sarah felt the flags of hope which had fluttered briskly for a few minutes again go limp, her stomach again go suddenly empty.

He had been here, talked to this man, lived if only briefly in this hamlet. Yet the land did not swallow people up. With a sudden flurry of panic she gripped the chair tightly. The priest noticed this and looked at her questioningly.

"It's nothing," she murmured. An abrupt, terrifying thought had flared up in her mind. *The bandits.*

The hills and woods around Feldkirch were infested with bands of these robbers. Who knew what happened in the depths of the forests; a man would never be found. She remembered the change in Bramante's attitude when her name had been brought up. Perhaps it was a sympathy for a dead man's sister which had brought the change about.

No!

She would not allow herself to think of Robert in such a way. He was alive. And well. And waiting for her. He was!

"Perhaps you would like to see the inscriptions yourself?" Father Bruno asked.

"Pardon me?" Sarah said softly. Still in her brain the blood surged, her thoughts racing in a hundred conflicting directions.

"I have an hour before confessions," Father Bruno said, pushing back from his desk. "Perhaps you would like to view the Avarian inscriptions yourself."

29

"Yes," she decided with a resolute toss of her head, "I would like very much to see them." Although, knowing that she would be unable to fathom the forgotten language of the Avarians, it was difficult to say what she hoped to gain from viewing the ancient inscription.

Still—there might be something, however slight, some whisper or spark of understanding, some clue to Robert's own thoughts as he studied them.

Father Bruno tugged on a worn green sweater and took an oil lamp from the hook on the wall.

"It's very dark in the tombs," he explained. "Very dark and quite cold."

"The *tombs,* you said?" Sarah asked, recoiling slightly at the bleak term.

"Yes," the priest mused. "Although I don't know exactly what they were, perhaps a redoubt, a final stronghold. But bones were once found there, and they've since been called the tombs.

"I lean toward the former theory myself," Father Bruno continued, "a redoubt. The hummocks were constructed with a mind to the view and the well. The same attributes the early fathers had in mind when they built the first church here in the twelfth century. The well is still sweet," he added.

The rising wind was chilly as Father Bruno escorted Sarah through the rose gardens behind the rectory; fleecy white clouds scudded across the pale sky.

The wind pressed Sarah's heavy skirt to her legs and drove the last fading petals from the yellow and pink roses. A single, glossy crow sailed curiously overhead before descending, cawing twice, to view them from the autumnal limbs of a massive, wind-torn chestnut tree.

"Here we are," the cleric said at last.

They had stopped before a massive earthen mound some seventy feet long, forty wide, and thirty high. In another location, with its grassy, contoured aspect, it might have been mistaken for a natural landform—perhaps on the steppes—but here it was anachronistic, obviously foreign, and a trifle bizarre. At this end there had been some excavation revealing uncut, poorly fitted stonework.

"The original entry was through the top," Father Bruno explained. "That's all caved in now."

He put the lantern down and fished in his cassock for a match. Shielding the flame with his hand he touched fire to the low wick.

"There."

A jerry-built plank door had been thrown up across the entrance and Father Bruno pulled it aside, panting a little with the exertion, his glasses nearly slipping off.

"The boys kept getting in it," he explained.

He thrust the lamp before him and, ducking to clear the low lintel, entered the dark entrance shaft to the Avarian tomb.

A rush of foul air wafted from deep in the interior, nearly overcoming them as they passed into the close confines of the burrow.

The lantern glow painted the priest's craggy face eerily. His lips, she noticed, were pressed tightly against his teeth . . . she was not alone in her discomfort as they pressed ahead into the constricting, airless tunnel.

There was a feeling she did not like . . . a feeling that caused her skin to go cold and crawl, especially her scalp.

In other places—Egypt, the caves at La Madeleine—she had toured the homes of peoples passed over by civilization, long dead, vanished without traces but for a broken pot, a fragment of bone, or an image scratched sometimes meticulously, sometimes almost desperately on walls; seldom an image of the men themselves, as if they wished for the anonymity of time. They were usually of items important to them—food sources, plant and animal, or nebulous deities, mythical creatures, or sun and moon.

There was always this musty odor, the eerie emptiness of such places which tightened the muscles, caused the mouth to go cottony, and sent unnerving impulses racing up the spine.

"I don't wonder you call it a tomb," Sarah remarked as they stopped to clear away some debris which had tumbled from the ancient walls. "These monuments to the dead, their ancient homes, battlefields," she went on, "it's difficult to remain skeptical of the mysterious in the darkness, the quiet . . ."

The passageway which had been only a narrow corridor barely wide enough to walk through, so low that Sarah was forced to bend slightly forward as she moved, now widened suddenly into an alcove, the floor of which was nearly fifteen feet below where they now stood.

"Be careful now, Miss Chamliss," the priest said, his voice echoing hauntingly through the alcove. "I believe there were once steps here, but they've long since crumbled away."

The changing lantern light bathed the alcove, casting long irregular shadows on the walls of the great dugout as they moved down into the pit below. It was shaped like a huge bathtub, and there were half a dozen smaller chambers hollowed into the earth around it.

A pervading, yellowish lichen clung to every conceivable surface. There were indistinct jumbled knots of mounds on the surface of the floor. Water seeped in from above somewhere and trickled down a stony wall, fuzzing the stones with slimy green moss before disappearing into the loamy soil without a trace.

There was a damp, raw odor to the room, almost like the smell of decaying fish, yet much fainter. A cluster of thumb-sized bats clung to the jagged outcropping just overhead.

"This alcove," Father Bruno said, helping Sarah around

32

a tight bend, "is the one with the inscription."

Unimposing, the whitish scratches were scribed unevenly into a rounded brown boulder half the size of a cart.

Father Bruno hung the lantern gingerly on a peg someone had driven into a cleft near the writing.

Here, some eleven centuries earlier, a band of cold, beaten barbarians had huddled, perhaps speaking in whispers as they worked or perhaps not speaking at all—watching the feeble fire smoke the cave ceiling as they pondered their imminent death, the extinction of their race.

"Can it be read?" Sarah asked, fingering the strange, blocky letters.

"By no one I know of. Perhaps your brother was making headway. He seemed pleased with the work he was doing.

"Legend has it that it is the tale of the Avarian's trial, of the kidnapped Frankish princess who had brought the doom down on their heads. There is a treasure associated with the tale—but all of this is merely folklore. No one knows."

"Look here!"

Sarah had crouched lower, examining the carving. Her fingers rested below two figures.

"Why, what is that?"

"Chalk," she said, looking up into the priest's eyes. "It is chalk. Someone has underlined these two symbols with chalk."

"Strange. Whatever for . . . unless it was your brother."

"It has to have been," Sarah said excitedly, a surge of buoyancy flushing her cheeks. "No one else would have . . . could have. Have you paper, Father Bruno? May I copy these figures?"

"Why, of course," Father Bruno said. Unspoken was the conviction that the girl was grasping at straws. She was tenacious, he'd give her that.

He watched as Sarah copied the ancient writing. Slowly, meticulously she worked, assuring herself that every line was exactly as it had been carved by the Avarians. Not knowing the language, she had no way of knowing which seemingly aimless line might represent a subtle grammatical variation, an inflection.

Finally, when she was finished she stood, gazing still at the chalk marks. It was little, but it was substantial—Robert had put them there. For a reason of his own. She had only to discover what his reason was.

"I've kept you too long, Father," she apologized. "Your confessions . . ."

"It's all right Sarah," he said a bit forlornly, "I only hope that this does you some good."

They walked from the cavern, resealing it as they came out into the cool, purpling evening.

"Father," Sarah asked. "The Frankish princess . . . did the old tales tell what happened to her?"

"Yes," he said thoughtfully. "Perhaps she fell in love with her captor or perhaps they felt that by her very capture she had disgraced her people . . . but the legend reports she and her Avarian husband were murdered with the same sword and placed together in an unmarked grave."

The wind buffeted the tall elms bordering the church ruins, the clouds were massing over the valley, highlighted by the silver rays of the hidden sun.

Sarah was intrigued by the tale of the kidnapped Frankish princess, her final violent end at the hands of her own people—a love story which would never be told, buried now beneath the layers of dust, the forgotten years.

Perhaps it was the visit to the hummock, but she felt close to the woman whose name she had not heard, whose face she would never see, whose time had melted away.

"It's going to rain," Father Bruno suggested. He had

been standing quietly by, watching as Sarah moved among her own thoughts.

"Yes," she said, startled by the sudden change in the weather. She watched the stacked, twisting clouds quietly. "But I'm keeping you, Father. You must already be late."

"I should be going," he admitted, running a hand through his sparse red hair before replacing his hat, "if you'll be all right."

"Of course."

"Please come back, Sarah, if I can be of any help at all," he offered, swinging open the rectory door for her.

"I will, thank you," Sarah answered. Then her breath was stolen from her; a man sat in the rectory, in the priest's swivel chair. It couldn't be, but . . . "Robert?" her voice quavered. She took a half step forward, then hesitated.

"Pardon me?" The young man turned around in the chair, blue eyes twinkling inquisitively.

It wasn't Robert, in fact he bore no resemblance to Robert—he was fair haired, small mouth finely molded, but in the deep shadows of the room there had been some suggestion of her brother in the line of the jaw, the way he rested in the chair, fingers thoughtfully intertwined.

"I'm so sorry," Sarah stammered. She felt her cheeks flush. Involuntarily she put her hands to her hair, removing the blue scarf she wore, tying it loosely around her throat.

"You needn't apologize. I remind you of someone you know?"

He rose from his chair, an engaging smile on his lips. His blond hair was cut short, tousled into vagrant curls by the wind.

"The Count von Steinbock, Eric Mann," Father Bruno said in introduction. "And this, Count von Steinbock, is a new friend of mine, Sarah Chamliss from America."

Eric von Steinbock bowed slightly, curtly, his eyes twinkling as he took Sarah's hand briefly in his. "I am so charmed," he said. "You are visiting Feldkirch? You will find it quite scenic. We are proud of our bucolic little valley.

"Father Bruno," he continued. "I am looking for our little Minna. Have you seen her? My sister," he explained to Sarah, "she gets off by herself now and then."

"The poor thing." Father Bruno added, "The Countess is not quite . . . well."

"I'm sorry," Sarah said quietly.

"It's the bloodlines," Eric said with an enigmatic smile. "The blood grows thin."

"She has not been here," Father Bruno said. "If she should appear, I'll send a man to report to you."

"Fine, Father," Count von Steinbock said, a trifle wearily, Sarah thought. "It would be appreciated."

"Now," Father Bruno said with a glance at his watch, "I really must be hearing confessions."

"And you, Miss Chamliss?" the count asked. "May I give you a ride somewhere? I am afraid the weather is turning nasty on us. If you intend to return to Feldkirch this afternoon, you are sure to get rained on."

"I appreciate it, Count von Steinbock," she said, "but really . . ." she hesitated.

"I assure you I am a gentleman, Miss Chamliss," Eric von Steinbock said with a quick, deep smile. "*Nicht wahr,* Father Bruno?"

"I would think you should accept the ride, Sarah," the priest agreed. Outside the wind played against the shutters and the long rolling peal of thunder funneled through the valley.

"Thank you," Sarah said. "I would appreciate it."

"*Sehr gut!* Thank you, Father. *Auf Wiedersehen!*"

"I hope I'm not putting you out," Sarah said, but the count denied it vigorously.

36

"*Nein!* Not at all. No. I must go anyway to Feldkirch village to seek my wandering sister."

It had already begun to rain, great irregular drops spattering the earth. The long Daimler-Benz automobile sat beneath the wind-ruffled cypress. The count opened the door, closing it as Sarah swept her skirt in.

"It can turn very angry in this part of the country so quickly," he told Sarah, stepping in to the driver's seat. He stepped down on the starter and adjusted the spark, gripping the huge mahogany steering wheel masterfully.

With a roar and a belch of smoke the great automobile rolled out onto the narrow lane. The rain had begun in earnest now, and the count switched on the wipers as he steered the Daimler through the iron curtain of the downpour, twisting along the tree-lined road.

"These roads," he said with dismay, "nothing like one finds in Berlin or Vienna—or in America, *nein?*"

Sarah agreed. "It must take quite a bit of skill . . . at this speed."

"I apologize," the count said immediately pulling his foot off the throttle. "I live at such a pace . . . it can become dangerous."

"I do appreciate this," Sarah said earnestly as the car slowed to a lazy pace. "Count von Steinbock . . ."

"*Ach!* Please," he implored her, "all of this business with titles and protocol! I have no use for it. I was raised with it, but I do not adhere to these archaic customs. Useless relics. I would wish, Miss Chamliss, that you would consent to call me by my Christian name, Eric."

"I would, gladly," Sarah said with relief. Titles have always weighed heavily on the tongue of an American, and for Sarah especially it was difficult to play the subservient.

Eric spoke easily as they wound through the forested hillside, his smile coming easily. He did not affect the manners of nobility, nor did he dress the part. Wearing a white, turtle-necked sweater, slacks and a chocolate sharkskin coat, he seemed to be what he wished to be—a gentleman of some means who did not choose to dazzle others with his possessions.

In a European man that was a rare quality; in a Teutonic male, unheard of in Sarah's brief experience.

She avoided speaking of Robert; perhaps she had no strength for it. Eric pointed out the various peaks, the crumbled Rugian fortress, the broken highway left to mark the Roman Empire's foothold in Austria.

Eric stopped the car near a toppled milestone. On it they could clearly distinguish Roman numerals, the marks chiseled by some forgotten craftsman on antiquity's brief page.

"All of Europe suffers change," Eric said slowly, meditatively. "And there will be more. Vast changes, enormous movements of peoples."

The clouds had sunk low over the valley, a gray shroud drifting slowly past the fogged windscreen of the car as Eric, arms draped over the wheel, spoke.

"At first there were the Illyric people. Then the Celts, moving restlessly across the Germanic nation. The Romans thrust their imperial sword deep into Austria before that civilized bloody grip was broken by the Goths, the Lombards, the fearsome Vandals. Ostrogoths, Huns . . . Slavs and Avars. Bavarians.

"Who will be next? Will they be conquerors or the defeated? The wheel turns restlessly, inexorably." He turned the key on once again and drove toward Feldkirch, lost in his own thoughts as was Sarah in hers.

"Where are you staying?"

"With the Huchtings," she told him.

"I know the place well."

They had entered the empty, cobblestone boulevard, the tires slapping on the roadway, spattering water in silver spurs behind.

Suddenly Eric stopped.

"Minna!"

A wretched woman in gray, head thrown back into the rain wandered past. A slender woman, not yet old, her eyes were sunken into deep sockets, her dark stringy hair hanging in rain-drenched strands.

"Minna! Get in here!"

Eric leaped from the car, grabbing her by the shoulder. Angrily she spun away from him, swiping his hand away.

"Go away!"

"You must come home. You'll catch your death!"

"What does not die?" She shrugged. "Perhaps I have chosen."

Eric held her with both hands now, and she gazed indecisively into her brother's eyes. "Eric?" she said dubiously.

"Yes. Come home now, dear Minna. Come home. Poor Mitzi will be wondering where you are. She's only a kitten, and she'll be wondering what has happened to you," he said, speaking softly as he guided her toward the car.

"Yes, you're right, Eric. Poor Mitzi, what have I been thinking of," Minna said, putting her hand in anguish to her head as she stepped into the rear seat of the Daimler.

Suddenly she saw Sarah. Her eyes opened fiercely, her jaw muscles tensed. "And what slut is this!"

"Stop it, Minna!"

"Stop what? What slut is this, Eric, you evil thing!"

"This is Sarah. A friend of Father Bruno's."

"That makes no difference. I can see it in her eyes."

"I am sorry if my presence . . ." Sarah began.

"Silence, peasant!" Minna shrieked. "I did not give you permission to speak, foreign slut. Wench!"

They were at the Huchtings' front door now. Hurriedly Eric got out, opening Sarah's door as Minna raved on.

"Miss Chamliss . . . what can I say . . .?"

They stood facing each other in the rain. Eric's hair fell across his forehead, his eyes pleaded for understanding.

Behind him she could still see Minna through the steamed window, mouth moving in venomous phrases.

"There's no need to explain anything to me, Eric. I thank you for the ride."

"But you . . . I do not want you to leave me in this way."

"I must," she said, adopting a quick, forced smile. "I hope we meet another day, Count von Steinbock, under other circumstances. Please take care of your sister."

"I beg you to understand . . ."

"I do understand. And please take care of her. She is not well, is she? Help her. As for me—I am not so easily offended. Thank you for the ride, Count . . ."

"Eric."

"Eric. I thank you."

She watched from the porch as the long gray automobile rolled into the mist, disappearing as it made the long bend at the end of the cypress row. Then, sighing as she scraped her boots clean, she entered the house.

Renate was at the window, peering through the chintz curtains while Hans drooped mournfully over his supper of bratkartoffeln and hard cased sausage. "Now this," the little man said morosely, poking at his fried potatoes without enthusiasm.

Renate clicked her tongue and wagged her head worriedly, glancing at Sarah with stern eyes.

"Count von Steinbock?" she asked, though she knew perfectly well there was no other car like that in the Tyrol, and she had seen the blond Eric Mann on numerous occasions.

"He gave me a lift back from the church."

"Ach!" Hans was disconsolate. "Now this—what will befall us, Renate?"

"You say 'Now this!' Has something else happened, Herr Huchting?"

"Yes. Something has happened. Look in your room, Fraulein Chamliss."

40

In puzzlement Sarah put down her coat and walked up the staircase to the loft. When she opened the door she found the room in utter disarray.

The bedding had been thrown on the floor. Her papers, including her passport and some sketches, were strewn about the room. Her clothing, some of it ripped apart, especially the linings, lay everywhere as if the room had been pillaged by a savage horde.

Drawers were pulled out, turned upside down on the bed, shoes scattered about, even her powder box had been dumped out, coating the wooden floor with lilac snow.

"What a mess, what a mess," Renate intoned, nervously rubbing her hands together.

"I assure you it will be cleaned up," Sarah promised her. "But who was it? What did they want?"

"I saw nothing. I was in the market. When I returned . . . Miss Chamliss, have you secrets you are keeping from us? We are simple people. Hans is frightened."

"I don't know what it is, Renate. I don't know what they wanted. Don't worry, please. If you like, I will move."

Hesitantly Renate considered it, finally answering, "No." She shook her head decisively. "You stay. I will help you clean up, if you wish."

"You have your own work," Sarah replied. "If you will give me a broom, I will clean up the mess."

While Renate went downstairs to get the broom, Sarah began cleaning up, gathering up the papers. They had crumpled a sketch she had made of the Swiss Alps. She straightened it out as best she could.

Downstairs she could hear the Huchtings talking.

"She doesn't know," Frau Huchting was saying.

"No?" Hans was dubious. "And what about that Count von Steinbock—that sister of his. Does she know what sort of place Steinbock is . . .?"

Their voices trailed off and Sarah could hear no more.

It was two hours before she had the room in an acceptable condition, although the floors did not sparkle as they did when Renate mopped them. Wearily Sarah sat at the little table, the lamp flickering low.

She took off her bracelet, let her hair down and for a moment rested her forehead on the table, trying to think of nothing.

"Oh, Robert—what have you gotten involved in? What is happening around me? I feel blind, a fool; it makes no sense."

Remembering, she took the piece of paper from her pocket. Carefully she spread it out on the table, staring at the meaningless figures written so many centuries ago by the Avarians, underscored by Robert.

For what purpose?

Did the two scratchy symbols signify blood, treasure, prayer, perhaps all of these? Was it a dirge, an instruction to those who would come after—those who never came?

Her eyes lost their focus and her head began to thrum faintly behind the left ear. It was all so hopeless. Without the key, the inscription was indecipherable.

Wearily she stretched her slender arms over her head, intertwining them briefly. She tucked the paper into her pocket and went to the window, the pale moonlight catching her hair momentarily through a break in the drifting clouds.

The earth was sodden, a freshet gurgled through the elm trees. The moon played hide and seek behind the thick clouds.

Just for a moment it flashed brightly, illuminating the bulky figure of the bearded man lurking under the trees.

"Go away!" she shouted angrily. Then softly, dismally she repeated, "Go away."

But the bandit, Ferrara, remained, lounging against the trunk of the rain-lacquered elm, a cupped cigarette in his hand.

Then the moon was gone once again, the night closing around the grove. Sarah waited a moment longer, the cool dampness flooding the room, before she closed the shutters and sagged onto the bed.

Four

Morning was lucid, brilliant. A wren perched momentarily on the window sill, then vanished. Sunlight streamed through the elm trees. Sarah washed and dressed quickly, before the orange ball of the coming sun had floated up over the treetops. The floor was cold underfoot, but Renate could already be heard downstairs building a fire in the iron stove.

"Fraulein Chamliss!" she called, hearing Sarah moving about.

"Yes, Renate."

"You have a visitor this morning."

"A visitor?" At this hour. It must be important. Hurriedly she drew on her boots, buttoning them quickly.

Only Renate was in the house when she came down the stairway. Eagerly she looked around, but the house was empty. Frau Huchting smiled.

"He is outside."

"*He?* Who is it, Renate?"

"A young man. A young man with blond hair who seems taken with you."

Eric . . . she pulled her coat on rapidly, straightening her blouse. He was waiting there, sitting on the stone wall of the garden. But it was not the Count von Steinbock.

"Rudi!"

"*Guten Tag*," the boy called cheerily, throwing down the pebbles he had been tossing. "Are you not so glad to see me?" he asked, frowning slightly.

"Of course I am, Rudi. I just wasn't expecting you. Shouldn't you be in school?"

"Not today," he answered. "It is a special holiday, you see. Don't you still need an expert guide?"

"I do," she said, "but I don't want you to get into trouble." She smoothed his pale hair, holding his head for a moment with both hands. "Special holiday!"

"Oh, yes." he laughed. "I have them frequently. I am sorry," he went on seriously, "that I am not the Count von Steinbock."

"The Count von . . ."

"You look so surprised. This is a small town, our Feldkirch am Tyrol. People look out their windows, and in the morning the whole town knows what has happened the night before."

"I met the count at the church. He gave me a ride home. Don't you approve, Rudi?"

"Oh, *ja!*" he said enthusiastically. "I approve so much. The Count von Steinbock is a *man!* Such a fine car he drives! Such manners. He is a great fencing master, you know, and a skier. Last year he was in Stockholm for the Olympiad, the javelin . . . unfortunately he had sprained his knee or Austria would certainly have won that event."

"The Huchtings seem to have little enthusiasm for the count," Sarah noted.

"It is only jealousy, I am certain," Rudi conjectured. "The jealousy of the peasantry. But really, the Count von Steinbock is not some ancient petty tyrant. He is such a modern man, a fine education at Cologne, I think."

As they spoke they walked along the hedge-bound path toward Feldkirch. Rudi was highly animated, moving his hands, walking backward as he faced Sarah, discoursing on what appeared to be one of his pet topics, the Count von Steinbock.

"What is it, Rudi," Sarah asked, "that people seem to fear about the count?"

"It is not him, Fraulein Chamliss, but Steinbock Castle itself. And his family—his sister, you have met." Rudi touched a finger to his skull, tapping it.

"Minna is not a well woman," Sarah suggested.

"No. But it is the grand duchess—Count von Steinbock's mother—who frightens them most. Iron, this one is iron. Of the old nobility. A close friend of the emperor, and the Archduke Ferdinand."

"She is stern?"

"Stern!" Rudi laughed. "*Ja! Sehr* stern. A woman of ice and fire. But there is more to it, I believe," he continued. "There are whispers." His voice fell off and he glanced around the deserted row.

"Whispers?"

"It's Steinbock Castle itself . . . it is quite enchanted. Cursed. Strange things have happened there in these last seven centuries since the Baron Huebner built the palace. He was driven from Vienna himself—no one knows why. A pirate and a brutal lord. The common memory is still strong in Feldkirch concerning this butcher."

"Butcher?"

"Yes . . . there are stories," Rudi whispered, "but I cannot even tell them to you. Horrible things."

They walked in silence the rest of the way to town, Rudi stopping once to pilfer the last blackberries from a tangled vine in a neglected garden.

The village was set along the uneven, narrow cobblestone street. The houses, half-framed with steeply sloping roofs, were generally two-storied, with living quarters upstairs over the various shops.

Overhead the wispy, pale clouds rushed toward the mammoth backdrop of the snow-crested Alps.

"What do you mean to do?" Rudi asked.

"To inquire—everywhere, and of everyone—for Robert," Sarah answered with determination.

"No one has seen him, Miss Chamliss," the boy insisted. "I have asked already about Mr. Chamliss."

"If Robert was here in Feldkirch, someone knows. And he *was* here. That much I know."

They began at the first shop—a cobbler's, with the tapping sounds of a tiny hammer, the rich, good smell of tanned leather, and a baldheaded mole of a man named Schmidt.

"He hasn't seen anyone like your brother," Robert said, translating the cobbler's response to Sarah's question.

"Is he *sure?*"

"*Nein! Nein!*" the shoemaker repeated impatiently. "*Kein Amerikaner!*"

"Thank you," Sarah said as the man turned to go back to his work. "But wait. Rudi—ask Herr Schmidt if he can read this."

Rudi glanced dubiously at the scrap of paper containing the Avarian inscription, but he handed it to Schmidt who pushed his glasses farther up his nose and shrugged, muttering something.

"Herr Schmidt does not even read German," Rudi translated.

Three small children, chattering excitedly, followed them from shop to shop. At the bakery, where a square-shouldered, buxom woman thrust loaves of pumpernickel into a vast stone oven with a huge wooden paddle, Sarah bought each child an onion roll, and they went away munching happily, calling back a cheery "*Gruss Gott!*"

At noon, no closer to an answer then they had been that morning, with fourteen shops and homes inquired at, they rested in the chestnut-shaded village square. Sarah cooled her feet in the bubbling fountain while Rudi stretched out on the grass.

Several children played tag, an old man rested on a

wooden bench, eyes closed, cane in his work-gnarled hands.

"It will be no different with the rest of the town," Rudi commented. His eyes too were closed, his hair nearly white in the sunlight. A tiny yellow butterfly hovered near his head.

"Perhaps not," Sarah agreed glumly. But everyone must be asked. Every stone turned. Robert had been here. He had visited the tombs, talked to Father Bruno—yet no one in Feldkirch remembered, or would remember having seen him.

"Why?" Sarah asked aloud.

"Excuse me?" Rudi said sleepily, stretching his arms.

"I said *why,* Rudi. Why are the people of Feldkirch behaving this way? Robert had to stay somewhere while he was here. He had to eat, to walk the same street we walked this morning, speaking to the same people. Yet they deny it. Why?"

Rudi could only shake his head.

In the afternoon they returned to the village. Herr Anderer, the blacksmith, was away on vacation. The tiny woman who operated the town's only inn was hard of hearing and could not enlighten them. Or would not . . .

That impression lingered on after several interviews, and it both bewildered and frustrated Sarah.

They found a friendly, dark-eyed young girl leaning over the bottom half of a Dutch door at the tailor shop. She wore a low cut blouse, exhibiting an ample bosom. "I am Helga Kroeber," she said, flashing a perfect smile. "Welcome to Feldkirch."

"Helga. I am Sarah Chamliss."

They fell to talking while Rudi ambled off after a school chum. The girl was vivacious, quite pretty and charming.

"No," Helga said with certainty, "I have seen no one like your brother. But I cannot believe someone in town has not." —

48

"Nor can I," Sarah said.

"I will ask around," Helga promised. "Perhaps they are only shy of strangers."

Briefly they spoke of Paris, of the coming Oktoberfest, which caused Helga's eyes to sparkle with anticipation, and of Steinbock Castle.

"It is an eerie place," Helga confided, her elbows still resting on the shelf of the Dutch door. "My cousin once worked there as a maid. She told me," she whispered, "that horrible things happen after nightfall. Sounds—of course it is haunted. Baron Huebner, the old cutthroat, walks the halls. My cousin could not last out the week."

"But the count. . ." Sarah began.

"The Count von Steinbock," Helga said wistfully. Her eyes focused on some indefinite far distant point and she smiled contentedly. "He is a man. Oh, to be his sweetheart."

"Do you know the count?"

"Me?" Helga laughed. "Oh, no!" She tossed her head regretfully. "He would not notice me if he passed by. Not a fine gentleman like the count. But I see him. It is a pity he was born to such a family."

"And what of this Carlo Bramante?" Sarah asked casually. "Have you seen him? Does he ever come into town?"

Helga's lips had fallen to a straight, hard line. Her eyes glared defiantly.

"Bramante!" she shouted. She strangled on a shrill broken laugh. "Do I know him? You ask me this?"

Suddenly she swung open the lower section of the door and stepped from behind it. It was only then that Sarah saw she was ripe with child, fully eight months pregnant.

"Bramante," Helga Kroeber said in a low, nearly animal voice. She patted her distended abdomen. "He did this to me—in the forest. He forced himself on me. Do you understand?"

Then the girl dissolved into tears and Sarah stretched out an apologetic hand. Helga turned away and rushed into the house.

Sarah stood a moment longer in the doorway, stunned, then she turned away. Upstairs a gruff, stout man with a drooping black mustache and thinning hair threw open the shutters and glared down at Sarah.

"Oh, Rudi," she sighed, catching sight of the boy. "I really put my foot in my mouth this time."

Rudi blinked and glanced tentatively at her feet.

"I mean, I talked too much," she said, explaining what had occurred.

"But you couldn't have known," Rudi said, "please don't feel bad. This Bramante is a thug," he muttered angrily as they turned and walked toward the Huchtings' house in the fading light of day.

"It happened while Helga's boyfriend, Fritz, was gone. Called up to Army service. That man upstairs," Rudi explained, "is Helga's Uncle Karl. Herr Karl Flaig is our police captain. He dreams of nothing beyond capturing Bramante and hanging him on the spot."

Sarah stood for a moment watching the pennants of cloud above the mountain peaks first purple, then fade to faint, fleeting orange, the countryside flooding with deep shadows which crept from under the trees and ridges. The high peaks still held a last, brilliant crown of reddish gold above the snow line.

She thought of Carlo Bramante as she and Rudi parted at the fork in the old road where the stone well stood.

Carlo Bramante was a thief and a thug as Rudi had labeled him. He had accosted Sarah and Hans in the forest; he had attacked a simple village girl and plundered the countryside at will.

Why then did she remember aspects of his personality fondly? She smiled briefly, ashamed of the pleasure it gave her to recall his dark curls, the indulgent black eyes, the vaguely cynical set of his fine mouth.

You are too much the romantic, Sarah, she told herself severely. Because the man is handsome . . . a handsome rogue is still a rogue, perhaps the more because of it.

The Huchtings were not at home when she arrived. It was an hour after sunset, and already the flagstone floor was terribly cold, the house utterly dark.

She struck a match to the candle on the plank table and found the note Renate had left beside the plate of cheese, bread, and fruit.

They would not be home until late—perhaps not until morning. A friend's daughter was being married; there was no telling how long the celebration would go on.

Wearily Sarah climbed the staircase, still thinking of the inscription. The Avarian notations had meant something of great importance once. Perhaps they did again.

She thought momentarily of the raven-haired, fiery Spaniard she and Robert had met at an exhibition. His work was being hooted down to the point where the manager of the gallery had asked him to remove his oddly shaped figures formed of irregular crescents and cubes, ovals and distorted features, some with eyes on the same side of the nose.

"It is there to see," this wild young man, this Señor Picasso had shouted, "for those who have eyes to see."

She swung open the door to her room and instantly a huge arm was thrown around her throat. A husky, hissing voice spoke.

"Leave. Leave Feldkirch now! Your life has no value here."

He pressed solidly against her, the bulk of his weight leaning on her shoulders, the smell of his perspiration clinging to her nostrils, the fire of his voice ringing in her ears.

"Do you hear me?" he demanded.

"I hear you," she gasped.

"Mind what you hear." For a second his arm tightened, then it dropped free and the man departed, his clumping footsteps echoing up the stairwell as Sarah sagged against the door, her fingers pressed to her throat.

He stood for a moment silhouetted in the doorway by the feeble starlight—a bear of a man with a thick, bushy beard. Then he was gone, the door slamming solidly.

"Ferrara," Sarah gasped. It had been Ferrara, of that she had little doubt. That beast of a bandit. She ran quickly to the window, but could see no one on that side of the house.

I'll leave, Ferrara, she swore, *when I have found Robert. When you are hanging from an oak tree or when I am carried away.*

They could all go hang! What did they want of her? All of them—they could go hang.

She vowed she would not cry, and she clenched her fists against it; but as she lay her head on the table in the darkened room, the hot trickles began at the corners of her eyes, streaming down her cheeks. She threw her head back, disclaiming the tears, proudly denying them. But still they came.

"Robert . . ." she said so softly that the sound barely passed her trembling lips. But there was no answer. No answer at all.

With a start her head came up. Daylight streamed through the window. But that wasn't possible!

There was a tiny sound at the shutters. And again.

I couldn't have slept all night draped over the table, she told herself. But she had, her clothing wrinkled, her face pressed red on one cheek told the tale.

There was a sound at the shutters again.

Ferrara!

No. Certainly not in the daylight. Hesitantly she opened the shutters. It was Rudi who had been tossing pebbles against her window.

"Rudi! It's so early."

"Too early?" he asked. "Not for this! Come down quickly, Fraulein Chamliss. I have found a woman who reads Avarian!"

Five

"She is an old woman. A very old woman," Rudi said. "It is a long way to where she lives. Far into the mountains. She never comes to town, despising the people."

"Despising them. Why?"

They had walked the better part of the morning already, climbing into the foothills now golden with stubble barley and autumn grass, sprinkled here and there with fire-red gillyflowers and the last of the chicory, blue as the far-reaching sky itself.

"She despises them because she thinks they are the enemies of her people. Descendants of those who slaughtered her ancestors. Her name is Senta, and they call her a gypsy. But she calls herself the Queen of the Avarians."

"A queen without subjects," Sarah commented.

For a time they sat beneath a massive spruce tree, watching a gray squirrel scavenge the ground for the last of the pine nuts, eating their own small lunch.

A wind came up early in the afternoon, carrying the threat of winter as they followed the road into the southern Alps. Up a narrow gorge, perched precariously on the lip of an outcropping of weather-scored white granite, they came upon the cabin.

A window opened and then closed hastily as Rudi led

the way up the narrow path to the tiny hut. At the door they were met by a slender girl with generous sloe eyes, straight nose, and obsidian black hair.

"Good afternoon," she said in perfect English. "I am Katrinka. My mother will see you shortly."

Katrinka's features could hardly be called Germanic. A beautiful girl with almost oriental eyes and high cheek-bones, and a broad, nearly petulant mouth, she smiled steadily.

Sarah smiled back, nearly gawking. The thought of the murdered Frankish princess flared up in her imagination. Was this a reflection of that ancient woman? Or her child—bred out of the Mongolian wilds.

A weak, unsteady voice sounded within the cabin. A tongue utterly unfamiliar. Katrinka nodded.

"Mother will see you now." Although Katrinka continued to smile, she did so rigidly, Sarah thought. There was a forced quality about it as if the smile was meant to conceal deeper, contrary emotions.

"I must ask you not to tire her," Katrinka requested as they moved into the interior of the dark cabin.

"Of course."

The floor was dark wood, polished to a luster. On the mantel above the stone fireplace there were several pieces of bric-a-brac and a pair of brass candle holders. There were no photographs in the room, no furniture but the table and the huge rocker with curled arms where the old woman sat peacefully, her head bowed.

She was at least ninety, wrinkled and thin to the point of emaciation. Yet there was fire in those eyes, and keen intelligence.

She spoke briefly in the dead tongue of the Avarians, gesturing faintly with her age-freckled hand.

"Mother wishes to know what it is you want," Katrinka translated.

"I would like to know if she can read an ancient Avarian

inscription," Sarah said.

Katrinka spoke again to her mother. The old woman's eyes brightened and she answered sharply.

"She says of course she can read it," Katrinka said with a fond glance at her mother. "After all—she is the Queen of the Avarian people."

Katrinka herself, Sarah decided, was less than enthusiastic after hearing what she wanted. Her forehead furrowed slightly and she turned half away from them as Sarah gave the paper with the inscription on it to Senta.

At a command from Senta, Katrinka opened the wooden shutters so that the light illuminated the characters on the scrap of paper.

The old woman nodded, smiled distantly, and handed the paper back. Then she replied in her ancient language.

"What does she say?" Sarah wanted to know.

"She does not know," Katrinka said.

The girl stood against the wall, the yellow daylight shading her fine features, her arms crossed below her breasts.

"She must know . . . you said . . . it is so important, Katrinka!" She stepped nearer to the girl, trying to impress the importance of it upon her.

"She does not know."

Senta looked oddly at her daughter, her eyes flickering from one woman to the other. She asked a question in Avarian which Katrinka answered with a staccato flow of words.

"Katrinka, I need to know. It may be a clue to finding my lost brother. If I cannot find out what the words mean, I am utterly lost. I believe Senta knows; why won't you tell me?"

Katrinka turned away, looking down the long mountain slopes to the valleys below. Feldkirch showed as a collection of patchwork green and gold farms, tiny red and white roofs for houses seemingly built for ants to inhabit.

"Ice Castle." Katrinka said after a long, studious pause. Her voice was faint so that Sarah could barely be sure of what she heard.

"Pardon me?"

"Ice Castle! She says it reads: 'Ice Castle.'"

"But what does that mean?" Sarah asked.

Katrinka shrugged. "Senta has read the words. She is very tired. Please go now."

"But, Katrinka . . ."

"Please go now," she said more strongly.

Puzzled by the translation, by Katrinka's sudden change of inclination, Sarah backed apologetically for the door.

The sunlight caught a gleaming, small object on the table. Katrinka's eyes met hers, fiercely. The Avarian girl's hand shot out and snatched up the bright object. But not before Sarah had seen exactly what it was.

A British gold sovereign.

"You are no longer welcome," Katrinka said tersely. "Please go."

Outside the day was a brilliant collage of blue, deep green, and stunning white. Yet Sarah found nothing uplifting in the sight. It had happened again. Another door had been shut in her face, another secret kept.

Rudi was sitting on a large, sun-bleached rock to one side of the path, building hurdles for a stream of red ants with blades of grass. He glanced up happily.

"Success?"

"I don't know," Sarah said dismally. "Let's be going, Rudi. It's a long way to walk before dark."

She turned back once more to the tiny hut, but the door was fast, the shutters pulled to. A thin curl of gray smoke rose into the blue and ivory sky from the stone chimney.

Something had been concealed. Once more.

Yet she felt growing within her a determination. If

there were something so worth concealing, it was worth discovering. Robert had not driven off the road on a sudden curve; he had not been thrown by a horse; nor had he been taken ill. Something quite unusual had occurred. People do not trouble themselves to conceal the commonplace.

That so many seemed to know the secret led her to believe that it could be discovered. Somewhere there was that one loose tongue.

"Let them try their best," she told Rudi as they strode through the long, bending grass, once flushing a partridge from cover. "They'll not beat me at this. Whatever their stake is, mine is greater."

They came onto the main road from the highlands, a winding trail used anciently as a war corridor from across the Brenner Pass. The day had turned suddenly cold, the gray thunderheads massing, the air filled with electricity.

The few splashes of color, the harebells gaudy blue, the occasional golden poppies, seemed unnaturally bright against the leaden skies and the shadowed grasslands.

The mist floated low across the blue spruce, shading the trees, fogging them with glistening dew. The long automobile waited at the side of the road beneath a lonesome, lightning-shattered alder.

Eric was there and he came quickly to up them, taking her hand lightly before releasing it as if it had been an impetuous gesture.

"I searched all around for you," the count said. There was concern in his pale eyes. The wind ruffled his hair. He took her hand again and this time he did not let it go so quickly.

"Don't wander these wild hills by yourself, please. There is too much danger just now."

Rudi hung back, awed by the presence of the nobleman who in his yellow sweater and white slacks appeared to him every bit as astonishing as an Apollo descended from the heavens. One did not speak to the nobility; and if one had the temerity to do so, one received no answer.

"And you, my young friend," Eric said turning suddenly to the boy, "you certainly should know better than to take a beautiful young woman into these mountains."

Rudi was crestfallen, he stammered a reply. Eric shook his head, but the reprimand was lighthearted and delivered with a rare smile.

"Come now," Eric suggested. "It looks like it will rain again. Let me give you a ride back."

"I would appreciate it," Sarah said gratefully. Her legs were not used to such long climbs and the threatening weather had been blotting out the skies, making the trip home an unwelcome prospect.

"And you, young man," Eric said to Rudi who had been standing to one side, hat in hand, "do you prefer to walk? I assure you my driving is safe, my car a comfortable one."

Rudi, who had never been inside an automobile, who had never spoken to a member of the ruling class, climbed into the rear seat of the Daimler with an awkward display of embarrassment and gratitude, feeling the leather upholstery gingerly with curious fingers.

"He is an admirer of yours," Sarah told Eric in a low voice.

"And you, Miss Chamliss?"

"I too, Count von Steinbock," she admitted.

In a foreign land, with all faces turned against her, he had been the one friendly face, the single person willing to help. To help without her request, without thought of reward, but only out of his own goodness.

The car started with a muffled, vigorous roar, and Eric shifted into low gear, following the mountainside road at an easy pace.

"You see, I have adjusted my driving habits," he said. "Miss Chamliss does not want me to kill myself driving an automobile, Rudi," the count said into the rearview mirror.

"It would be such an incredible waste," Sarah said.

"But soon I will be in more danger," Eric said in an uncharacteristic, pessimistic tone. Sarah glanced curiously at him. "The war—it will come," he explained. "Brother against brother. Perhaps it will be a war such as the world has not seen before. A war which will involve the entire world."

"Let us pray not."

"Prayer is all very fine. But it will not stop this war. There are too many who wish for war desperately. And they win out—always."

Around a tight bend in the road they came suddenly upon a procession of ragged, slowly moving goatherds. There were women in tattered shawls, nursing babies, and old men with staffs.

"Who are they?" Sarah asked, struck by the pathetic aspect of the band.

"Trentinos," Eric told her. He stopped the car for a moment while the old men herded the goats from the roadway. "We are into Trento now," he said.

"Are they Italian?" Sarah asked.

"Yes. Most of the people in the south Tyrol are of Italian descent. Though the Trentinos have at various times been under the French flag, the Italian, the Austrian. The dual monarchy of Austria-Hungary is composed of many diverse peoples," he explained as the goatherds moved on and the automobile rolled past, pressing northward toward Feldkirch through the deep high forest.

"Much like the United States," Rudi suggested.

"Yes," Eric agreed. "There are these people of the south Tyrol, the Trentinos; there are Czechs and Poles, Slovenians, Croatians, Slovaks and Serbians, Italians.

"We would like to believe we can all exist together peacefully," the count went on, "as they do in your country, Sarah. Yet we are plagued by dissenters, anarchists. Like our friend Bramante."

"Bramante is a Trentino then?"

"Yes. He wishes . . . who knows what he wishes, but he has convinced himself and others that he is fighting for the freedom of Trento. He wishes it ceded to Italy. An impossibility, of course. Can Arizona be ceded to Mexico? It is folly. These things can be worked out, but the man is not a man of reason. He is a simple bandit.

"It is people such as Bramante that will lead the empire to war," Eric conjectured morosely. "They feed on dissatisfaction, nurturing it for their own benefit."

The discussion seemed to have disturbed Eric. He drove silently on, dropping into the low country, past the trembling ranks of elm along the roadside. It had begun to rain, large, scattered drops of water exploding on the windshield.

"The woman"—Eric said abruptly—"did she help you at all?"

"Very little," Sarah admitted.

"You must let me help you, Sarah. The people are wary of strangers. They trust me and will tell me whatever I ask. Besides, I have the automobile. It will be so much quicker. And safer."

"I would be grateful," Sarah answered. Then abruptly she asked, "Do you know what the Ice Castle is?"

"The Ice Castle?"

Eric turned perplexed eyes to her, rubbing his chin briefly. "No. I know nothing of such a place. Though in winter," he added with a laugh, "our Steinbock might be described so."

The rain had begun in earnest now, leaden sheets of wind-twisted water slanting against the fields. Eric stopped the car in front of the Huchtings' house. A small wisp of smoke rose from the chimney before being swallowed in the deeper gray of the skies. Thunder growled up the long valleys, lightning flared up briefly in the distance.

"Rudi," the count offered, "I should take you home. You'll be drenched."

"No, sir. I thank you. I will get out here."

Sarah, surprised at the boy's reluctance to travel a ways more with his hero, glanced at Rudi.

"The rain is quite heavy, Rudi," she said.

"Come on, I'll take you," Eric said, smiling at the shy boy.

"No, *danke,* sir. I will get out here."

Eric shrugged, sliding the car into gear as Rudi leaped out, slamming the door. They stood beneath the eaves, watching as the automobile raced out of sight through the mist and rain.

"You'll have a long wet walk, Rudi."

"Yes."

Rudi was lost in his own thoughts. Twice he started to speak before he managed it.

"He knows very well what the Ice Castle is, Miss Chamliss. Everyone in Feldkirch knows of it."

The rain dripped from the eaves, the wind cutting at their flesh. Sarah could only stare at the boy.

"If the Count von Steinbock knows—why—?"

"I cannot say," the boy answered in a lowered voice. His hands were thrust deeply into his coat pockets, his teeth chattering with the cold. His normally affable, boyish face was shadowed with apprehension.

"But I can assure you, the Count von Steinbock knows very well what the Ice Castle is. But he did not wish to tell you. Nor," he added ruefully, "did he wish to have me or anyone else tell you of the Ice Castle."

The wind had abated, but the temperature dropped swiftly. The driving rain turned into heavy sleet and then to drifting snow. Rudi looked once more at Sarah, then almost mournfully he trudged off through the weather, hands still deep in his pockets, snowflakes clinging to his shoulders and cap.

What then had she stumbled into?

If it were true the count were lying, for what reason? She had no inclination to doubt Rudi, but Eric had not seemed capable of lying, of deception. Seldom had she met a man with such an open face, as if guile were beyond him. Yet the question lingered.

Was this Ice Castle such a grim secret that no one could bear to speak of it? She remembered the sudden fury on Katrinka's face, the stony reluctance.

Yet Robert had gone there, probably.

Leaving a message behind him. But for whom? Surely he could not have foreseen Sarah's coming. Then for whose eyes had the message in the tombs been meant? And if she had seen it, how many others for whom it was not meant knew of it? How many who meant Robert harm?

It was a puzzle of such complexity that the pieces fit nothing, not even one another, let alone the whole. Robert was a simple scholarly man. Who would wish to harm him at all?

But if what Rudi said was true, and she believed it was, someone meant to conceal the very existence of this mysterious Ice Castle—whatever it was.

And not only Sarah, but a shy, cheerful little boy who meant only to help might be in terrible danger.

Six

For days the snowstorm, like some forbidding spell, hung over the valley, the people moving glumly in their necessary travels, shuffling to shops and barns, watching the total bleakness of the skies, cursing and shaking futile fists at the snow-laden clouds which now seemed eternal in their blackness.

Sarah, with no way to travel about to make her inquiries, spent much of the time in the Huchtings' kitchen, chatting with Renate, helping with the cooking, assimilating much of the local gossip.

"If this continues," Renate said with disgust, gesturing angrily at the gloomy skies with her paring knife as if to puncture the warp of winter's weave, "there will be no Oktoberfest this year. All the planning will be for nothing."

The Oktoberfest, the last defiant celebration before winter's lock barred the Austrians into their houses, was uppermost in all their minds.

"There will be the band from Landeck—they have a handsome fellow with a great black mustache who blows the tuba with pipes a blizzard would envy." Renate put down her knife momentarily and was lost in reminiscence, perhaps of her girlhood when some faceless, broad-shouldered youth had whirled and danced with her until the orange midnight moon had risen over the mountains.

"Such cider. All year long the cider is discussed. Who will have the best? Well, it's always Fromm, of course, with his artesian water and sheltered orchard, but the Lebers have fine apples too. And better pears, if you ask me.

"Then the folks from the high valleys will be down with their cattle festooned with late blossoms, their colorful carts decorated with wildflowers—don't ask me where they find roses this late in the year, but they mingle the deep purple of the wild roses with edelweiss. It's all so lovely, Sarah," Renate sighed, leaning across the sink to gaze out into the melancholy skies.

"But perhaps this year there will be no celebration," she anguished.

Sarah too watched the closing skies with concern, but not for the lost Oktoberfest. If winter closed the high country, her search for Robert would be terminated as surely as if she were shackled with irons.

None but a fool, they said, walked the high slopes after snowfall; and none but a saint could survive.

As if heeding some human plea, the winter turned charitable after five days and withdrew into the high reaches, leaving the valleys free of ice and snow for a few compassionate weeks.

Now Feldkirch came suddenly to life, the rosy-cheeked maidens laughing as they raced by in wagons or sleighs, furs wreathing their faces as they called out to the boys. The pavilion beyond the square was decorated with fresh paint and garlands, the icy clear blue sky roofing the world with goodwill and encouragement.

Hans found an ancient side saddle in the livery barn and lent Sarah his roan mare. The horse was slow, patiently inclined and inelegant in its heavy winter coat. Nevertheless Sarah was grateful for its use.

She rode the side paths, asking everywhere for information, but gathered very little. She had not seen Rudi since the day they had gone to visit Senta. When she called at the Uhlmann house, Rudi's mother, a timid, dumpy woman with small eyes, would not even open the door. She only peered uncertainly through the narrow opening, repeating over and over again: "*Nein, nein, nein!*"

Finally, out of desperation, she rode out to visit Father Bruno once again—on the same day the band arrived from Landeck, playing their instruments in the back of a green sleigh heaped with furs. The pavilion was decorated lavishly with hothouse blooms, crepe, and Japanese lanterns. Oktoberfest was here.

Father Bruno was in the garden, gathering the last of his apples in a wicker basket. He glanced up smiling at Sarah's approach.

"Miss Chamliss, welcome back." He put down his apple basket and wiped his hand apologetically on his cassock before taking her hand. "Will you have an apple?"

Sarah thanked him and took one, biting into the cold, sweet pulp, enjoying the juices accumulating in her mouth, the sweetness of the last spring and summer captured within the fruit to be given back when the weather had chilled and the ice formed on the ponds.

"Delicious. Superb," Sarah said, obviously pleasing the priest with her remarks.

"They are good this year, if a trifle small. But not good enough, I'm afraid," he said with a shake of his head.

"Herr Fromm will capture the prize again this year?" Sarah asked, surprising Father Bruno with her knowledge of local proceedings.

"I fear so," he answered with a heavy sigh. He rested on the low stone wall, mopping his head lightly. "I have no time to tend my earthly garden," he commented wistfully.

"Every apple is perfect, Father Bruno."

"Ah—just so! Just so," he nodded, accepting the philosophy.

"Everything seems to be ready in the village," Sarah remarked.

"Yes, it should be ready. It is a joyous occasion for us, Sarah," Father Bruno said. "I am sorry your joy will not match ours during this festival. That is unless . . ."

"No. I have not yet found my brother. That is why I returned to see you, Father. No one, it seems, will help me in Feldkirch. No one, if not you."

"No? Odd," he said distractedly. "That is not like our usual gossips. Do they say what the reason is?"

"No. They say nothing." Sarah waited as the priest gathered up his garden tools and put them away in his shed. He wagged his head as he moved about, obviously talking to himself.

"I can find no reason for it," he said finally. "Our people have always been kind, helpful. It is totally out of their character to refuse assistance to a young woman."

"I have had the inscription from the tombs translated, Father."

His head snapped up. "You don't tell me! Did it help at all, Sarah? What did it say, for heaven's sake?"

The priest was as excited as Sarah was—or as she had been before finding the translation was worthless to her.

"This is quite intriguing, Sarah, you must tell me all about it. I am a mystery fan, you know. But this—this is our first in Feldkirch, and it seems to be thickening daily."

"I found a woman called Senta," she began. "She calls herself the Queen of the Avarians. A gypsy, I believe, most people call her."

"Senta, yes. I should have thought of her. But I hadn't seen her in many years. I thought perhaps she had passed on."

"She translated the inscription for me. I don't know if she did so correctly or not. Or if it was passed on to me correctly through her daughter."

"Yes? And what did she say?"

"Ice Castle. She translated it to read: Ice Castle."

"You don't say?" Father Bruno stood, waving a finger in the air for a moment. "Yes. That could be. The Avarians might have known of it. The Ice Castle. It could even be there that the Avarian soldiers secreted the missing treasure—if it existed.

"At least one part of your theory must be correct, Sarah. If Robert believed the inscription to read Ice Castle, he would have gone there. For an archeologist, the lure would have been overpowering."

"And that is where I will go," she vowed, "to the Ice Castle. Yet the people in town will say nothing of it." She looked squarely into the unwavering eyes of the ruddy-faced priest. "And you, Father, will you withhold the information from me?"

"Of course not," the priest said, looking slightly wounded and surprised. "But, Sarah, I must absolutely beg you not to go there! It is far too dangerous."

"Exactly so."

Both of their heads snapped around at the sound of the strange voice. Eric Mann, the Count von Steinbock, stood at the garden gate dressed in a long gray coat with a narrow mink collar.

Sarah stepped involuntarily toward him then stopped. "Eric!" she managed to gasp.

"Fraulein Chamliss," he said formally, bowing with just his head; but despite the formality of it, he was smiling generously with his eyes, more faintly with his mouth.

"I beg your forgiveness," Eric said, striding toward them. "I know it has been difficult for you here. I hated to have you think I was a part of the general deceit. Yet, Miss Chamliss—Sarah—I could not have you searching for your brother in the area of the Ice Castle.

"It is," he said grimly, "a place set against man and his dominion. A treacherous, quite deadly arena where man and nature must encounter one another on the most savage of terms." The count glanced at the priest.

"Do I exaggerate, Father Bruno?"

"No," the priest said soberly. "Unfortunately, you do not exaggerate in the slightest. I know of ten men who have been killed there. Six lie buried on the knoll beyond the elms. Four more will never be found. I suppose," he conjectured, "that they might have been treasure seekers—from my recent information," he finished without revealing exactly what he had heard from Sarah. The priest was a man skilled at maintaining confidences, it seemed.

"I want to know all about it, this Ice Castle," Sarah said quietly. The wind rattled in the dark trees, the chill had come back into the air as day rapidly declined, the sun showing only as an orange ball through the silhouettes of the bare walnut trees along the lane. The glass of the church sparkled with yellow and bluish highlights, the steeple catching a last golden adornment at its pinnacle.

"Let us go inside to speak," the priest said. He put his arm around Sarah as they turned to go in. He did so naturally, without thinking, giving her shoulder an affectionate, slight squeeze. And the action brought tears to Sarah's eyes.

How long it had been without family or friend! With no one to hold her or take her hand when she was most in need of a kind touch.

They settled into the soft, worn chairs as Father Bruno prodded the embers of the hearth into life. The flames danced at the instigation of his poker, leaping instantly to the kindling as if he had disturbed some slumbering hill of fire ants.

"Perhaps Eric Mann should explain the Ice Castle to you," Father Bruno suggested. "I have been there only twice, and then only to its mouth. Each time to administer the last rites."

Eric nodded agreeably. His face, contoured by the

firelight, was sharp and thoughtful. He was apparently searching for words. His long-lashed eyes probed the firelight for a long minute before he spoke, his hands pressed together, his shoulders bent slightly forward toward her.

"It is an ancient and massive cavern," he began, "voluminous beyond description. A dreary, labyrinthine chamber." He paused a long while. "I have visited the Ice Castle frequently. Just to the anteroom, the great vaulted mouth of the place. It is not far from Steinbock."

"Then I would like to . . ." Sarah interrupted, but Eric cut her off.

"No," he said positively, "you would not like to go there. Water seeps into the cave from somewhere above, in the heart of the Alps. It has been so for eons. As the water trickles into the cave, it freezes against the ice already locked into the stone.

"But first it runs in bizarre fashion, forming stalactites and stalagmites of greenish ice, creating great frozen arches, bridges and turrets, spires and battlements as if carved by some insane, demonic artist. There are gloriously beautiful vaulted ceilings of blue ice, marvelous as any in a cathedral, rows of massive icy girders given to collapse and deep, black pits with mirror-smooth chutes underfoot which lead . . .

"The ice never melts, Sarah. It rearranges itself, but it never melts . . . except to thunder down upon an intruder to this dominion of cold and death.

"Inside the Ice Castle," Eric went on, "are a thousand corridors leading to nowhere or worse. Great blocks of ice clog the passageways. There are huge chambers within. Some have names, like the Napoleon's Tomb where a long, perfectly translucent bench fits neatly into a dim alcove like a gigantic coffin.

"The Satan Room is by far the most terrifying. The wind squeals and growls from some invisible ice organ, deep

70

within the bowels of the place. There the ice has sculpted itself into grotesque forms—gargoyles perch along massive, jagged walls. And all of this is in the cold, the intimidating darkness, only to be seen by flickering torchlight."

"But you have never been far inside," Sarah said. "That is what you told me. How can you know all of this?"

"I know," Eric replied wearily. His hands rested limply on the great wooden arms of the chair he rested in.

"But how? I mean to go there, Eric. If Robert has gone in, so shall I."

"You shall not!" Eric Mann said so fiercely that Sarah, despite herself, trembled. "No one ever shall again."

"She does not understand," Father Bruno put in.

Eric fingered his forehead nervously, finally looking up into Sarah's eyes, the firelight shadowing his face. "I had a brother. Helmuth. Only a year younger than I. Helmuth was possessed, Sarah."

"Possessed?"

"Yes. By some ice demon which called him to this place—this Ice Castle. As a boy he used to sneak away. He was whipped, fearfully, for sneaking into the cavern. Yet he always returned. He knew every inch of it—he told me fantastic tales which we kept secret as children . . ."

Eric took a deep breath. "I used to beg him to stop. But always he went back. It was two years ago that he returned from the university, a finished Austrian gentleman with his books and pipe, easy charm and dueling scar . . . and the same old passion!" Eric slammed his fist against the chair.

"A madman! A madman! He took his climbing boots out one morning, a rope, iron spikes, two lanterns, a box of matches, a volume of Goethe to read . . . just think! And he went exploring."

"Helmuth is one of the men who never returned," Father Bruno said. "The count has sent others into the cave looking for his brother. Two of them also were lost. Do you understand now, Sarah?"

She watched Eric who sat slumped limply in his chair. It was no wonder he had fought to keep her from knowing of the Ice Castle, to keep her now from going there. His only brother, one he had loved very much, had been lost there. And there were the others—men he had commissioned to search and who had also been lost.

"Dear Sarah," Eric said in a tone much more familiar than he had used before. He put a hand on her shoulder. A gentle hand, a hand that possessed great strength. "I will not have you die there. No one must go to the Ice Castle again. I cannot carry the burden of another soul lost to that frozen inferno. No one must ever go again."

Sarah placed her hand on Eric's. Looking into the depths of his fire-bright eyes she asked, "Would you go again, Eric? If you believed you could find Helmuth even now?"

His eyes raised questioningly.

"I have lost a brother too, Eric. And I believe Robert is in the Ice Castle. How can I do less than you have done? I loved my own brother no less."

Before they left the church, while Eric warmed up the Daimler, Father Bruno took Sarah aside once more.

It was full dark now, with only the faint moonlight beyond the valley, but still Sarah knew the priest was worried. She felt what she could not see etched on his face.

"What is it, Father?"

"A man came today." After a pause he added, "He wished to see the tomb."

"You showed him the inscription?" she asked.

"What else could I do? But I did not like doing it."

"Who was he?"

"He did not give his name, Sarah. He was not an Austrian, and his English, as near as I could tell, was perfect. Perhaps an American or an Englishman. Or a well-educated man."

"Surely he said something! How he came to know of the inscription, why he had come."

"He said nothing."

"Could he read it?"

"I do not think so," the priest answered doubtfully. "But this man—he is the sort whose face tells no tales." He paused again, as if starting to add something, but he said only, "I thought you should know."

Eric tooted the horn on the automobile. Sarah thanked Father Bruno quickly, and gathering up her skirts ran to the waiting, sputtering automobile.

"The pony will find its way home?"

"Yes. It has a will for the barn at feeding time."

They did not speak of the Ice Castle. The Daimler puttered merrily along the winding, now familiar lane, the headlamps flashing on the rows of trees, shadowing the ridges of the rough road.

"What did the priest want?" Eric asked.

"It was nothing," she replied with the slightest hesitation which caused Eric to purse his lips and shrug. To speak of the visitor would be to speak of the Ice Castle, and she wished no more talk of the place.

"Do you know a man with a huge black beard?" she asked abruptly. "A brawling, broad-shouldered man with the look of a fighter."

"No," he replied, taking a tight turn easily. "Why do you ask?"

She told him then of Ferrara who had been lurking outside her window, of his entry and threat. Eric's mouth tightened into a grim frown.

"You should not have delayed speaking of this. I shall speak to Police Captain Flaig about this immediately. He will post a man near the Huchtings'."

The moon had found a break in the clouds and it

showed silver as it followed the car over the gradually flattening terrain.

It was pleasant in the closed automobile, warm and soothing with the sounds from the engine compartment muffled to a quiet hum. Sarah felt her eyelids grow heavy, and without realizing it her head touched Eric's shoulder and rested there. She made no effort to remove it.

"This Ferrara business is bad," Eric said as if speaking to himself. "I will not allow it. Bramante and his crew . . . no good."

"It doesn't worry me," Sarah said, her eyes still closed.

"It worries me. Very much. I would beg you to stay at Steinbock Castle . . . were it not for Minna." His voice faded away.

"Poor Minna," Sarah said drowsily. She felt Eric's hand drop to her arm and she opened her eyes for a moment. His hand gave her a gentle stroke and then rested there.

"I don't want to speak of it anymore," Eric said. He had stopped the car near the Huchtings' house, leaving the engine running. It was warm there, snuggled against Eric, and quiet, and safe . . . yes, it was that feeling of being safe, a feeling long absent that she craved just then.

"I'll be at Oktoberfest," the count said, sitting her up. Sarah's head bobbed lazily and she had to rub her eyes.

"I hadn't thought about it," she replied. "It would be fun."

"It will be great fun," he told her. "The people in costume, music, dancing, the cider of course. Such happy traditions. Traditions, I think, born out of the unhappy lives of the peasants of old. Small occasions to brighten their hard lot. And we—the so-called nobility—sat stiffly in our castles, missing all of life."

"But you go?"

"Yes," he laughed, "like a thief skulking about. With everyone in masks, I think they never know it is I. I am not totally sure they would welcome me. During Oktoberfest

I am like every other young man in the valley. And so it will be this year. Except I will have my own girl this year. I apologize . . . if . . . I said what I thought, not what was proper."

"I am entirely flattered, Eric. Entirely so that you would think of me in this way," Sarah said sincerely. "But what shall you be? What mask will you wear? How will I recognize you?"

"Ah," he said, wagging a gentle finger, "that is not fair. It is the sport of Oktoberfest. Our masks make us invisible to those we do not wish to see. Or to have see us. You will play the devil recognizing me, Sarah."

"All right," she laughed. "But I'll know you, Eric. It would take more than a mask to hide you from me."

Quickly then, and unexpectedly, he bent his mouth forward and kissed her, and she in return kissed him. Gingerly their lips met, exploring another person, another world. The two worlds met briefly, warmly, and then they drew apart.

"I must be going," she said, her eyes cast down.

"Yes." He understood and allowed it, but there was no shame in his voice or in his cool blue eyes. "Go tonight, Sarah. But come back to me."

Then he was gone, the warmth, the safety dissipated in the night, and only the cold wind remained, the swaying trees before the frigid moon. She drew her collar tightly around her throat and gathered up her skirts, walking briskly toward the Huchtings' door.

For a moment as the moon waned and hid again behind the constantly shifting clouds, she felt a touch of near panic as she failed to find the key. Finally, triumphantly her fingers closed around the key and with worried fingers she managed to let herself in.

Your nerves are shot, young lady, she told herself. She pressed her back to the door, letting her eyes adjust to the dark, antiseptic interior of the house. The embers were still glowing faintly and Renate's head poked around the door to the bedroom, her hair stuffed into a nightcap.

With a sigh Sarah took off her coat and trudged up the stairs to her loft. The wind rattled at the shutters as she hurriedly got into her gown. Then, on impulse she opened the shutters. Nothing.

Thank God! she thought. He is gone. Perhaps Eric had stopped by the police station, perhaps he had simply quit watching, but there was no Ferrara lurking under the dark trees.

Suddenly the moon broke free again and in the light she saw him.

My God, my God! What do I have to do?

She closed the shutters deliberately, the hot tears on her cheeks streaming down, having broken free of the dam of self-control.

She blew out the lantern and covered herself with the thick down comforter. Then she tried counting sheep, thinking of nothing, and talking to herself calmly.

He is nothing. A nasty, huge man. So what? He dares not come in. And tomorrow Eric will notify Herr Captain Flaig. Probably he already has and the police will come and find this beast, Ferrara.

Her eyes opened once, wide and suddenly with the creaking of the house, but there was no one there.

Just a dark, empty room. That is all, she encouraged herself. And finally she fell off to sleep.

But her dreams were tormented.

She found herself inside the Ice Castle, a terrifying mammoth dungeon of ice and darkness. Gargoyles with bearded faces flew from the high reaches, tearing at her clothing.

Deep within the icy tomb she heard his feeble voice calling. Robert—he was calling more weakly and more desperately, but the hands of ice held her tenaciously and a blood-soaked king, sword in hand rose up before her, calling for her blood.

Eric—he was in the mouth of the cave, his strong hands stretching toward her, but his reach was too short, the sucking maelstrom forces inside the Ice Castle too powerful.

She was torn from his grasp, the ice crashing around her like shattered mirrors, spinning deeper into a black, frozen abyss. And the face of a shrieking harpy, Minna's face, cackled with mad pleasure before the world went dark and the Ice Castle in a cataclysmic shuddering tremor collapsed totally, burying her forever in the frozen heart of the earth.

Seven

Renate was up early. To Hans's dismay, breakfast was merely milk and cheese.

"I haven't time for it today, Hans," she scolded teasingly. "Sarah and I must prepare for the feast and the dance at the pavilion. We have our secret admirers to think of," she told him.

Dejectedly Hans shuffled toward the door, muttering something about romantic women.

"Wait until midnight," Renate laughed. "He'll be joyous as a boy at Christmas. And probably more than half drunk. It's not this year's cider the men to go taste—it's last year's," Renate confided with a wink.

Renate was baking apple tarts. There were easily ten dozen already on the table, and she added to them, using her apron for a hot pad as she slid the steaming hot tarts onto the huge platters.

"You watch," she said, "this year I will bring home the cup. Frau Shirer took the first prize last year." She made a sour frown and shook her head. "Too sour. They were far too sour, those tarts. And too much nutmeg. But the judges had been into the cider and had no palate left."

The pungent aroma of apple tarts filled the cottage. Hot juice bubbled from each light pastry. Sarah could no more resist tasting of one with a finger than a child could.

As if she were a child Renate scolded her, but she smiled proudly. "You see—no one can resist my tarts. I have to watch Hans. He'll gobble them up by the score. Frau Shirer!" she muttered again.

Sarah first cleaned off the table where Hans had hurriedly eaten, then cleaned out the fireplace. Then, when the air was warmer, she boiled water and poured the first real bath she had had for days.

A long, slow, soothing soak in the wooden tub filled with water so hot it turned her skin red. It worked into her muscles, warming her thoroughly. She dozed idly in the water, scented with Renate's essence of rose, her hair piled up on her head, her mind empty of all thoughts, all care. There was for that little while only the pleasant scent of the water and the surrounding, liquid warmth, so that she felt only a creature of flesh, mindless, without thought or knowledge of tomorrow or yesterday.

Afterward she toweled off in the cool room, dressing hurriedly in the flowered cotton yellow dress, brushing her hair until it crackled with electricity, shining in the brilliant cold October light.

Renate had finished baking when Sarah came down. Sarah put the iron on the stove top and spread out the ivory chiffon dress she planned to wear that evening.

"It's lovely," Renate said, noticing the dress. "I've never seen one so beautiful except perhaps on Minna von Steinbock before   "

"Before she went mad?"

"Yes. Before that."

"When did that happen?"

"She was always a shy, nervous girl," Renate confided. "But it was two years ago. After Helmuth von Steinbock was lost."

"In the Ice Castle."

Renate's eyebrows raised, but she only answered, "Yes. That was when it happened."

"She went to pieces completely when her brother died?" Sarah asked.

"Oh, yes, Fraulein Chamliss! After all—she witnessed it."

"Witnessed it? Deep inside of the Ice Castle. Minna von Steinbock was there too?" The idea seemed incredible. A girl of seventeen—as Minna would have been then— following her brawny, athletic brother deep into that frozen hell!

"Yes, Fraulein. All of the townspeople know of it. But we do not talk of it to outsiders. But since you knew of the Ice Castle . . . I thought you knew about Minna."

"No, I didn't," Sarah answered, shaken. Nor, she thought, had Eric seen fit to mention it. Why? Perhaps it had simply not come up.

"Here, Renate," Sarah said, "you wear this dress. We can take the hem up easily."

"I couldn't," Renate replied, but her eyes told a different story.

"Please." Sarah pressed it on the Austrian woman. "It suits you, besides I have the dress I'm wearing."

"*Danke,* Fraulein Chamliss. *Vielen Dank!*" Renate rushed upstairs to put the dress on. When she returned, beaming with pride and pleasure, Sarah helped her hem it up.

"Renate!" Hans came in the door hastily, then stopped, taken aback at the sight of his wife, standing on a wooden chair as Sarah adjusted the hem to the chiffon.

"What is this?" he asked, stepping forward, tugging thoughtfully at his bushy side whiskers. "Renate, you look . . ."

"Don't start, you old rascal," Renate snapped. "Don't you think a woman gets tired of wearing the same dress? For five years," she said, holding out her spread fingers, "I have worn the calico to Oktoberfest. Miss Chamliss has given this handsome dress to me. Say nothing!"

"I only wanted to say that you look pretty—quite pretty, dear Renate. It makes me think of the Oktoberfest you and I met. Those long years ago. I shall be proud of you this evening."

Renate's face had softened as he spoke, now she could barely manage a surprised thank you. She said nothing even as Hans pilfered one of the forbidden tarts and sat at the table, watching Sarah's deft fingers pin up the hem.

"Outside," Hans said with a nod of his head, "I met Herr Police Captain Flaig prowling about."

"Herr Karl Flaig? And what did he want, Hans? Have you been up to something?"

"Me? Me, *Liebchen?*" Hans said, his round face a display of wounded innocence. "Certainly not." He took another tart, seeing that Renate had not scolded him for the first.

"Then what was it?"

Sarah glanced up into Hans's face. The old man was looking at her oddly. "Bramante," Hans said.

"Ach! That bandit. No wonder Herr Flaig came himself."

"No wonder," Hans agreed. "I would like to be there the day our police captain lays hands on that scoundrel."

"Yes, and I too . . . after what happened to poor Helga Kroeber."

"Herr Flaig has not forgotten," Hans said. "It inflames his hatred of Bramante. His own niece."

"What makes him look for Bramante here?" Renate asked. "And no more tarts!"

Hans sheepishly withdrew his hand from the platter. "There was a report," Hans told her. "Of one of Bramante's lieutenants being seen here."

He glanced secretively at Sarah who had finished her pinning.

"A man named Ferrara," Sarah said. "He was prowling around the house. The night you and Herr Huchting were out, he actually broke in."

"Was something taken?"

"No," Sarah assured her. "Nor anything bothered. He came to threaten me. To tell me to leave Feldkirch."

"In our house! You should have told us, Sarah," Renate scolded her.

"Don't worry. Herr Flaig will take care of this," Hans assured her.

"I'm not worried," Sarah said. "Not now, at least," she smiled.

Renate went to finish sewing the hem, and Hans went to the barn. He must have had a jug hidden there from the eagerness he showed.

Sarah went outside for a breath of air and was greeted immediately by a cheery, familiar voice.

"*Guten Tag,* Miss Chamliss."

"Rudi!" It was good to see the boy, and she walked over to him. He was proudly displaying a new barbershop haircut. When she commented on it, he answered with embarrassment.

"It is for the dance tonight. I am taking Greta Kleinschmidt."

"I see. And is she pretty, Rudi?"

"Not so pretty as you, Miss Chamliss. But it seems you have found a sweetheart already."

"Perhaps so."

Sarah climbed onto the stone wall next to Rudi. "You stayed away so long," she scolded him with a smile. "What else was I to do? You did not want to come by."

"Oh, no!" he answered seriously. "I did not want to stay away. It was because of Count von Steinbock. He spoke to my mother, telling her that you might wish me to take you to someplace very dangerous, and I was not to do so on any account."

"The Ice Castle?"

"Yes, I suppose so. But you know of it now!"

"Yes. The count told me about it. And about his brother.

And I learned that Minna was there when Helmuth met his fate."

"Yes—this is all true. You see? You will find out everything you wish to know in a little time."

"Yes, Rudi. But there is nothing more I can learn in Feldkirch of Robert."

"You're not thinking of going to the Ice Castle!" Rudi shouted, jumping from the wall to face her.

"Yes."

"But you must not! Perhaps they did not tell you what sort of place it is. My own cousin, Johann, was killed there."

"It was explained to me," Sarah said quietly. "But let's speak no more of it today. It's Oktoberfest, and everyone is so jolly."

They made it a pact, and together wandered the countryside, watching the brightly decorated carts of the peasants pouring into Feldkirch from the surrounding mountains—perhaps the last time they would be able to make the trip before winter closed the high passes.

They called out merrily to the passing parade. Children sat on the tailgates, waving back, singing festive songs.

Some of the carts were heaped full of apples or pears; Rudi pointed out the wagon of Herr Fromm whose apples always won the competition.

The people wore the colorful Tyrolian traditional costume, the girls in laced bodice dresses and fur caps, most carrying huge bouquets of wildflowers. The men, leading prize livestock behind them, wore green felt caps, coats, and flowered vests.

The cattle, many of them, were decorated with flowers sewn onto their bridles. A yellow-haired girl tossed Sarah a bright bouquet as they passed in their cart.

Red gillyflowers, yellow John's-worts, and vivid blue harebells made up the bouquet, along with sky-blue chicory and hundreds of blackeyed susans. Sarah waved a thanks and cradled the flowers to her.

The streets of Feldkirch were filled with visitors. Some of the shops, like the Bruenigs' candy shop, were taking advantage of the influx of people, others had closed early, not wanting to miss the festivities.

The band had already arrived from Landeck and had set up on the pavilion. Long strings of Japanese lanterns stretched across the dance floor.

The tuba player with the black mustache—the one Renate admired so much—played a few practice notes on his instrument, but declined to strike up the band, to the disappointment of the crowd which wandered past.

"Tonight, my friends," he called out, answering a few groans. "You may dance all night. Until we are out of breath and your feet are worn off!"

"Step back!"

Rudi's warning came just in time. For a huge Hispano-Suiza motorcar came racing around the corner. Sarah jumped backward, her bouquet falling into the gutter to be crushed beneath the automobile's wheels.

Rudi waved a small threatening fist after the car. Sarah only stood, catching her breath, watching after it.

There had been four men in the car, all in blue-gray uniforms, wearing spiked helmets.

"Who were they?" she asked breathlessly.

"Germans," Rudi said with disgust. He stooped to pick up the battered, bruised bunch of flowers. He handed them to her, mostly stems with their heads missing, bruised and flattened. Sarah had to laugh as she accepted the flowers from Rudi.

He laughed as well, shaking his head. But he promised seriously, "I shall get a new bouquet for you. A bigger one, prettier yet."

"It's all right, Rudi," Sarah said, wiping a tear of laughter away from the corner of her eye. "It wasn't your fault."

"These Prussians," he said angrily. "As if they had been

put on earth for the benefit of the rest of mankind."

They walked on. Now that it was late afternoon, Sarah wished to return to the Huchtings'. Renate wanted her to help with her hair, and Sarah wished to clean up herself.

"But where would they have been going?" Sarah asked thoughtfully.

"The Germans?" Rudi blinked. "I don't know. The way they were going leads to Steinbock Castle. Perhaps to visit the Count von Steinbock, or the grand duchess. She sometimes has visitors—important visitors. But never before German officers, I do not think."

"I know Eric attended the university at Cologne," Sarah said, blushing slightly as she recognized that Rudi was smiling. "I mean the Count von Steinbock," she said hastily.

"I am happy that you know him so well that you call the count by his given name," Rudi shrugged.

"And I believe that Helmuth was also educated in Germany. Probably, as you say, they are friends of the Steinbock family."

"Rude friends," Rudi commented. "They might have killed you. These gentlemen!" he made a sour expression. "But not Eric Mann," he added quickly. "He does not ride over his people's backs like some feudal lord."

"No. But I wonder, Rudi, will you save a dance for me tonight? My partner may not show up, if he has company."

"I will save a dance, Fraulein Chamliss," Rudi promised sincerely, "but I would not worry. He will show up. No man would keep you waiting."

With that Rudi was gone, and Sarah turned to the Huchtings' door.

Renate wore her hair in a popular style, long braids, which swept past her waist nearly eighteen inches, were coiled on top of her head in intricate design, interwoven with delicate yellow and white edelweiss.

Freshly bathed in rose water, wearing the ivory chiffon,

she was still a handsome woman. At least Sarah thought so, and so did Hans. More than once he gave his wife a secret kiss.

"It's the cider he's been at," Renate said.

"You can't attribute it all to the cider," Sarah replied. "You'd better be careful tonight."

Renate laughed. "And you, Fraulein Chamliss. Whatever I bring out in an old man like Hans, you are sure to bring out in the young men."

"It is a long winter ahead," Hans said, having just come in the door. "These young mountaineers grow bold, wanting one sweet memory to warm the long nights."

"But she may have an escort, one they will not trifle with," Renate said.

"Rudi Uhlmann?" Hans laughed.

"Someone of slightly more stature," Renate said, enjoying the teasing.

"Oh, I see," Hans said.

"But how will you know your sweetheart tonight, Sarah? All of the young men will be in masks?"

"I think I will know him," she replied. "Besides, there was something he said. A hint."

Renate smiled and continued packing her tarts into the wicker basket, humming an old Tyrolian folksong.

Eric had said nothing really. *You will play the devil recognizing me.* She felt certain that he would be wearing a devil's mask. Anyway, there would be no mistaking him. That long-striding walk, the set of his broad shoulders, the graceful movements of his hands, the tilt of his head. Things no mask could hide.

By nightfall the town had filled to overflowing with visitors. So many that it seemed incredible the surrounding mountains could have hidden them all. There was much loud laughter, yodling, and singing. Maidens danced arm in arm, three abreast, down the main street, their cheeks flushed with the cool air, the excitement.

A glorious sunset played among the wide stretching clouds, long strands of orange and purple bleeding across the broad valley. Here and there a brilliant star peered hesitantly through the deep violet of the sky. The white buildings of Feldkirch took on a dreamlike aspect, deeply shadowed, tinted rose on the western walls.

Masked men and women danced by, some drunk, all merry, their inhibitions shattered by liquor, their confidence bolstered by the concealing masks. But there was no ugliness, no fighting. Just a letting go of those burdensome emotions too dangerous to be pent up the winter long.

The pavilion sparkled with the paper lanterns; red and golden, green and blue, they swayed in the gentle breeze. The dancers swirled in close, hectic circles as the band blistered an intoxicated, charging polka tune.

Feet trampled the wooden dance floor, skirts flew wide in dizzy spirals, the tuba carried above it all—the man with the black mustache, true to his word, and his formidable reputation, blatted through his bulky instrument, cheeks and forehead red and perspiring, eyes distended as he gave them all their money's worth and more, the constant beat of the tuba setting the frantic pace for the brass band, and for all of the celebration.

"I must go see the livestock," Hans said. He wore a monkey's mask back on top of his head. His gait was already unsteady, and Renate warned him.

"See that the livestock are not in a cider jug."

"How you scold me," Hans said. Then, impishly he pulled down his mask and went off, dancing as he moved, through the crowd.

"I'll not see him again," Renate said disapprovingly, "until the farewell dance. Or until Karl Flaig brings him home."

Rudi came past, partly proud, partly red-faced with a slender, tall young girl on his arm. He nodded to Sarah, but seemed incapable of speaking. His cheeks were quite red.

"Renate!"

A huge, straw-haired man wearing a bull mask lumbered up to them. He pulled up his mask. "It is I, Karl Kesselring."

"Karl," Renate said nervously, her hand going to her throat. "It must have been . . ."

"*Vierzehn Jahre.* But don't say how long it has been. Tonight it seems those fourteen years have never passed. You will dance with me, *nicht wahr?* You look so pretty tonight, Renate, and for one night let us be young again. I mean no disrespect; I ask only for one dance."

"Sarah?"

"Dance, Renate. I have seen a friend I wish to talk to. Dance," she responded.

Together they whirled away, Renate and the hulking mountaineer. Whatever their past might have been mattered not, but now they danced, happily, caught up in the color and sounds of the night.

Father Bruno stood near the cider table, chatting with a thin, red-haired man. Sarah went up to him.

"Fraulein Chamliss! So good to see you here," the priest said, giving her his hand.

"And you, Father Bruno."

"Excuse us, please, Herr Langer," Father Bruno said, bowing to the red-haired man who stepped away, hoisting a cider mug.

"Won't you have a glass of cider, Sarah?" the priest asked.

"If it won't turn my feet to stones," Sarah answered, undecided. "I mean to dance before the night is through."

"No," the priest laughed, "you see I indulge myself. A quart may turn your feet to stone, but a pint will grow wings on your heels."

He gave Sarah a pewter cup filled with warm cider. Topped with cinnamon and nutmeg, it warmed her throat and heart as she drank it. The night had come in suddenly, and now there were no lights to be seen beyond the pavilion. Briskly the dancers spun and floated across the floor. The tuba man worked more fluidly now as the band played a Ländler.

Rudi danced by awkwardly, with Greta Kleinschmidt. Beyond them, wistfully, Helga Kroeber, her belly ripe with child, watched the dancers.

"A sad story," the priest said, nodding toward Helga. "But with a happy ending, I hope. Soon her boyfriend will be granted leave from the army. They are to be married."

Sarah nodded dreamily. The cider had warmed her completely, and she smiled mildly at Renate who danced by with a man she did not recognize. Several times, lurking around the perimeter of the pavilion, she noticed Herr Flaig, the police captain, keeping watch on the wild mountaineers.

"But I forget," Father Bruno said suddenly, "I wished to tell you something."

"Of importance?"

"I can't say. But the man who came to look at the inscriptions. He is here tonight. Just over there, near the bandstand."

Sarah turned and peered into the lights, past the moving crowd of dancers. For a moment she saw him, and then he was gone.

"Did you see him? Do you know him?" Father Bruno asked.

"I did see him, but I don't know who he is," she answered.

But she had seen him before.

But where?

And then she had it—in Liechtenstein, and again on the platform at the border. The Englishman with the sharp nose, large dark mustache, and constant pipe. He had spoken to her then, warning her—was it a warning?—that she would find it "quite chilly in Feldkirch."

Now he was here. And he had studied the inscriptions. Who then, was he?

"Sarah?" the priest said, studying her questioningly.

"I'm sorry. I believe I might have seen that man before. Did you see where he went?"

"No. He seems to have vanished."

"I would like to have spoken to him," she said regretfully.

"Enjoy the dance, Sarah. I'll look for him, and alert some of the men."

"No," she said hastily, "perhaps we had better not. This is all suddenly complicated to me, Father. Too much has happened and continues to happen. I think before we bring others into our mystery we should understand what purpose we serve."

"I will look around then," Father Bruno agreed. "But discreetly."

Before she had a chance to answer, a great, thick-chested mountain man had taken her hand and whirled her onto the floor. Laughing he spoke to her as they danced. She understood not a word of it.

It felt good to dance, she had to admit to herself. The lights were spinning. The cider may have affected me some, she thought. Renate danced by, hardly noticing her.

The music seemed overwhelming, the press of the crowd annoying as she tried to free herself of the wild mountaineer. He was having none of it, so they danced again. Sarah kept her eyes away from the floor. She thought she saw the Englishman once again. Then she saw the long, familiar shape of the Daimler automobile up the narrow alley to one side. Eric had come, then.

She wished desperately for him. The mountaineer spun like a dervish, guffawing heartily as he clumped like a madman across the dance floor, the music spinning in her ears. Then it stopped.

The tempo of the music altered and broke. He walked across the dance floor, a red devil's mask on his face, his lean body moving lithely. Then she was in his arms and they swayed together to the lilting melody of a waltz, Sarah's heart pounding violently.

It's the cider, she thought. But it wasn't.

In the embrace of this man she felt a thrill of electricity, a racing impulse which caused her blood to pound and then seem to drain from her head, making her giddy, uncertain. She tried to speak, but her mouth made no intelligible sound. Never before . . . never.

They danced the waltz, and another, silently, the music bonding them together, their feet in perfect, unpracticed coordination.

The Japanese lanterns glowed now with a soft haze. Everything was as if seen through a thin film of gauze. The stars, far above, glinted brilliantly through the open pavilion roof.

There was nothing she could have done if he forced her to dance forever in that way. Nothing at all. His strong arms were at once overpowering and yielding, every motion deft and exactly patterned to hers. They danced, and without a word being spoken she was conquered. Totally.

Finally the music halted, the spell collapsed.

"I must speak to you," he said.

"My God!"

Sarah drew back, her hands to her face. It was not Eric von Steinbock. Who then?

She stood numbed with humiliation and confusion. Then some glimmer of recognition flared in her memory. Eric was coming now, striding angrily across the pavilion. She reached out suddenly and threw up his mask.

"Bramante!"

Whose voice it was, she never knew. But there could have been no greater panic if the pavilion had caught fire.

Carlo Bramante did not hesitate. With three leaps he was to the cider table, and over it in an avalanche of tumbling cups and jugs.

Eric glanced quickly at Sarah, then lunged after the bandit, a handgun filling his fist. There were shrieks and cries of alarm. Frau Shirer fainted dead away.

The band had never stopped playing, but for a single moment, and now the brassy sounds continued to ring out as the bizarre chase continued.

Men in masks, goats, devils, bulls and clowns stumbled over each other in a frenzy to run down Bramante. Police Captain Flaig appeared out of nowhere, with two uniformed police at his side. He shouted directions out frantically, rage streaking his features.

Helga Kroeber shouted over and over again:

"Kill him! Kill him!"

Bramante was out of the pavilion and into the shadows before anyone had truly reacted. In seconds he was up a nearby alley, dancing past a couple secluded in a doorway. Shocked, they peered out in time to see him cut through the hostelry at the end of the street, and they pointed him out to the pursuit led by Eric and Herr Flaig and his men.

By now the band played to an empty floor as half the town streamed out into the alleys and avenues, some snatching up pitchforks and clubs. Torchlight filled the sky, and violent curses sounded.

At the edge of town, near the mill, there were dozens of haystacks, and Bramante dove into one.

"There!" Flaig shouted. He had seen the desperate move of the bandit and he at once lined his officers up.

"Fire! Fire at will!" he shouted recklessly, himself waving a revolver. The policemen filled the night with the thunder of their volley. The haystack was peppered with gunshots.

"Look out!" Flaig shouted. The haystack had burst suddenly into flame, which then spread to a nearby haystack and another until six in all formed crackling bonfires, sparks dancing high into the air, the entire north end of town illuminated with the deadly light.

"Where is he?" Eric panted.

"In there, sir," Flaig said, gesturing with his pistol. The firelight glistened on his perspiration-soaked face, drawing a waxen mask—an ugly, distorted mask of hatred. "At least I hope so. I hope so."

At the first volley Sarah had rushed toward the mill; already the fires lighted the black night with golden sparks, the flames roaring ominously.

She became lost at first and had to backtrack. Working up a narrow alleyway she passed a cart. The driver called out to her.

"It's nothing, Fraulein! Do not hurry."

She looked up to see the black bearded driver snap his whip and urge the team away, rolling rapidly across the cobblestoned road.

She knew him immediately. Ferrara! And the irregularly shaped canvas package in the wagon bed? She watched after the wagon until it disappeared around a bend in the road, then she walked slowly toward the fire.

It had nearly gone out. Men with pitchforks searched through the ashes, the heat blistering their skin, soot covering their faces and festival finery.

"Sarah."

Eric was beside her and he put an arm around her.

"You're trembling, dear. It must have been awful for you."

"There's nothing here, Herr Captain Flaig!"

"Look again then!" the police captain sputtered. "He was there, I know it! Look deeper!"

The worker shrugged and turned back to the smoldering haystack.

"Nothing," he said after five more minutes.

Sarah stood rigidly, her head swimming, her heart

pounding violently. Bramante was not there. She had seen him make his escape, but she could not bring herself to say anything. That feeling still lingered. That feeling as they danced, as they touched. But it was nonsense. He was a criminal, a thug. She supposed one could be attracted in that way to a criminal, a beast. Yet . . .

"They will find him," Eric promised her.

"Yes."

"But your hands are icy," he said, lifting her chin. "And you tremble still. This does it! You cannot stay here in Feldkirch any longer. You will stay at Steinbock. Minna will just have to sulk."

"I could not, Eric."

"You must. This is too dangerous. These Trentinos grow too bold."

"It would not be proper."

"Of course it would. Mother is there, and we have friends visiting. It would be entirely proper," he said looking into her eyes, smiling slightly. "I promise."

"I can't . . ."

"Think on it," he said, putting a finger to her lips. "Only think on it, Sarah. Please?"

"All right," she nodded.

Then for a moment Eric was gone, speaking quietly to Herr Captain Flaig, gesturing back toward town. Sarah hardly heard her slip up beside her.

"I would accept the invitation," the somehow familiar voice said. "Go to Steinbock Castle. That is where Robert went."

Sarah's head came around suddenly, but already the girl had slipped off into the shadows—a familiar shape. It took Sarah awhile to place the figure, the voice.

It was Katrinka, the Avarian girl.

Eight

As if the festival had broken a spell, or some lingering prayer had ended, winter came suddenly upon Feldkirch. Snow slanted through the gray, outstretched arms of the elms, filming the ground, the roadways, and fields with white. There was no more talk of cider or dancing, flower arrangements or dresses, beaux and song. But only of survival.

The winters come in hard in the Tyrol, snow accumulating slowly in the high passes, building avalanches, lying in wait along the flanks of the Alps. Wood for fires is difficult to find, and forage for the livestock, and food for the children. The time would come when the villagers, and especially the mountain folk, would huddle together near cold hearths, cursing the everlasting gray sky.

It was still early in the winter cycle. This snow was the first to stick, and there was no weight behind the high clouds. The thunder, far from being a menacing roar, was a chuckling deep in the soft gullet of a nearly windless storm.

Sarah walked the bare knolls, the hood of her coat dusted with snow, her eyes searching the Alps through the whey of the morning.

Through the drifting swirls of snow she watched it suddenly appear, silently, then again be enveloped by the closing curtain of white. A key? An open door? Or a blind alley? Steinbock Castle's slender spires cut the pennants of low-lying cloud. A fortress which had outlived its time, a cold and cheerless home.

The girl, flitting like a shadow to her side, had said—Go! That is where Robert went. But could there have been truth in her words?

Eric had no qualms about her visiting Steinbock. In fact, he had insisted on it, even asking her to stay. But then, perhaps it was not Eric she had to dread. There was Minna, her coal-black, fearful eyes flashing as she cursed her. And the grand duchess, of whom she knew next to nothing. Except that there was steel in her, and a fierce aristocratic stance.

There was one other thing to be considered. A very simple item, yet one inexplicable. A gold British sovereign.

The coin had been in the hut where Katrinka and her mother lived. How had it come to be there? A poor Austrian gypsy—no matter how royally blooded—had no means of obtaining such a coin. Yet Katrinka had one. She had concealed one. She had been angry at Sarah's discovery of it.

There was, however, a Britisher at that moment in Feldkirch. A secretive, will-o'-the-wisp man without a name, without a reason for being in Feldkirch.

Could there be a connection between the man with the pipe and the Avarians? If so, what could it possibly have to do with Robert?

As she strode the long hillsides, the snow drifting in soft whorls, she became certain of only one point in this maze of inquiry—she had to go to the Ice Castle. Robert had gone there. All of the clues pointed in that direction, and toward Steinbock.

There could, therefore, be but one course of action. And then again it appeared, punctuating her decision . . .

baroque spires, frosted with blue-gray snow, long, tedious battlements useless for defense, absurd as decoration, bold in design, but lacking in architectural execution— Steinbock Castle. It seemed to be peering oddly through the parting snow flurries, then withdrawing, as if it wished to do so. Frightening, gargantuan, utterly weird in the whiteness—what was its real character? She meant to know. She meant to know before the snows came again.

Deep in the sheltered valley called Semmering, the small band of men huddled around the open fire, blankets thrown over their heads, rifles across their laps.

Silone clambered up onto the lookout point at the Emperor's Nose and relieved Rovato. The slender man's teeth were chattering; he nodded a head toward the fire below.

"Anything to eat?"

"Not much. Goat meat," Silone shrugged.

"In Naples right now," Rovato began, but the look on Silone's face caused him to shut his mouth. As he climbed down he continued his thought, however. In Naples it would be warm. And Anna Ghiberti would be drying her long dark hair on the balcony, watching the fishing ships in the harbor, their multicolored sails billowing in the soft breeze . . .

He pulled his collar more tightly around his neck. That bear, Ferrara, glanced up as he came into the camp. Bramante kept his head down, speaking softly to his chief lieutenant.

"You must not have made it clear, Mirko," he muttered to Ferrara.

"I made it clear, Carlo. Perfectly. The girl has more spunk than good sense."

"It cannot continue," Carlo Bramante said, rising suddenly.

"No," Ferrara agreed with a heavy shake of his head. "I

have heard that she may go there."

"To Steinbock?" Bramante shouted.

"Yes."

"That will not do . . . no! If the girl will not see things sensibly, we will have to explain things more definitely. I will not have her in Feldkirch, especially not in Steinbock."

"She will not go," Ferrara shrugged.

"I would hope you are wrong, Mirko. It would not do to have her witness the murder." The bandit chief turned suddenly to face the other man, the one who sat silently near the trunk of the lightning-scarred, broken spruce, his eyes watching Bramante. "Would it, Robert?" he demanded.

But Robert Chamliss did not answer; there was no answer he could make. He only bowed his head more deeply, praying that she would go herself. Go before it was too late, the unwinding of events trapping her inextricably, crushing her.

Suddenly he cast his head back, Bramante and Ferrara watching him. But he did not speak, he only cursed the cold skies, the Avarian inscriptions, and that damnable inspiration of a crazed nature—the Ice Castle.

Nine

Two matched grays, each with a white splotch on its flank, drew the phaeton along the winding road between the long colonnades of Italian cypress trees. Sarah rested comfortably in the back seat, a lap robe over her knees, enjoying the brisk ride through the Austrian countryside. Eagerly she anticipated the end of the journey; yet she also feared her arrival at Steinbock Castle. What she would find, how she would be received, she could not say. At least, she thought, her search had motion now, direction, and a point of concentration.

The driver was a slight, wooden-looking man who had taken her baggage with hardly a word. With gloved hands he guided the magnificent horses stiffly. Patches of blue snow still filled the deep vales, and lay on the shadowed side of trees and huge boulders.

They passed a dilapidated farm where a woman, bundled heavily in wool, lifted a weary head from her chores to watch the phaeton appear, flicker through the long, crooked shadows of the cypress along the roadway, and disappear over the crest.

One turn and then another, a dip through a deep, wooded dell, the clatter of the horses hoofs across a covered wooden bridge, the sudden flash of color and sunlight as they emerged, and they were there.

It hardly seemed forbidding this close and in daylight, but it was much larger than she had imagined. Steinbock Castle—aloof, massive, a whitish pink in the oddly filtered sunlight. It sprouted from the earth like a monument to a forgotten age of chivalry, of knighthood, barbarity, feudal oppression.

The courtyard was muddy, the roses, unpruned, forlorn around the high white wall. The coach clattered on a ways farther, passing through a great, iron-grated portal, and beyond to the massive, oaken door of the main house. No one came out to greet them, no face showed in the empty windows towering overhead.

"The count . . .?"

"The Count von Steinbock has departed for the day," the driver responded in a voice so dry, it seemed it might crack from long disuse.

Hurriedly he unloaded her baggage, and, leaving Sarah to watch, he whipped the horses around the long stone building which once had been a winery, and disappeared. A fine welcome. But what had she expected? Whatever she was, she was no welcome visitor. That had been made clear to her. Taking in her breath she marched to the door and rapped loudly, three times with the heavy knocker— an odd, twisted brazen eagle.

There was no response. Sarah stepped back and looked up into the high reaches of the castle. Nearly fifty feet above her a small window filled for an instant with color, then emptied once more.

The hillsides beyond the castle were bleak, barren, snow clinging to the craggy reaches, filling the clefts. A vineyard, long untended, filled several acres on the lower knolls. A pine forest closed in the valley to the east; several crows could be seen wheeling in the clear sky, cawing hoarsely to each other.

100

The door burst open with a creaking thud.

Minna, eyes wild, hair tangled, wearing a red silk dress half unbuttoned, stood there.

"You!" Minna panted, hunched forward like an old woman. Her eyes moved constantly, searching Sarah's face and dress. She touched her tongue to her lips.

"Hello, Minna," Sarah said mildly, though her heart was pounding. The young noblewoman was a pathetic sight. She doubted Minna had washed since their last encounter.

"Go away!" Minna stood suddenly straight and added haughtily, "You will not call me Minna. I am the Countess von Steinbock."

"Yes, Countess. Forgive me."

Over Minna's shoulder Sarah saw an older woman, apparently a servant, rushing to the door. She had a kind, round face, and a look of consternation played on her small, pursed mouth.

"Countess Minna!" she called, hastening to the door. "Dear Countess, you should not have come down." She seemed suddenly aware of Sarah's presence and glanced at her quizzically.

"I am Sarah Chamliss. The count . . ."

"You are she?" the servant said oddly. "I expected . . . never mind. We beg your pardon, Miss Chamliss."

"May I come in? Is the count here?"

"Please, please come in. I am Gertrude," she said, backing out of the doorway, still holding Minna, whose eyes blazed.

"You know what she is?" Minna hissed. Gertrude paid no attention to her, however.

"The count has taken his other guests hunting, Miss Chamliss. He apologizes for not being here; however, he could not delay the expedition and did not wish for you to travel our roads at night."

"Otto!" Gertrude called into the interior of the house. "Otto!"

After a minute a thin man, hobbled by a bad leg, arrived.

"The countess, Otto!" Gertrude said. Then she whispered something to the man.

"*Ja! Natürlich!*" He glanced casually at Sarah, his pale eyes blank, then turned to Minna. "Come, my Minna—you must go to your room now."

"She's Eric's harlot," Minna confided. Then she shrieked it: "Harlot!"

"Minna. Please." Then the girl broke into tears, sudden pathetic tears, and she allowed Otto to lead her away as docilely as a child.

"It is one of her bad days," Gertrude apologized with a shake of the head which seemed to indicate that most of Minna's days were bad days.

Sarah started to answer, but she became aware of another figure. On the long, curving staircase to the left of the massive foyer a woman in blue silk stood perfectly erect, her silver-blue hair exactly arranged, her eyes utterly cold as she examined Sarah minutely.

The grand duchess carried herself with all of the centuries of dignity her bloodline had infused. That she was nobility no one could doubt. Her face was seamless, yet rigid; haughty yet intelligent. She wore a single, massive emerald ring on her left hand, a matching necklace flowed down across her breast.

Sarah searched for words. She had begun to curtsy, to introduce herself, yet the grand duchess's sudden, electric voice cut her off.

"The Czar Nicholas room, Gertrude."

"Yes, Your Grace," Gertrude replied. She quickly picked up Sarah's luggage and moved to the smaller stairwell at the rear of the foyer.

As Sarah followed Gertrude, she looked back. The

102

grand duchess stood stock-still, as if, cast of marble, she could remain that way forever. From upstairs a sudden, terrible scream echoed.

"Minna," Gertrude said under her voice.

Sarah went quietly up the staircase which was bordered with miniature paintings from the fifteenth and sixteenth centuries.

"What is the Czar Nicholas room?" she asked as Gertrude paused on the landing to catch her breath.

"Just a bedroom, Ma'am. The Czar once slept there. The old Czar, Nicholas I. In 1849, I believe. The castle is full of history, excitement, Miss Chamliss," she paused thoughtfully, "though not much recently."

"Does no one come now?"

"Few, Ma'am. Very few." Gertrude continued up the staircase to the third story where a narrow, elbow-shaped hall bent to the south. There were no windows but those high on the wall where once there had been scaffolding for archers.

Suddenly she swung the heavy, black door open, and Sarah found herself in a rectangular, arched-ceiling room with an oval window. An oversized, posted bed sat against one wall, a bureau against another; and over the fireplace a matched, crossed set of swords with Toledo steel blades, fully engraved with figures of combatants and wild game. Another door beside the fireplace was sealed off.

Sarah waited as Gertrude unpacked her luggage and put the clothing, carefully folded, into the massive bureau, which was made of birdseye maple. Shutting the door quietly, she asked the maid:

"You say there are few visitors to Steinbock Castle. Then you must remember my brother Robert?"

"Why no, Ma'am," Gertrude said definitely. "There has been no one here for over a year but these Prussian gentlemen who are visiting now."

"A tall man, dark haired, soft spoken. An American?"

"No." She said it positively, looking Sarah directly in the eyes. "No one like that. Not ever. And I've been in Steinbock's service forty-three years, Ma'am."

"I'm sorry. Perhaps I was wrong, Gertrude," she said, remembering that time to pronounce the final "e" in the maid's name as the Germans do. "It was an impression I had been given."

"I am sorry. But he was not here. No." She shook her head again. "Now—by your leave? I have other tasks."

"Certainly, Gertrude. Please go about your business."

The maid smiled pleasantly, but there was a lingering hesitation in her eyes even as she closed the huge door to the room.

Perhaps she should have said nothing. But after all, there was nothing to fear. Nothing at all. Minna's hysterical cries again echoed through all the vast palace until finally a door was closed, and the sounds muffled.

Shaken, again disoriented, Sarah went to the window. Oval, set in leaded partitions, it was ancient and quite beautiful, catching the late light and transmitting a peaceful blueness to the interior of the room. Perhaps the czar had gazed from the window, toward the beautiful, gurgling rill which ran through the apple orchards; the Emperor of the Russians might have studied the looming Alps meditatively himself, letting his gaze fall to the valley where the broken cider press, the dilapidated, tumbled stone mill sat among the imported walnut trees. Where . . .

Robert!

She looked again, clutching the curtains, her eyes closed. When she opened them again he was still there. The tall man, dark hair mussed by the wind, his eyes on her window . . . or so it seemed.

"Robert!"

She called from the window, and her heart went with her words. "Robert!"

The man turned slightly away, looking inquisitively into the orchard. Then, slowly, without concern, he began to walk away.

"Robert!" she called once more, and it seemed the man far below stiffened once, nearly stopping, then went on.

Not waiting to snatch up her coat or hat she sprang from the room, her feet echoing through the narrow hallway. Then she was at the steps, and she fairly flew down them, looking neither right nor left. She burst through the foyer. Otto, who had been returning from somewhere with an empty, silver tray, stepped quickly from her path, his eyes wide.

Sarah burst into the open air of the courtyard. Which way now? Left—she turned and ran, her feet burning, her chest tight with the exertion. She found, at last, a low gate leading into a garden, and beyond to a path which wound past the wall of the outer ramparts toward the orchards.

She ran, the tears stinging her eyes, her heart a pounding sledgehammer, her legs growing rubbery, her lungs burning caverns, until she came around the corner of the granary. Then she stopped, terror-stricken, exhausted to collapse.

The stranger was before her, rifle in his hands, a cruel-looking, blond man with a savage scar across his cheek from eye socket to jawbone. He blocked her path.

"What is this? Hold up here!" he commanded.

Then another armed man appeared. A square-shouldered, stocky man with the coldest eyes Sarah had ever seen, he wore a blood-spattered white shirt.

"What have we here, Hermann?"

"Please," Sarah gasped. "My brother."

The shorter man stretched out a hand toward her shoulder. There was dried blood under his fingernails, a splotch of red on his forearm.

"What have you done!" she cried. The day spun crazily, the sky turning dark, the turrets of Steinbock flashing past as her legs collapsed beneath her and the faces of the men, wide-eyed, filled the sky.

And then Eric was there. Strong, tender, he went to his knee and lifted her head, placing it gently on his knee. "My God! Sarah, what is it? Dear Sarah!"

There was another long minute when she felt she would cave in completely; the whirling star-bursting sky blackened, but she held Eric's arm and he drew her from the abyss of her dark mind.

"It was Robert," she said quietly. "He was in the orchard." Again she became aware of the two blood-stained men beside her. Her head snapped up, her eyes searching.

"My friends," Eric said. "Hermann Glick and Herr Field Marshal Klaus Eisner. But what has happened to worry you so, Sarah? I am sorry our hunt was delayed."

Slowly the haze cleared from her consciousness, and Sarah perceived the two men, and the others of their retinue more clearly. Six other men waited, their faces faintly amused. They had five great stags at their feet, trophies of the hunt. And the blood on the arms of Glick and Eisner was only the blood of the magnificent Steinbock stags.

"When we heard you calling," Hermann Glick explained, "we came running with our weapons. I am afraid we frightened you still more. If so, I apologize."

"But you spoke of Robert," Eric said with concern, helping Sarah to her feet. "What have you seen?"

"In the orchard . . . I saw him, Eric. Truly."

"The lady's brother is missing," Eric explained to the Prussians. "In the orchard, you say. But where?" His eyes searched the hillside carefully.

"He left. He walked away. Please don't think me foolish, Eric! But I know it was Robert. I saw him from my window."

"I don't think you foolish," he said gravely, "yet I wonder why he would walk away from you, Sarah. Perhaps you would like to look closer."

"Yes," she said breathlessly. "Please."

They walked to the orchard, the leaves crumbling underfoot, Glick and Eisner still carrying their hunting rifles.

"Here!" Sarah said suddenly. Eric came up to where she stood, trembling finger pointing at the footprints in the soft, dark earth. "He *was* here."

"Someone . . ." Eric agreed. Carefully he turned and followed the footprints. Then the tracks faded out, near a ramshackle hut on the edge of the orchard grounds.

"Wait here," Eric said, but he had taken no more than two steps when the other man appeared.

Slight, dark haired, dressed in baggy trousers and white shirt, the man carried a pruning saw in one hand.

"Ernst!" Eric laughed. Startled, the man stared at the count, eyes agog. "This is our gardener," Eric explained.

"Sir," the little man said, bowing. Unused to such attention, he watched the other men and their weapons apprehensively.

"Were you in the orchard just now, Ernst?"

"Yes, sir. Of course! That is where my work is. In the orchard. Have I done wrong, Herr Count Mann?"

"Of course not, Ernst. Not at all. Don't worry. The lady thought you were someone else. Did you see her?"

"Yes, sir. Yes, sir. I heard her calling and I saw her in the house. But she was not calling to me. I saw no one else, so I turned and came back to sharpen my saw."

"But it couldn't have been you," Sarah said passionately. "I was sure . . ."

Eric took her gently by the shoulders. "Sarah. Once, when we first met, you even thought I was your brother. Remember? At the church rectory. It is simply your imagination, your tired eyes and mind, your strong desire to see Robert everywhere."

"That is all?" Field Marshal Eisner asked jovially. "The end of our little mystery?"

"Yes, Klaus," Eric replied. "So it seems. Miss Chamliss has been somewhat overwrought. Her stay in Feldkirch has been something of a trial."

"I am sorry to hear it is so." He straightened his tunic and pulled on his mustache. "For myself, it has been most enjoyable in your little valley. A fine hunt, a friendly host. But now, you must excuse us, Eric, Miss Chamliss. We must bathe and prepare for our journey home."

"Certainly."

Sarah watched as the two Germans walked back to Steinbock, laughing heartily over what she could not hear. The gardener, Ernst, still stood there trembling.

"Go on about your work, Ernst," Eric said. "I did not mean to interfere with your work."

Ernst bowed curtly, eyeing Sarah curiously once more before departing.

"I am sorry we began your visit in such a way," Eric said. "Come, let me show you the true hospitality of Steinbock. For tonight, put away your worries, and enjoy my wine, my food, my home."

Gratefully Sarah allowed him to put a steadying arm around her as they walked back toward the high bleak structure, Steinbock Castle.

Yet her mind was hardly at ease. Her eyes had not been so anxious to see Robert that she had invented his presence in the orchard. At least she did not think so.

She said nothing of it to Eric, yet she had not failed to notice one conflicting particular. Ernst, the gardener, wore round-toed, worn brogans.

The footprints in the orchard were those of nearly new, pointed-toed military boots.

Ferrara's report was terse, sharp. Bramante listened attentively, eyes closed, hands clasped as the bandits clustered around the fire. When Ferrara was finished, Bramante sighed heavily.

"Well?" Ferrara asked.

"There is no choice," Bramante said. The bandit leader's eyes went again to the American. "Robert Chamliss must die."

Ten

It was a bitterly cold night, but in the stately royal dining room of Steinbock Castle, a great oak log roared in the mammoth fireplace, lighting and warming the deep room.

Sarah was seated at the center of the twelve-foot table, directly opposite Minna. At the head of the table was the grand duchess, at the foot, Eric Mann.

Otto moved silently around the table, filling the wine glasses, then departing as Gertrude arrived with the vichyssoise.

"Had I known she would be here," Minna said flippantly, "I would have eaten in my room. I don't care for this one, Eric."

"Why don't you go to your room then, dear Minna," Eric suggested wearily.

The grand duchess, elegant in silver brocade, said nothing as she watched the interplay.

"It's cold up there," Minna said, pouting.

"Then be good, dear," Eric said in a low voice. He glanced at Sarah in obvious embarrassment. "This is one of the original rooms of Steinbock," he said. "It dates to Baron Huebner's time—the thirteenth century."

"It's impressive," Sarah answered, studying the great stone arches, the three-foot thick timbers strung between the flared trusses.

"It's falling apart," the grand duchess said dryly, sipping her claret.

"It's cold," Minna complained.

"A part of the price we pay for our station," Eric said with a smile. "The peasants live in cozy, warm cottages while we shiver the winter long in this stone icebox. Ah, rank," he sighed, finishing his own wine.

"Eric imagines we shall all one day be of the same class," the grand duchess said. With the faintest of smiles she added, "We would be no better than you."

"Not I!" Minna exclaimed, her voice frightened, defiant. "I shall never be a peasant."

"It wouldn't be so bad," Eric told her. "In America everyone is a peasant, isn't that so, Sarah?"

"We prefer to think we are all royalty," Sarah replied softly.

"There," Minna complained bitterly, "one is even denied by law the right to a title! Think of it—it's in their . . . constitution. What rot."

Minna's hair dipped into her soup as she hunched over the table. Someone had buttoned her dress and attempted to comb back her hair, but it had all come loose again.

Otto brought in a rack of lamb and Eric carved it deftly, the knife flashing against the steel, then moving as a surgeon's scalpel in neat, practiced cuts.

"My son is too modern," the grand duchess lamented, her breast heaving with a sigh.

"Not I, Mother," Minna hastened to say. "I would never bring peasants to dinner."

"No, of course not, Minna," the grand duchess said frostily, looking at Sarah who blushed slightly and cut her meat.

"If this is going to continue . . ." Eric said hotly.

"What, dear Eric?" the grand duchess inquired innocently. "Minna simply said she would not dine with peasants."

111

"Not willingly," Minna said with a snort, throwing back her hair as she pushed her soup plate from her. Her fingers drummed on the table as she watched Sarah eat.

"No—you would not dare be too modern," Eric said evenly. "You would rather turn to dust in this motley, rotten collection of stone and timber, your mind rooted firmly in the past, your eyes refusing to see."

"You grow too bold, Eric," the grand duchess cautioned.

"I see nothing so fine about modernity," Minna interjected.

"Aeroplanes, autocars, wireless telegraphs . . ." Eric began insistently.

"All nonsense," his mother said with a dismissing wave of the hand, "lacking in gentility. The modern world will be a hectic jumble of automated creations dashing here and there to no purpose whatever."

"I am sure Sarah does not feel that way," Minna prodded.

"I am only sure that progress will occur," Sarah replied. "Change is the only certainty."

"Yes . . . a modern woman," Minna sniffed.

"In a sense. What else can I be?" Sarah asked.

"Nothing good," the grand duchess complained. "Nothing at all will come of it."

"But much has," Sarah said eagerly. "People can communicate with one another. Children may safely drink milk thanks to Monsieur Pasteur. In Vienna, Herr Freud . . ."

"I have heard of Herr Freud!" the grand duchess interrupted. "And wish to hear no more. He is a madman, and a degenerate."

"Not at all," Sarah continued. "Herr Freud seeks to explain the causes of problems. He does not advocate them."

"It's filth and nonsense," the grand duchess commented shortly.

"I have not heard of Herr Freud," Minna said. "Who is he?"

"No one, dear."

"But I want to know? Am I a child?"

"Yes."

"I want to know anyway. If I am a child, I'm a precocious girl. Do tell me, Miss Chamliss."

"She will not!" the grand duchess decreed with all the authority of her rank.

"Please." Minna was sulking. She literally pawed at the tablecloth, her dark eyes wide, damp.

"Miss Chamliss," the grand duchess went on, ignoring her daughter's pleas, "we are used to such situations as Herr Freud examines. Insanity is in our blood. Obviously."

Minna fell back as if struck.

"We pay it little mind," the grande dame went on. "There is no need for concern as long as the individual is harmless. If he—or she—is not harmless, it is best for everyone if that individual is simply confined."

"Locked up!" Sarah said angrily.

"Yes."

"Or placed in chains?"

"If necessary."

"Beaten?"

"Perhaps. Yes."

"I cannot see . . ." Sarah began, her blood rising. She wanted no argument here, now, with this woman; but certain attitudes could not be brooked. This concept was one which she could not let pass without argument.

"I do not wish to discuss it further," the grand duchess snapped.

"But I do."

"Perhaps," Eric said, "we should let it drop." Yet in his eyes there was a strange mingling of pride and amusement as Sarah rose to the bait.

"Minna needs help," Sarah insisted. "To let her live out her life in this manner is a crime."

"Enough."

"It is not enough. Not until she *is* helped. Forgive me— another nasty tendency of us Americans is our insistence on being heard.

"You mock Herr Freud, yet admit you would beat or cage your daughter."

"I hardly said that, my dear."

"As much."

The grand duchess sat rigidly in her chair. In her entire life no one had spoken to her in this tone, certainly no guest, no foreigner, no peasant.

Minna, elbows on the table, dark eyes on Sarah asked thoughtfully: "How does Herr Freud help people?"

"In a variety of ways," Sarah replied. "Hypnosis, I understand. Analyzing one's dreams."

"My dreams are much too carnivorous," Minna said.

"Eric!" the grand duchess said, folding her napkin. "I will stand no more of this. My nerves . . ."

"Perhaps," Minna said, suddenly changing expressions and demeanor, "our guest would like to hear some of the history of Steinbock." She smiled eagerly—and—Sarah thought—quite carnivorously!

"It is growing late," Eric submitted, but the others ignored his observation.

"The Baron Huebner, of course, is well known—even in America, Miss Chamliss?"

"Word of some of his actions has reached me," Sarah admitted, restraining a shudder. The Butcher of Steinbock, they called him. His atrocities would have filled a book.

"He was Mama's first husband's ancestor. Quite a colorful man," Minna said, her neck stretching out toward Sarah. The girl's eyes positively glittered.

"In those times there was much cruelty," Eric said. He

114

was obviously uncomfortable with this discussion of Minna's.

"But none so refined as our ancestor's," Minna objected. "So practiced, so artful. He was a villain of the extreme proportion."

"He was a disgusting beast," Eric said. The grand duchess nodded amiably, taking no offence at the characterization.

"Perhaps," the older woman suggested, without a trace of a smile, "Miss Chamliss would like to see the torture chamber, Eric. Some of the accouterments are still in working order."

"The baron was no egalitarian, Miss Chamliss," Minna said, peering hotly through her tangled hair. "He did not dine with peasants, but *on* them."

"I think our guest has had enough of this lunacy," Eric said, standing abruptly. "Sarah?" He offered his arm to her.

"I thank you for the dinner," Sarah said to the grand duchess. Then with a bow to Minna, she added, "and for the entertainment."

The grand duchess nearly smiled, her eyes vaguely amused, studying Sarah's face more deeply now. The girl was not upset, or if she was, she had a tremendous ability to conceal what she felt. Minna was crestfallen.

As Sarah and Eric walked from the room Minna began suddenly to cackle wildly, then fell into a deep, unintelligible muttering. "I'll show her the pike!"

"Shut up!" they could hear the grand duchess command.

"I beg your pardon," Eric said as they came into the main hall. The dark, austere room was hung with portraits. It was frigid, breezy. They may as well have been outside where the wind groaned in the elms.

"You need not apologize," she told him. She meant it as well. She had come there at his insistence, but only to be secure from another form of harassment at the hands of Bramante. In no way could she be considered a welcome guest. Eric had warned her of much of this. Minna's derangement was no secret to anyone in Feldkirch—nor was the sinister reputation of Steinbock.

They had come to the open arch at the north end of the vast hall. The moon, frosted, pale rose through the trees, was beautiful if haunting in its liquid appearance.

They stood close to each other and Sarah felt the count's arm around her waist. Together they watched the moon rise, filling with deep golden hues. She gazed at the man briefly—a serious, troubled young man with the manners of a nobleman, the heart of a democrat. He was handsome, nearly beautiful in the moonlight. Yet she found herself thinking of another, a man she hated, feared, mistrusted—Carlo Bramante.

The electricity of the evening at the dance pavilion had not waned. It remained a contradictory, discomforting puzzlement. To love what one hates—that is life's most acid torment.

"There's the old rascal," Eric said.

"What?" Sarah's head turned around slowly, in perplexity.

"There."

Eric's raised finger pointed to the old portrait now bathed in revealing, grotesque moonlight.

"Baron Huebner."

The portrait revealed a man of utter baseness and cold depravity. It was a wonder the baron had not destroyed the artist and portrait both, so succinctly did it reveal his crippled character. Yet such people do not see themselves in that light; perhaps he had thought it quite flattering.

A tremendous red beard framed a malicious tiny mouth. Fierce, obscene eyes glared out across the centuries from above rounded, high cheekbones. A ringed hand was raised in haughty contempt. Beneath it all, after all this time, there was the unmistakable essence of evil.

"He was a filthy man," Eric offered.

"It's horrid. Why don't you have it burned?"

"Impossible. Mother would never hear of it. Besides," he laughed, "by now it's absolutely valuable. The painter, as so often happens, has become more famous than his cretin subject."

They walked quietly toward the staircase, the cold of the house enveloping them. "What was it Minna shouted?" Sarah asked.

"When was that?"

"She said, 'I'll show her the pike!' What did that mean?"

"A part of her illness," Eric said, shrugging it off.

"But surely it had a meaning. To her, at least." Sarah insisted.

"Yes. To her." Eric drew in a deep breath as they stood on the lower landing. "The baron discovered his son with a harlot one winter's night. He watched as they rendez-voused and as the girl slipped off to her own room. He followed her to that room and beheaded her. Then, as a lesson to his errant son, he had the head impaled on a pike and set before the gate. The son, Roland von Steinbock, my ancestral uncle, discovered it as he left the following morning riding to the hunt."

"How ghastly!"

"The Baron Huebner did not think so. It is said he stood on the balcony and laughed until the tears filled his eyes as Roland pawed at the blood-soaked earth, bemoaning his peasant girl's death. And now," Eric said, deeply abashed, "I must go off to sleep. Sarah . . ." He said no more, but his eyes seemed on the verge of tears which he could not allow himself. Eric turned slowly and heavily trudged up the stairs as if the weight of his family were on his shoulders.

After a moment's silent watching, Sarah followed, turning the opposite way at the head of the staircase.

Someone had removed or neglected to replace the hallway candles, so Sarah was forced to grope her way along the stone corridor. After a moment she became aware that she had passed her room, but in the utter darkness she could not be certain by how much. There were one hundred and sixteen rooms in Steinbock Castle, thirty-four on the third floor, nineteen in this wing.

"How could you have done this?" she asked herself angrily. "One doesn't simply begin opening doors." Yet no one else was housed in the wing, or supposed to be. So what did it matter?

Gingerly she stretched out a hand to the doorknob of the room she found herself before. Locked.

All right. She worked her way back toward the staircase. The next room was also locked. The third was open, but the room empty, a vast hole gaping in the roof, allowing cold starlight to filter into the room, which had obviously once been burned. Rubble littered the floor. A rat scurried away at her entrance.

Shuddering, she closed that door and worked her way onward.

A light.

She hesitated. Light bled through the crack of the iron-strapped door. Voices, muffled by the thick walls, could be heard indistinctly. Hesitantly she held the knob without turning it.

"Well, who can it be? I'll simply explain that I've lost my way. In a home this size, it must have happened frequently."

But still her hand refused to turn the knob.

A voice was raised angrily, and she recognized it. Field Marshal Klaus Eisner. But the Prussians were to have left early in the day. Perhaps they had missed connections, or simply changed their minds. Yet Eric had said nothing of it. Perhaps he knew nothing of it.

She recalled with sudden, intense apprehension the bloody hand of the savagely scarred blond German.

But you are a silly girl, she admonished herself. *Everything has become mysterious to you. They are simply friends of Eric.* Yet her hand refused to twist the brass knob.

A voice belonging to Hermann Glick was suddenly raised in heated argument, a rapid spate of German too muffled and run together for her to understand fully.

One word she had heard clearly, too clearly: *Mörder!* A murderer—whom did Glick refer to? *Mörder.* Without any doubt the serious little man had said that word, and no other. Sarah's hand retracted slowly from the knob. She stood, fixed a moment longer.

Surely, she told herself, it is imagination. Has everything become altogether sinister? She had nearly decided that it was only imagination, that if the word had been spoken it could crop up in any number of places in ordinary conversation.

Summoning up her courage, she lifted her chin and stepped toward the door. Then footsteps echoed in the chill hallway. The measured footsteps approached evenly, accompanied by the dimmest flicker of light.

Instinctively she pulled back into the recess of the opposite doorway, her heart racing as the footsteps drew nearer, the faint reddish light of a glowing candle painting the cold stone walls eerily. He brushed by within inches of her, but he did not see her in the darkness. Eric!

He rapped twice on the door which opened immediately.

"Ah, Eric," Glick said. "We thought for a moment there was someone else out there."

"But who?" Eric asked as the door closed once again. "The girl?"

"Perhaps." Their voices again came indistinctly ". . . are you sure about her? . . . no trouble." Then again: *"Mörder!"*

Sarah waited only a moment. The word rang in her ears

as she rushed forward through the gray corridor, finally, desperately finding the Czar Nicholas room.

Inside, her mind lightened by the feeble glow of her own candle, she determined to lock the door. Only the key, which had rested securely on a hook, was now missing! She undressed, her teeth chattering with the cold, and crawled into bed after first drawing a heavy chair before the door—silly precaution; yet she did it.

The moon painted the gallery of the room. Sarah found her eyes going to the crossed swords above the fireplace. Perhaps, she thought, I should have one. And what would you do with it? she demanded sternly of herself.

A murderer . . . who? And of whom? Herself! She sat bold upright at the notion, but it seemed ludicrous. Whatever for?

Yet, she supposed, people had been murdered before without understanding the reason for it. She closed her eyes, stilled her heart with self-persuasion. Yet she prayed the night would be a short one.

From deep within the dank bowels of Steinbock a shrill, wavering cry sounded. Only Minna shrieking, poor thing . . . or was it? Perhaps some unavenged soul called out from the damp, black hole of the torture chamber. *Mörder.*

Restlessly she slept. Off in the woods an owl hooted impatiently. The moon rose to full prominence, a hard silver gleam filling the night.

Once she heard a distant creaking sound and her eyes opened fully, but there was nothing to be seen. It was long past midnight, the castle utterly dark, icy with the freezing night. Again, with determination she closed her eyes, throwing an arm over them, snuggling more deeply into the eiderdown.

Silently the door opened.

Sarah's eyelids flickered, then opened wide. There was no light but the silver moon. No sound but the footsteps.

Sarah rolled from the bed in an instant. Over her the poised figure loomed. Menacing, wide-eyed, the moon glinted on the flashing silver of the weapon in the intruder's hands.

"Minna . . . don't!" Sarah stepped quickly to the corner, her voice choked, shrill. "What are you doing?"

Minna lunged forward awkwardly, the long deadly spear in her hands. Did she mean to kill, to frighten, to mutilate? Sarah was never to know. As the girl swept forward with the murderous pike she swung aside, grasping desperately for the shaft of the weapon just behind the iron head.

Minna's voice gurgled oddly. She tripped, fell, and slumped to the floor, the pike clattering free of her trembling, thin hands.

Sarah snatched up the weapon first and threw it aside. Then she lit the candle.

"Minna? Are you all right? Did it cut you?"

The girl was pressed to the floor like some crushed lily. She did not speak; she did not move. Her white gown was spread out across the floor. Probably she had tripped over the excessive material of the long gown.

"Minna?" Sarah said softly. She lifted the girl's head gently. "Please get up. You're all right."

"I wanted to show you the pike," Minna said mechanically, taking Sarah's hand, following her to the bed where she sagged against the post. "I only wished to show you the pike."

"Yes." Sarah glanced at the ugly weapon on the floor. It was the weapon Baron Huebner had used to behead and then display another woman's head on its point, like some trophy of the nobility.

"Did you want to kill me, Minna? Did you see me as some threat?"

"As my brother's concubine . . ." Minna shook her head as if she were coming out of a daze. "Murder. My God! I murder. Like the baron." Wonderingly she dwelled on that.

"Is that what you came for?" Sarah asked, sitting beside Minna on the bed, putting an arm around the shivering girl. "Or did you just want to frighten me."

"I only wanted to show you the pike . . . but there's blood in our line. We're all murderers. Doomed by it. The baron was a killer. I am too. It will only be a matter of time. Perhaps I have already killed . . . it's in the blood. It is in the blood."

The girl's voice ran rapidly, sobs breaking her words. Now she fell utterly to pieces and fell against Sarah's shoulder, clutching at the material of her nightgown, crying as if she would never stop, as if she had never cried before and had simply saved this torrent up for night upon night.

"It's not in the blood," Sarah said sternly. She hugged Minna tightly then lifted her chin once more. "Don't you believe it, and don't let anyone tell you differently."

"They say . . ."

"I don't care what they say," Sarah said as sternly as a teacher lecturing a wayward youth. "Insanity does not run in the blood. More likely than not it is this house that keeps you in this state!"

"Steinbock?"

"Yes."

"It's my home," Minna insisted.

"A fine home. Dungeons, legends, cold forbidding spaces. And what company do you have? Who speaks with you but your mother—if she?"

"It's lonely," Minna admitted. She had softened so, especially in the eyes, that Sarah could hardly find the same Minna in them. She allowed Sarah to comfort her as if she were a lost and lonely child.

"You run away, Minna. Where do you go?"

"I don't know."

"And why do you think you run away? You're not happy here. You know Father Bruno, don't you? And you like him? Why don't you talk to him. Let him help you."

Minna stiffened suddenly. The spell was broken, and she came rigidly to her feet. "I won't. Besides," she said with a toss of her head, "it wouldn't do any good. None whatsoever. It's in me to kill, and I know it. It's in the blood."

"It's not in the blood! You must believe me, Minna. It's not in you to kill!"

"But Helmuth . . ." her voice faltered. "If it's not . . . what of poor Helmuth?"

"What do you mean? What of Helmuth Mann?" Sarah reached out toward the girl, but Minna backed away defensively, her arms behind her, groping for the door, eyes flashing sparks.

"I might have killed you," she said in a strained, singsong voice. "Easily. And Helmuth . . . it's all in the blood, you foolish wench!"

Then her mouth opened in a fierce, derisive laugh. Angrily she swung open the door. "I fooled you, Miss Chamliss. You thought you enjoyed you petting me so! You thought I did not come to kill you at all. You stupid . . . pathetic . . . wench!"

She screamed then, from the bowels of her tormented self, a rolling, spine-tingling scream that echoed through the castle.

"Minna!"

Sarah rushed to the doorway, but she was gone, running through the black hallway, her voice filling the night.

"Helmuth!"

Eleven

With the first morning light Sarah was up and dressing. Gertrude, bearing a tray with coffee, rolls and marmalade, and a single red rose in a silver bud vase, knocked tentatively and crept in, her honest face wearing the burden of worry.

"A small breakfast, Ma'am." Hurriedly she put the tray down, her eyes eluding Sarah's. "The mistress and the master are both off early."

Sarah paused a moment from pinning her chestnut tresses up. Putting down her brush and hairpins she pushed back her chair and stood up.

"The rose," Gertrude said, wiping her hands on her apron, "is from the master."

"Thank you, Gertrude," Sarah replied.

There was so obviously something further on the maid's mind that Sarah waited patiently for Gertrude to find the words she searched for.

"You've been kind, Ma'am," Gertrude said finally.

"We've hardly spoken."

"Not to me. To the young mistress. To Minna, I mean." The honest soul clutched her apron nervously.

"She needs help," Sarah said.

"Yes!" Gertrude answered, nearly shouting. "Yes, that's what I mean entirely. She needs someone, and you've tried to help despite her manners. I've tried, too. God knows it, Ma'am. I've begged the mistress to find a doctor for her. I brush her hair and try to keep her dresses shut . . . but it's a miserable, thankless battle, Ma'am."

"If only her mother would see that something is dreadfully wrong."

"Oh, she sees it. But she thinks it can't be helped. Or she doesn't want it so." Gertrude looked astonished at her own impudence.

"It does seem so," Sarah said.

"I don't believe she wants Minna talking about it. That's what they have to do, isn't it? Talk about her problems?"

"Yes. It has to be brought up, worked out."

"I don't think the grand duchess would like that," Gertrude said, wagging her head. "No, not a bit."

"They say it dates to the death of her brother, Helmuth. They say she witnessed it."

"I should not talk of it," Gertrude said, glancing warily toward the door. "But, yes. She saw Helmuth's accident . . . she came back screaming, raving mad. And there was no consoling her. Since then she's gotten worse.

"She runs off," Gertrude confided, "to visit Helmuth's grave, she says."

"Where is that?"

"Ma'am." Gertrude's eyes were wide as she leaned closer. "There is no grave. Helmuth's body was never recovered from the Ice Castle."

There was no one at all in the great castle. Or if there were, they kept themselves hidden.

After the short breakfast, Sarah went to the stable. Otto provided her with a horse and wagon, though uncertainly. His great cow eyes rested on the young woman as he scuttled about, hitching the harness.

She gave the man a silver twenty-pfennig piece which he took as if it were contraband and slid surreptitiously into his pants pocket.

Sarah slapped the reins against the pony's flanks and he stepped out nimbly, seeming to enjoy the prospect of exercise.

As they passed through the garden Sarah heard a shriek from high in the castle. Minna, no doubt, enraged by some imagined slight; or perhaps haunted even in the brilliant light of day by Helmuth's ghost.

Sarah found herself urging the pony on even more quickly, as if trying to escape from the long shadows cast by Steinbock Castle.

Soon she was out into the open countryside, the wildflowers had now passed, buried beneath the first snows, but still the countryside was pretty, the tall, mournful pines craning toward the sun, the tiny cottages set at long intervals against the rolling knolls. And above, beyond it all, the brilliant snow-clad peaks of the thrusting Alps, tearing at the fragile robin's-egg blue sky.

In Feldkirch she stopped first at the Huchtings' house. Several items had been left behind in her hasty departure, and she found them neatly bundled on the bureau. She left five marks for Renate and went outside.

"Renate! Hans!"

She called out repeatedly, walking back to the barn, but neither of them was there.

It was odd, this time of the day, but after all she knew little of their habits. The tiny cottage was neat, with no indication of any trouble.

Sarah again snapped the reins, urging the horse to motion. He seemed not to mind, trotting easily, the steam blowing from his muzzle. He towed the cart readily.

Ahead she spied a familiar figure, though in unfamiliar dress. She halted the wagon near the rushing weir at the mill.

"Hans!"

He turned to greet her stiffly, self-importantly.

126

"Yes, Fraulein? May I be of assistance?"

Despite herself Sarah smiled. Hans was wearing the uniform of the district police, and he stood proudly erect, arms straight at his side, his hands clad in white gloves.

"Why, Hans, you look so handsome! But what are you doing in a police uniform?"

"I am a special officer," he said, his spine and neck so rigid that it seemed he must be suffering to stand so. "Herr Police Captain Flaig has appointed me to this position."

"But is there trouble?"

"I cannot discuss this," Hans said professionally. "I must refer you to Herr Captain Flaig."

"You will tell Renate that I got my things?"

"If the occasion arrives," Hans said formally. "However, one never knows in my profession when one will see one's loved ones again."

Proudly the little man strode off, and Sarah moved along. It was impossible not to notice that there were several more of these special police in Feldkirch. Some of them she recognized, some she did not. Mostly middle-aged men without weapons they stood along the main boulevard impressing one another with their tailor-new uniforms.

Rudi was not at home when Sarah reached the Uhlmann house on the far side of the marsh ponds. Incredulously, his mother reported that the boy had gone to school.

"Will you give him this note then?" Sarah asked.

Frau Uhlmann looked suspiciously at the note which was in English.

"And give him this." Sarah gave the woman ten marks, at which her eyes brightened.

"*Ja, Fraulein. Ja, sicher!*"

It was late afternoon when Sarah reached the church. A wedding party was only now dispersing, the men loosening their ties, slapping each other on the back as the women chatted merrily, some of them red-eyed still.

She waited under the elms, which swayed gently in the breeze, solemn as nuns at their prayers, until the last well-wisher had gone. Then she entered the churchyard and found Father Bruno, feet propped on his desk, eyes half-closed.

"A wedding is a joyous occasion," she ventured.

"*Ja*, but a wearying one for the man who must shake hands and give the blessings, ignore the imbibers and fainting overwrought ladies . . . but a joyous occasion," he said with a vastly satisfied smile. He scratched his head vigorously, pushing his glasses back on his nose.

"You seem especially pleased," Sarah said.

"Yes. It was Helga Kroeber, Sarah. Her boyfriend came back on leave from the army. So happy they seemed. I only hope they have a few days together before the baby arrives," he said with an odd smile.

"They were happy?"

"Utterly."

"But the circumstances . . . Bramante's assault in the forest. The young man was very noble. Helga was so unhappy, I'm glad for her," Sarah said sincerely. Yet a question formed itself in the back of her mind.

"Father Bruno," she began, "the baby . . . ?"

"Sarah, please," Father Bruno said, sitting erect. "Anything I would say might violate the privacy of the confessional. But," he went on, "in confidence, I would venture an observation."

"Which is?"

"Only a general observation . . . which many in Feldkirch might offer. The young man and woman were in love. She has an uncle who is also a police captain. Youth can be a frightening time of life. Panic sometimes takes over. Let us just be happy that the young man came back from the army to claim what is justly his . . . Helga Kroeber, I mean."

Sarah did not answer. The priest had not meant to say so

much perhaps, but as he said, such conjecture was probably a part of the common gossip in Feldkirch.

A young man and a young woman in love. Fear, then panic. The boy runs away to join the army. In utter distress perhaps Helga invented a story. Who better to implicate than the known bandit, Bramante?

"But you have come for something in particular," Father Bruno said.

"Yes," Sarah said, her thoughts suddenly breaking off. "I have come for Minna von Steinbock."

"At her request?" Father Bruno's eyebrows arched slightly.

"No," Sarah replied. "You know that would not happen. Although, if she could . . . I think she prays desperately for help she dares not ask for."

"Yes. Like so many of us."

"Her mother does not feel she needs assistance."

"No," the priest said with a heavy shake of his head, "she would not. But then the Steinbocks have lived with insanity for centuries. In the early days there was so much intermarriage in a feeble attempt to keep the blood 'pure' and noble. Such an idea," Father Bruno went on sadly, "but by pursuing it they themselves spelled the ruin of their kind. Hemophilia, odd spineless men, spoiled, sterile women . . .

"I apologize, Sarah. It is something I have thought on often. This idea that the blood can be kept from contamination. Each man is new, his world a new world to do with as he may. Each woman comes to her feet of her own will, not because of her noble ancestors' helping arms. Yet the idea remains fixed in their minds. Perhaps without such ideas they have nothing," he pondered.

"Yet we have a chance to do something for one person. Now," Sarah said.

"Minna." The priest sighed. "Do you know how often I have tried? She used to come now and then to Mass, and afterward to chat with me. Yet they would not allow it. And Minna could not understand it at all. Her poor confused little mind troubled with black thoughts, tales of murder and insanity, taught, no *commanded,* to despise all but nobility, all but Steinbock. The family! And what a family it has been."

"I feel there is light in her darkness," Sarah insisted. "If only we could open the door, she would come through into the sunlight."

"If only. Yes. But I am no longer allowed at Steinbock Castle, Sarah. Nor is Minna allowed in Feldkirch. Save her? Yes—pull her from that accursed dungeon she lives in."

Father Bruno sagged back into his chair, his fists clenched with the same frustration Sarah felt.

"Then I will find a way," she said quietly.

The priest looked up at this sturdy, proud woman. Up against amazing odds, nearly overwhelmed by her own problems, she still had the compassion to think of another.

"Do." Father Bruno said it almost prayerfully. "To save another's soul is to save one's own."

The shadows had grown long, the sun flashing through the elms as Sarah left the church. She was absorbed in her own thoughts so that she did not see the man beside the cart until she was nearly to it.

"*Abend!*" he greeted her, but his accent was so ludicrous that she knew instantly that he was not a German speaker.

She peered closely at the man in the shadows. "You!"

"Yes. Me, Miss Chamliss," the Britisher said. He nodded amiably and struck a match to his constant companion, the pipe.

"And just who *are* you?"

"Me?" He acted surprised by the question, a mocking smile ripening on his mustached mouth. "Why, just a traveler, as yourself."

130

"A strange traveler who spends the bulk of his time in concealment."

"I am a private person," he said, hooking his thumbs into his checkered vest.

"Sir, whoever you are, I have little time for puzzles."

"Indeed? It seemed to me that was how you spent *your* time. But I will not banter with you. I have come to appeal to you—go home! You will never find your brother here. Go home before you are struck down by tragedy."

"I will not!" Sarah said emphatically. "I am tired of that suggestion. I am tired of being bullied and threatened, tricked and deceived, lied to and ignored! Whoever you are, sir, go home yourself if you are of a mind to do so. Leave me to my fate whatever it might be!"

"I can say no more in the face of such an explosion." The Englishman shrugged. "I do admire your courage, young lady. Let us pray it does not bring you to an untimely end."

Having said that he turned and started off as if on a Sunday stroll. Sarah watched him for a moment. "But wait!" she cried. "Don't you owe me an explanation? What do you know of this? Was it you who gave the Avarian girl money? What do you know of Robert!"

She shouted after him, but with a wave of his hand he simply continued on his way, disappearing finally into the shelter of the trees.

"Englishmen!" she shouted, unable to think of a suitable expletive. Yet it made her wonder more. There seemed to be so many people interested in her search. Why? And why would not one of them step forward to help her?

She saw no light in Steinbock Castle as she returned from Feldkirch just as the last violent splash of crimson faded to a washy gray on the high, broken clouds to the west. A lamp burned low in the orchard cottage where Ernst, the gardener, lived. But aside from that feeble glow

131

the bizarre form of Steinbock lay mummified in silent, black sleep.

But wait—a light seemed to flicker ever so briefly, then be extinguished in her room. Yet there were so many rooms . . . had it been hers?

A rap at the outer door brought no response. Where were Gertrude and Otto? For that matter where had the grand duchess, who seemed never to travel, gone? And Eric? She ventured a call.

"Eric? Gertrude?"

There was no answer. She found a candle on the nearby sideboard and lit it, walking through the foyer to the dining room. Empty. There was no one in the main hall. Sarah shuddered as her candle caught the features of Baron Huebner still malevolently gazing down at all of humanity from his portrait on the wall.

"Eric!"

Nothing. The night did not respond to her questioning voice. She moved toward the staircase, her skirts rustling against the marble of the floor. She had placed a hand on the bannister, her foot stretching for the first step when the cry sounded.

A cry was it? Or a demon gasping! It was a low, woebegone, incredibly hollow sound, like an animal sounding its death song to an empty night. Again it came. She started to turn and rush to her room. But the thought came suddenly—Minna!

She was certain that it was Minna, appealing to the dark world for help, her soul pleading. Sarah listened again, but no sound came.

"Minna?"

She stepped down from the staircase and moved uncertainly across the room, finding a door she was unfamiliar with and, beyond it, a dank, cold set of stairs leading downward. They were ancient steps, carved from gray granite, chipped and seeping water—a ruin built around, pushed from the mind. She knew suddenly what the steps led to—the dungeon. Baron Huebner's torture chamber. The cold bowels of Steinbock Castle. The stony, damp heart of the house itself, remnant of a bloody, bygone era, perhaps stained with the blood of the baron's victims.

Cautiously she inched her way downward, once nearly tripping at a place where a step was missing. Her flickering candle caught a tapestry of spiders' webs, an empty, wrought-iron torch holder, an iron ring projecting uselessly from the cold stone. What had it once held?

A cold draft filtered through the stonework, or perhaps seeped from below, from the heart of the mountain beside which Steinbock nestled. Suddenly she was down under a high arched stone ceiling of ancient origin, standing on a chipped, stone floor, cold as ice. Here and there apparatus of no certain origin cluttered the floor: rusted red iron, wooden yokes or tables with splintered legs. It seemed some fury had once destroyed all of these implements of torture. Yet probably, it was only time, inexorable, heartless, unforgiving, which had wrought the havoc.

Where her light could not reach, long corridors led off into the darkness, stretching perhaps back into time. A sudden movement caused her breath to catch; something rubbed against her leg. A rat scurried off excitedly.

Get gone, devil, she breathed.

Again a whisper of sound came to her ears. But what sound?—a whistle, a gasp, a croaking, desperate noise. Sarah stepped forward cautiously, past a pit which seemed to have no bottom. She did not wish to speculate what use it might have once seen.

Again the sound . . . she moved forward tentatively.

If Minna was here, she needed to be taken out. What sort of black magic could this work on her mind? If it were not Minna . . .

Cautiously she chose the corridor to the left, the first of five deep tunnels. A corroded, broken chain lay on the buckled stone floor. A bat screeched once and was silent, winging off through the blackness.

What was it like, she wondered, to live one's life out in such surroundings?—in black, tormenting caverns, real and imagined, where love and light are hopeless dreams, where death haunts the corridors of stone.

The tunnel opened onto a huge cavern—a cavern because there was no longer ceiling or walls, just native stone hollowed into the heart of the earth. Yet there were rooms—or dungeons, whatever one wished to call them. Dank, decayed closets with rotted planks hung to the walls. Once they were pallets for the prisoners of Baron Huebner, places where men waited to be tortured or to die.

Quite suddenly she found herself before a different sort of alcove. There were iron bars fixed to the ceiling, but the door was open. There was a bed of a more modern sort, stuffed with straw, supported by legs of new wood. A small table sat near the bed, and on it a coal-oil lamp rested.

Carefully she moved into the room. On the tiny table was a book. A volume of Goethe's works. And beside it a tray of half-eaten food.

Someone was living here! In this dungeon, black pit, in the entrails of Steinbock a person lived without light, sound, company!

She backed from the room, her eyes sweeping the darkness. Someone was here. It was not only the evidence that told her so . . . a certain feeling pervaded the cold gloom. Someone was here. The being who lived in this icy blackness, the person who belonged to darkness.

Backward she moved, her hand feeling the wall, her eyes searching for the sound which came again, even more faintly . . . but it was not Minna.

134

She became lost and disoriented, and the candle, waning in the thin oxygen, threatened to go out. Hurriedly, her heart beating, she searched one corridor, then another. A sound followed her retreat, a rasping, metallic sound. Chains, illness, death—the images flared up in her mind's eye until finally her foot found the stairs and she raced upward, the candle falling from her hand, the night closing to blackness. With relief her hands stretched out and found the door. Closed. Locked!

Locked behind her . . . and the sound grew louder behind her. Furiously she pounded on the door, the sound of her falling fists making hardly a whisper of sound against the heavy planks. How many prisoners had beaten uselessly against the enormous door?

Then another sound met her ears, from through the door—a giggling, a mad cackling.

"Minna! Is that you? Let me out!"

"Harlot . . . do you like my dungeon? Shall I leave you there with . . . *what it is?*"

"Minna," she said as calmly as possible, "you must let me out. You must."

"No," a quiet voice said. "I must not. Rot, wench. It does me no harm."

Then her footsteps retreated, a merry little tune sounding faintly. Sarah rested her head against the door. Again she pushed, as hard as her muscles would permit. Again the door stood firm. Again the scraping, metallic sound echoed behind her, seeming nearer, more ominous.

"Minna!"

The door suddenly swung open. And Eric was there, in the light, in the fresh air, his hands taking her strongly, gently, his lips once touching her forehead, as he held her to him.

"Whatever are you doing there, poor Sarah?" he murmured. "Darling, what are you doing in such a dreary

135

place?"

She could not answer at first, but simply clung to him, taking a measure of his strength into her own heart. There was nothing, nothing at all in the night he could not dominate, no danger too great for him to face evenly, and now he held her.

"Minna," she said, her voice a grating scratch in her throat. "I thought heard her crying down there. And when I went to help her, she shut me down there."

He said nothing for a moment. He locked the door with a great brass key and together they walked to the terrace where the cold, utterly fresh, utterly invigorating wind washed over them, restoring her spirits as it chilled her. Eric stood firmly by her, yet there was a tension in him she could feel.

"Such a joke . . . such a macabre joke. This life, this place. I feel at times like destroying the temple of Steinbock. This mockery. This monument to unhappiness."

Then he fell silent. Sarah watched him, the way his mouth pressed against his teeth bitterly, the searching eyes seeking the far peaks, the moon dancing on the snowfields.

"I should have stayed in Germany, in Cologne. Helmuth should have stayed away . . . we are trapped by some magnetic force. Some evil magnetism calls us home to Steinbock and devours us."

"Eric . . ."

But he would not let her speak. He bent down slightly, his mouth meeting hers, his arms holding her so tightly that the breath went from her and sent her senses reeling.

"If I could only leave now . . . if only you were free to go with me. Lord, Sarah, if we were two people free to live our own lives—would you go?"

He asked her, and she did not know. Eric perhaps wished for no reply but the one she gave. A short, tender kiss, a moment when their eyes met, a brief encounter before the night forced them back into the sterile shelter of Steinbock.

From the upper reaches, Minna's convulsive shrieking rolled through the empty, loveless cavern.

Twelve

Otto tapped lightly at her door before the first gray of dawn. Quickly Sarah drew on her wrapper and went to answer.

"There's a boy here to see you."

"Thank you, Otto."

The man's eyes posed an unasked question. He dangled the lantern he carried at arm's length.

"Please, Otto—it's most important—please don't tell a soul that I've gone out."

"No, Ma'am. I won't." He answered with the blasé, world-weary air of one who has spent a lifetime among secrets and mysterious movements.

Rudi perched on the seat of the one-horse cart uncertainly, his eyes taking in the awesome sprawl of stone, timber, and grounds which was Steinbock Castle. With relief he smiled as he saw Sarah burst from the front door.

"I always hoped to see this place," he confided, "but now I wish to see no more."

"Did you bring everything?"

"Yes, Miss Chamliss. I was so surprised when your note came for me. But I have everything."

"Then let us be on our way quickly. Before someone else knows you are here."

Rudi frowned curiously and shrugged, but he slapped the pony's rump and drove from Steinbock. The skies were rolling gray, bulky and heavy with moisture. It would certainly snow.

"But you have not told me where we are going," Rudi said. He had his hat tilted back jauntily, but for all of his airs, there was the mark of worry on his pleasant, smooth face.

"I thought you would have guessed. The place I must go now. The Ice Castle."

"But you must not!"

"But I must, Rudi, and you know that," Sarah said positively. "Since I first heard of the Ice Castle I have been told over and over again that I must not go there. But I must. That is where Robert went, I know that. For whatever reason, he visited this hole in the mountains where men go only to perish or become lost, wandering in this icy dungeon without light or warmth. And so I must go."

"Very well," Rudi said pessimistically. "I am not sure of the direction from this side of the mountain, however; I shall have to take the longer route."

"That's fine, Rudi. I am in no hurry. But tell me, can we see it from here?"

"No, not exactly, but I can show you the peak." He drew up a moment, his finger pointing to the saw-toothed, snow-dusted crag which loomed up nearly behind Steinbock Castle. "There is the Eagle's Nest, that is what they call the peak. On the other side is the Ice Castle."

"So near? Why it practically sits atop Steinbock."

"Yes, Miss Chamliss. That is the mountain. But you cannot reach it from this side, as far as I know. There is no trail."

Eagle's Nest was indeed sheer on this side, and there seemed to be no way to cross the scarred, bluish mountain to where Rudi said the Ice Castle was located. Although she wondered . . .

Rudi drove on, yet he fidgeted in the seat until Sarah finally had to ask what was wrong. "You're not frightened, Rudi?"

"Oh, no, Fraulein Chamliss. Not I. Not at all," he said bravely. "But there is very big doings in Feldkirch. Much excitement and I hate to miss out."

"What is happening there?" She remembered Hans Huchting in his police uniform, the other men she had seen standing in the streets.

"You mean you have not heard! I thought surely you would know, since you are at Steinbock. The Count von Steinbock and the grand duchess come nearly every day to town to buy this or that, to make arrangements . . ."

"For what, Rudi?"

"The Archduke Ferdinand is expected," Rudi said, astonished that Sarah could know nothing of it. "The town is alive with the news. It is said he will be the next Emperor of Austro-Hungary. The Emperor Franz Joseph is an old man."

The emperor's nephew!

"He is coming here? To stay at Steinbock? But why?" And why, she thought, had Eric not informed her?

"Oh, *ja! Natürlich!* He is an old friend of the grand duchess. The Archduke Ferdinand is returning to Vienna. He will stay and hunt with Eric for Steinbock stag. They are famous for their size and great racks of antler. And the archduke is a superb sportsman."

They wound slowly upward through the dense forest, the Eagle's Nest towering over them, seeming to grow ever larger as they found the trail up the white flanks of the massive peak. Now they found snow in the passes, deep in the cuts where the rock had splintered and fallen. Dead trees lay like bleached bones beside the trail where landslides had carried whole forests away.

Still higher they climbed, until the timber fell away and the landscape presented only barren white rock, broken ridges, ice-clogged clefts. They passed over a fragile, swaying bridge. Beneath them white water surged over massive boulders, churning wildly, white froth cutting at the channel walls, spray exploding high into the air, catching the color of the sun in a miniature rainbow before washing over the bridge. Deep green velvet fern grew in the shady depths of the canyon and one last delicate harebell produced a splash of fading blue against the white rock.

Then they were before it. Around a tight turn in the road they came upon a gaping black hole bored into the side of the mountain. All of fifty feet high, the yawning cavern caught the wind and gave back an echoing, growling dirge like the protesting voice of a battle-scarred giant.

The Ice Castle. The devouring mouth. The killer of men.

"I will get your supplies," Rudi said. He jumped from the cart, but unsteadily, his hair lifting from his scalp as the wind tore at it. He pulled the burlap sack from the wagon bed and began sorting through it.

"It will be better," the boy said, "if I carry the second lantern." His hands drew forth the lanterns, matches, coils of rope, short-handled pick, and chocolate bars.

"Rudi," Sarah said quietly. "You cannot go."

"*Nein! Ich muss* . . . I must go. I cannot allow you to go alone! A woman."

"But you must not. I will go alone, Rudi."

"No, Miss Chamliss . . . I am not afraid," the boy protested.

"I did not think you were, Rudi," she said, patting his flaxen hair briefly. "But if something were to happen to you, I would not forgive myself. Think of your mother. No," she repeated, "you will not go."

"All right," Rudi said calmly. "I will see you on your way, then I will go."

"No, Rudi. You will go now. I will stand and watch you go. You are foolish enough to follow me into the cave."

"I? I would do such a thing . . ."

"Go, Rudi. Thank you for thinking so much of me. But go. I would do anything to keep you from being hurt." She bent down then and kissed him on the cheek. It turned instantly red and Rudi backed away, his eyes large, astonished.

Again he began to protest, but Sarah would have none of it. Slowly he clambered into the wagon and turned the horse around. He started, stopped, then finally disappeared around the bend in the road, still looking mournfully back.

She was alone—in this foreign land, atop this wind-swept mountain, before the gaping mouth of an infamous cavern. The wind twisted her hair, flattening her clothing against her. Alone, but for the spirits which haunted the mountainside: Helmuth von Steinbock's spirit, those of six other men . . . or ten? How many others without name or memory since the Avarians had passed across the land?

They had come there looking for the treasure of the Avarian king. Come to die, to lose their way in the icy blackness. And now another had come, for a different reason—for love.

She waited alone, summoning the courage of her indomitable spirit. Softly it had begun to snow. Fleecy eiderdown floating through the air, melting as it touched her cheeks.

Alone. She moved toward the mouth of the cave, lantern in hand, rope slung across her shoulders, matches secure in an oilskin wrapper. Alone . . . but there were signs of another.

Who? The snow was beaten down by the passage of other feet. Melted to indistinctness, still the footprints could not have been older than twenty-four hours or the new snow would have covered them. Perhaps they had been impressed there even more recently, that very morning, possibly. But whose foot had made them? Man or woman, there was no telling. They were simply formless holes in the four inches of new snow, leading into the Ice Castle.

She hesitated. Her pulse pounded in every artery of her body, her legs faltered of their own volition.

If the fear of being alone in such a forbidding place had been intimidating, the knowledge that she was not alone was horrifying. She struggled but a moment with her fears. Probably it was nothing. A mountaineer, a treasure seeker, an explorer—nothing more sinister. Surely nothing more sinister. . . .

It was the need to know which finally caused Sarah to move forward, her feet taking tiny strides, her heart palpitating wildly. The need to know about Robert, to know the worst, or the best. To find that delicate, gentle man with whom she had played tennis on a summer afternoon, ridden with on horseback through the wild, colorful American desert, clung to when the news of Mother's death had come that rainy, dark December night, loved and looked up to—and been ever glad that such a man was her brother.

That mild, yet strong dark-eyed man was in Austria, probably in Feldkirch, possibly in this Ice Castle. The lanky boy who had shown her how to make a whistle with a blade of grass held between the thumbs, who had brushed her hair and braided it when there was no one else to do it, who had shown her for the first time books which opened the windows to the world, and doors to the past.

Outside the wind had shifted. It came from the west with an awful vengeance. Inside all was cold, bizarre, dark.

The gigantic anteroom, caught by the glimmer of

torchlight, was all they had said of it—a frozen cathedral, with alcoves and crystalline images formed of bluish ice. Underneath the footing was utterly treacherous already. Sarah changed into the spiked shoes Rudi had purchased.

The footprints which had preceded her into the Ice Castle disappeared entirely, ghostlike on the marble hard surface of the ice underfoot. The footing was easier with the climbing shoes, and she inched her way forward. In her hand she held the small vial.

Behind Sarah, as she moved into the maw of the place, tiny specks of red appeared on the ice. The vial in her left hand contained simply red food coloring, yet it marked her trail distinctly. She had no intention of becoming another victim lost in the Castle. As long as she had light, she could find her way out no matter the twists and turns she would be forced to make.

The cavern funneled down, then split into two separate channels, both leading slightly downward. She stood at the base of this "Y" for some time, hesitant. Which was the right tunnel? Or was there a right and a wrong to it?

She chose the one to her left finally, for no particular reason but that it seemed slightly less treacherous, the footing sounder. She moved forward, the tunnel constricting rapidly. She was forced to hunch forward slightly, creeping slowly past three-foot-long icicles which hung in clusters from the ceiling in this chamber, like the spikes in some fakir's coffin.

Abruptly the tunnel opened, the light spilling into a great room. The Satan Room! It had to be, by Eric's description. A cold breeze moved through the massive chamber, but it did not emanate from above; from somewhere far below it came, stale, nearly putrid. The moving air murmured through the honeycombed blocks of ice, like some great demonic calliope sounding an atavistic dirge.

The trickling ice-melt had formed incredible shapes

on the ledges above. Distinctly she saw small figures with popped-out eyes, horns on their heads, lashing tails, pointed ears, and mocking, broken-toothed grins. Perched on the shelf of ice were gargoyles, griffins, trolls, and kelpies. Each waiting, or so it seemed, for flesh, for lost travelers to lower their guard for one fatal instant.

Shuddering, she moved forward. Suddenly her feet went from under her and she slammed against the stony ice, sliding fifteen feet downward into a narrow depression before her clutching fingers could stop her descent.

She reminded herself to be more careful. This is no time for sightseeing, for imaginative flights, for carelessness. There is time only for the business at hand. Painfully she stood, her shoulder throbbing, her hands torn raw. She dusted the snow from her dress and continued, scrabbling out of the depression onto firm ice.

Deep in the gullet of the Ice Castle a rumbling began. A tremor growing in strength as it traveled, it surged through the frozen interior of the Ice Castle. It shook the pillars of ice beside her, toppling a grotesque little demon from his ledge. It landed beside her, shattering against the floor.

The ever-changing ice was constantly shifting. It growled and creaked, moaning as it moved. The build-up of ice became too heavy for the supporting keys in certain areas—then tons of ice broke loose without warning, crashing against the earth beneath it.

There was an arched doorway in the wall near a large altarlike formation, and Sarah took it, grateful to be out of the Satan Room; yet she was going deeper into the mountain, and every step was toward the unknown, the depths of the cavern.

She passed a series of minor chambers, then found a trickle of living water moving through a serpentine channel of uncertain depth. The cold had begun to work on her—she moved more slowly, breathing through her mouth. Her legs were leaden and the hand which held the waning lantern trembled.

The lamp she carried flickered dully and went out. Immediately she struck a match and turned up the wick. The oxygen was nearly absent from this chamber. Ahead the tunnel deadended in a sheet of greenish ice.

A wrong choice then. Very well, she would return to where the tunnel branched. The lantern fought to exist, the flame withering then flaring up as it caught a breath of oxygen from somewhere deep in the cave.

The lack of fresh air had caused Sarah's head to swim. Tiny dots of red and yellow swam through the air before her eyes. Dizzily she moved backward, following the red dots of her food coloring past the many tiny, black branch tunnels.

She had difficulty in thinking. Her lungs burned, but the red dots showed plainly. She followed them into a narrow tunnel. She had no memory of passing that way, but the dots indicated she had.

She lurched forward, stumbling headlong through the tunnel. Once she fell, the frozen floor of the tunnel coming up suddenly to slap her in the face. Again. She scratched her way forward. Here was a red dot. There another. She had not lost her way. But the close confines of the constricted tunnel seemed utterly unfamiliar.

Her head swam, her eyes caught nothing but shifting, fuzzed forms carved of blue ice. The entire world was ice, cold, blue, slick; she moved steadily forward. Almost frantically.

Stop. Take a deep breath. You are not lost.

The cold numbed her muscles. Water trickled from above, running in icy rivulets down the bare walls. Her hands, she noticed for the first time, had little circulation, appearing blue; they were stiff with the cold. I should have gotten gloves, she scolded herself.

But I am not lost . . .

The dots still showed before her. Now she was crawling, however, and the ceiling of the tunnel was so low she could not have stood if she had the strength to do so.

Somewhere deep in the bowels of the cavern the ice shifted, sending a grating, creaking tremor through the Ice Castle.

On hands and knees she rested, head hanging, eyes unfocused. There—right before her was a red dot! She was not lost. Soon she would be back in the Satan Room. She fingered the red splotch childishly. As it painted her finger she was numbed with shock—it was not her dye! It was thick, more purple. Placing it to her lips she tasted salt. It was not her trail she had been following back. The spots were something else altogether.

Blood—it was blood on the ice. Showing here and there in large splotches. An animal. Some wounded animal had dragged itself in here to die, but she did not believe it for an instant. It was human blood.

The tunnel narrowed even more. Still Sarah moved forward, following the trail as if there was no other choice. Perhaps there was none.

The fuel in her lantern had burned low. With a start she realized the second emergency lantern had fallen from her pack somewhere below. Her own trail lost, she followed this bloody track desperately.

It may be nothing, she thought—an explorer who has scratched himself, a treasure hunter who has taken a fall in one of those razor-edged ice pits. Yet she did not succeed in comforting herself.

Truthfully perhaps she no longer cared. Any company, even a bloody stranger, seemed preferable to these endless, frozen corridors. Her hands had absolutely no feeling in them now. Her muscles responded to her

147

wishes only with the greatest concentration.

Then it ended. The tunnel broke off, widened.

The chamber was twenty feet high, dry and a hint of a breeze, fresh air, wafted up from below. The lantern gasped, caught the oxygen and blazed cheerfully in this deep, unnamed, undiscovered pit. Sarah's lungs too swallowed deeply of the fresh air, her blood racing, her head clearing as the life-giving oxygen reached it.

The bloody trail had utterly disappeared. Somewhere in the tunnel it had given out without her being aware of it.

There was nothing at all in the chamber; or there appeared to be nothing at first glance. Then slowly her eyes focused on an unusual formation—a bench with a block of ice cut from it, square as a block formed for an igloo. A saw had been used to cut the cube free.

Curiosity took her to the odd formation. Carefully she removed the block of ice. Inside was an iron box. Empty. But what could it have held? It had been recently placed, recently removed. No Avarian treasure had been deposited in such a modern contrivance—what then? There was no clue at all.

It's better to be moving, she convinced herself. To remain inside the Ice Castle after the fuel in her lamp had been depleted could be deadly. There was another way out, straight ahead she saw a narrow, square tunnel. It almost appeared to have been carved by human hands. Examining it more closely, she was sure it was so. Human hands with tools had carved this tunnel. Cautiously she moved onward, deeper into the Ice Castle. How far had she come? There was no telling; it was an endless world of ice and darkness, trickling melt and biting cold. Yet it seemed easily a mile. If she knew her direction. . .perhaps she had passed through the mountain known as Eagle's Nest entirely. She had come at least that far.

She found, suddenly, a silver twenty-pfennig piece, half-imbedded in ice. So someone had been this far. But who, or for what reason, she could not guess. The coin was of the old type, no longer in use. Yet here and there one saw a few. It meant nothing—yet.

Her lantern suddenly caught the form—in the second chamber. She stood, horrified, yet drawn magnetically to it. Standing at peace, frozen into a block of nearly translucent ice—Eric! No, it was not Eric, yet he had the features of the von Steinbock family. His dress was out of date. His eyes, open to the dead world, were the same clear blue. Helmuth von Steinbock!

Fascinated, she stood transfixed before the macabre form. Mummified in ice, he appeared perfectly lifelike, preserved wonderfully. It was as if Helmuth had not been dead for long enough that death could corrupt his handsome features. Yet they said it had been two years.

There were two remarkable features which Sarah noticed immediately. Helmuth had not died accidentally! A dagger with a handle of silver still protruded from his breast. He had been murdered, then left to the mysterious Ice Castle so that the murder might go undiscovered forever. The second item was more pathetic. A rose, a red bud, lay beside the figure. Yet it was not frozen in ice. It had been placed there quite recently. In the last day or so, she guessed. The stems of other roses were there as well. Someone remembered Helmuth's dying, knew where he rested eternally.

Minna? It had to be. Yet how did she know? They said she visited Helmuth's grave—a grave no one else was aware of, presuming the Steinbock brother lost without trace in the Ice Castle. They also said Minna had been with him when he met his fate. But that fate had been murder!

Again. The first time she had not been sure. Now she was. A scuttling, small sound reached her ears. Someone was there now—in this frozen Hades!

He rushed past rapidly, his eyes open with fear, mouth wide in a sound he never made. A squat little man with glossy black eyes, wild curly hair. Shorter than Sarah, he was square shouldered, thick through the chest.

She gasped, pressed back against the wall, lantern raised to strike down. But he did not even hesitate. He ran past, squirming like a rat through a crawl hole, disappearing into a half-hidden tunnel as suddenly as he had appeared.

Sarah turned and scrambled toward the tunnel she had come in by. The little man had been bleeding from the arm. It was his blood she had seen on the ice. Whoever he was, whatever his motives for being in the Ice Castle, she did not wish to ascertain. She wished only to be out of it, into clear air, above the ground where the fresh wind whistled through the pines, where the earth retained its natural, familiar form.

She tried one tunnel, then another as the first reached a cul-de-sac. There, before her eyes, was a drop of red. Not blood, but dye. With relief she moved along the blazed trail, hands and knees scraping against the icy floor. She recognized a bend in the trail, a knob-shaped form; then she could stand and she fairly leaped across the narrow ribbon of moisture.

The Satan Room! Fearful, diabolical hellhole, it met her eyes and she felt tears well up from the joy she felt at seeing the dreadful place. Now! Now, she knew the way to the cavern mouth.

She ran, slipped, stumbled, fell, rushing through the corridors into the massive anteroom. Outside the pale orange of a bleeding sunset shone as brilliant and as welcome as the first new light of day. She struggled toward it, bursting through the clawing grip of the Ice Castle into the open air.

He waited there.

"Rudi!"

The boy stood shivering beside the cart.

"I did not follow you," he said uncertainly, fearful of a

scolding. "But I could not leave you here."

"You are a dream," she said. Sarah moved to the boy, her weary arm resting on his shoulder; her clothing was torn, her hands scraped. Rudi gazed worriedly at her.

"Your brother . . .?"

"Not a trace," she told him.

"Then you will not go back into that place?"

"I cannot say." Sarah looked back at the massive, grinning chasm. It mocked her smallness, invited her to return to its fearful labyrinths. "I cannot say now."

"But for now?" Rudi helped her into the cart. He watched her face forlornly.

"But for now, you are a vision, dear Rudi. Take me home. Take me to Steinbock Castle."

Rudi looked at her oddly, and she realized why. Home—she had called Steinbock Castle "home."

The wind was icy, a fluffy, light snow swirled in the faintly orange sky; yet she was happy, hardly feeling the discomfort. She sat beside Rudi, gripping his arm as he guided the cart down the long winding trail toward Steinbock.

Thirteen

Steinbock Castle was ablaze with white light. Brilliant, nearly dazzling, the castle dominated the mountain scenery, spewing forth light and gaiety. And for Steinbock to do so was striking, breathtaking. This ominous, dark fortress turned suddenly as bright as the Vienna Opera House on premiere evening!

"He is here," Rudi breathed reverentially.

"*He?*"

"The Archduke Franz Ferdinand."

The boy was right. Fifteen automobiles were scattered about the front garden grounds. Soldiers of the honor guard, resplendent in brass and plumed hats, stood stiffly near the main entrance to Steinbock.

"Go on down, Rudi," she told the hesitant boy.

"But I . . . if you say so."

The cart moved on through the darkness, the trees swaying rhythmically in the slight breeze. Such a transformation! She had never seen anything so beautiful as Steinbock just then, and she had hardly imagined such beauty. The lights caught the angles of the ramparts, the smooth contour of the spires, and shone through the arched, narrow windows. Inside the main hall was magnificently illuminated with glittering chandeliers.

No sooner had the clattering of the horse's hoofs on the

wooden bridge died away then they were challenged. From the side of the road an immense guard with a great flowing mustache and holding a bayoneted rifle emerged.

"Halt!" he bellowed once, and Rudi, quaking violently stopped immediately.

Instantly three other uniformed men appeared, all massive, stern soldiers. "What have we here?" their sergeant demanded. He studied the two of them minutely.

"I am a friend of the Count von Steinbock," Sarah said. "A house guest."

"You say so?" The sergeant's eyes narrowed slightly. "Englishwoman?" he asked, stepping nearer.

"American."

"American?" he scratched his head thoughtfully. One of the men whispered something to him quickly.

"Yes. I am a house guest here."

"Certainly. I can see that you belong here. By your fine manner of dressing, your coiffure," he said, walking around her.

She realized suddenly what he meant. Her dress was torn from the scrambling in the Ice Castle, her hair windblown and snarled. Smudges of lampblack spotted her hands, and she imagined her face as well. She laughed and glanced at Rudi.

"Look at me, Rudi! It's no wonder."

But Rudi was too astonished to laugh. He only wanted to be away from Steinbock. He had wished to see the archduke's company, but not from so near.

"Turn around, boy. Go home!" the sergeant commanded.

"Perhaps I should go," Sarah said, "but I won't. What I am telling you is the truth. Anyone in the house knows who I am. Send a man."

"You are ordering me?"

"I am telling you that you will be very sorry if Eric von Steinbock hears that I have been treated this way."

A shadow of uncertainty crept over the Austrian's features. He pondered the thought momentarily. "All right. Jurgen! Go to the house and ask someone to come down."

"The count?" the corporal asked, eyes wide.

"No, fool. Bring that maid, or the butler. Don't bother the count. If this were for nothing . . ."

It was some time before Gertrude arrived, holding her skirts high.

"Miss Chamliss!" she gasped, holding her throat breathlessly. "I'm so sorry. I knew it had to be you, Ma'am."

"She is a house guest?" the sergeant asked.

"Yes."

"I would suggest, Fraulein," he said with a brusque gesture, "that you remain nearer the house. At least assure yourself of a more suitable escort."

Rudi blanched, his hands still tight on the reins.

"I could hardly imagine a more suitable escort than this young gentleman," she replied. The sergeant shrugged, allowed his mouth a brief sour expression, then waved his arm, allowing her the grounds.

"Don't blame him so much, Miss Chamliss," Gertrude said as they turned from the guard post. "These are perilous times. He is protecting the archduke to the best of his ability."

"I know," she replied. It was true. She had no business being short with the soldier. It was only the overpowering weariness in her, the exhaustion of a demanding day.

Sleepily she followed Gertrude to the kitchen entrance where a dozen white-shirted men worked hurriedly, rushing here and there with sauces and salads, great silver trays piled high with shrimp and pork dressed with orange slices, garnished with parsley. Steam filled the massive kitchen, the smell of soap was strong; in the corner two men with brass brushes worked furiously on five-quart copper kettles. They scarcely glanced at the women.

A little man with a pointed black mustache waved a wooden spoon briskly in the air, shouting commands; he resembled some frantic orchestral conductor in chef's hat.

"They have taken over," Gertrude said above the clamor. "It is a madhouse. Well," she added, "it saves me the work."

"You'd think they were feeding an army."

"They practically are. Such a retinue the archduke has! And the count has some more guests . . . but they tell me this is nothing.

"Tomorrow night is the grand banquet—a state function nearly. Though how they will be able to eat again is beyond me." She added in a low voice, "Look here."

With little interest as her weariness overwhelmed her, Sarah followed Gertrude to the door which was open a crack and allowed them a view of the royal dining room. The long table was set magnificently with lighted candelabra and linen. Crystal sparkled, catching the light from the gold and crystal chandeliers. There was the subdued tinkling of silver and low voices.

Eric sat beside the archduke, handsome and natural in a black suit, flowing ruffled shirt, a ribbon around his neck from which some decoration dangled. The archduke was a florid, portly man with an affable expression, pouched jowls and shy, small eyes. His wife, the Countess Sophie Chotek, Duchess of Hohenberg, was at his left hand. She was a sturdy-looking woman with a high forehead and the strong hands of a peasant. She seemed slightly out of place, vaguely unsettled against the display of aristocratic formality.

Whatever incongruity or remoteness Countess Chotek radiated, it was completely negated by the submersion of the Grand Duchess von Steinbock in the dazzle and pomp of the affair.

155

Eric's mother held forth regally. She might have been the empress herself. Diamonds sparkled on every finger, a massive diamond necklace dripped from her throat. She wore a small tiara woven into her silvering hair. Gracefully she moved, balancing conversation with slight motions of her hands, which instructed the help. No glass was left unfilled, no course served a fraction of a minute late, no guest within range of her deep voice allowed to feel apart from the general company.

"Minna is not there," Sarah commented.

"No." Gertrude looked at her as if she had blasphemed. "How could she be? The daughter of the grand duchess would hardly fit this affair."

"She might spoil the occasion."

"She would definitely spoil the occasion," Gertrude said. There was an acid edge to her voice. "Yet I imagine she would hardly miss it."

"And where is she, Gertrude? Chained in the dungeon? In that cell?"

"Miss?" Gertrude removed her hand from the door and faced Sarah. "I don't understand. The countess is in her room, as always this time of the evening."

"When I was down there—in the dungeon—I saw a cell with a bed made and with food half-eaten. With a book . . . Goethe."

"But you couldn't think . . . ! Oh, no! Minna would not be tortured so in her own home."

"The grand duchess said something. About the way the insane should be treated."

"You must understand the grand duchess," Gertrude said. "She has a dry sense of humor. She is also an aristocrat in every sense of that term. She sometimes fabricates opinions in order to shock those who are of more common birth. But she loves Minna. I swear it is so!" Gertrude's eyes pleaded for belief. "I have been with this family since Minna's birth. Her mother would die for her.

156

She speaks as she does to cover her heartache."

"Who then, Gertrude? Who could have been living down there?"

"No one could. It's completely impossible, Miss. No one has taken a tray. How would anyone come in and out without being seen?

"No," she repeated, her expression one of great puzzlement. "Perhaps your imagination, Ma'am. In a place like that, it could happen."

"Perhaps so," Sarah said, although she did not believe a bit of it. Gertrude went away wiping her hands on her apron. Sarah turned for the staircase.

From the dining room the general murmur continued. But she was in no mood for such doings, even had she been presentable. Probably the grand duchess was relieved that she had not made an entrance. An unfamiliar gentleman in uniform, eyes quite red, brushed by, stopped, and nodded, his gaze curious; then he went down the stairs.

Several doors were open. The castle was filled to overflowing with guests. She prayed that she could at least get to her room without anyone else catching her in the state of disarray she was now in. With relief she found the handle to her room, the Czar Nicholas room and went in, closing the door softly.

Minna was there on the bed. Her hair was incredibly tangled, her eyes more lusterless than usual, sunken deeply into black sockets. Her hands were thin, the skin translucent so that each blue vein showed. There was hardly an ounce of flesh on her pathetically thin arms, it seemed.

But it was her eyes that held the gaze, deep, searching dark eyes which seemed to see only what Minna wished to see.

"I wasn't supposed to be out," she said in a frail voice. "It was Mitzi."

"Mitzi?"

"My kitten. Mitzi wanted some milk." She held out a blue bowl which Sarah took, placing it on the bureau.

"I'll have Gertrude get some milk," she said.

"Don't tell her it's for Mitzi . . . I don't think Gertrude likes cats," she said with a tiny shake of her head.

"I won't," Sarah promised. "But you will let me change my dress and brush my hair first? I've been wandering."

"Where?"

"All over. In the country. Then I went to Feldkirch," she said as she slipped out of her dress. "I saw Father Bruno recently. He wishes he could see you."

"No," Minna said, her voice a barely audible squeak. "I'm not allowed."

"That's a shame, Minna." Sarah buttoned her dress and shook out her hair, brushing it vigorously. Minna slipped up beside her on the settee, gazing vacantly at her own image in the mirror.

"I was a pretty baby," Minna commented blankly, touching her hair with her hands, withdrawing them quickly as if in astonishment.

"And you're a pretty woman, Minna. But you must take care of yourself," Sarah scolded mildly. "Let me brush your hair, won't you?"

Minna protested slightly, but she seemed not to have the energy for one of her violent outbursts. As Sarah brushed her dark hair she stared at the mirror, enjoying the nearly feline stroking of the brush, yet not quite comprehending what it was.

Sarah noticed this detachment. Then she noticed the other thing—tiny marks on Minna's arm, inside the elbow. She studied Minna's eyes in the mirror. Abruptly with a shock of realization, Sarah saw what she should have seen before. Minna was being drugged! Habitually, deliberately sedated.

Perhaps the girl *was* mad, perhaps she needed to be

tranquillized to suppress her fits of violence. Perhaps not
. . . perhaps it was only a way of chaining Minna up
without using manacles to do it.

She decided then what she had considered often
before. She would see that Minna had professional help,
no matter if helping her offended the grand duchess's
sensibilities or even forced Minna to reveal something she
did not wish to—the fact that she had killed.

"I will speak to Eric," she said out loud. "He will realize
the need for it."

"I was certainly a pretty baby," Minna repeated. Sarah
had finished her hair and Minna's hands touched it
gingerly.

"Minna? Did you know someone was living in the
torture chamber?" Sarah asked suddenly.

"Yes. I knew it. I saw the cot when I went to visit
Helmuth's grave."

"Helmuth's grave?" But Helmuth was locked in a frozen
tomb in the Ice Castle.

"Yes." Minna spun around to face her. "But I don't want
to talk about that," she said scowling.

"Doesn't it worry you?"

"At Steinbock!" Minna began a laugh, but broke it off
suddenly. "No. It wouldn't surprise me if there were
dozens of men down there. Anything can happen here . . .
Helmuth . . ."

The girl's forehead wrinkled up and her eyes focused
strangely as if she were being assaulted by a memory
which would not come.

"What about Helmuth? What of your brother, Minna?"

"I don't have to tell you. I'll never tell anyone." Minna
was suddenly on her feet, her arms moving in crazy arcs as
if she were a windmill before a gale. "I'll never tell that!
You!" she shouted. Her finger came level with Sarah's
eyes. "You always want to trick me. You filthy thing." Her
voice was utterly virulent. She backed toward the door. In

a defiant gesture she placed her hands to her head and tore wildly at her hair.

"Minna . . ."

"I knew what you were the first time I saw you. Why do I let you trick me!" Her fists were clenched tightly, and tears welled up in those hollow eyes. "Why do you make me see Helmuth die all over again!"

Then Minna rushed from the room, careening against the walls, stumbling and screaming. Several guests opened their doors to peer out. Sarah could only watch the girl run to her silent, empty room.

Perhaps she was wrong. Yes, she forced Minna to talk about Helmuth's death, and invoked her tantrums. Perhaps, after all, the grand duchess was right in merely tranquillizing the girl and keeping her in the house where she could be watched. Yet something in her heart rebelled against the notion. There must be a better way. There must.

At that moment she glanced up to find Eric standing in the doorway. His eyes caressed her and he smiled.

"You know how to worry a man," he said, stepping into the room. "Where have you been?"

"The Ice Castle," she said simply. The words weighted his expression with concern.

"But I asked you not to. Such a monstrous place. I bring you here to keep you safely from this rascal Bramante, and I have brought you to other hazards." He shook his head worriedly and moved beside her, taking her hands. "You must not let anything happen to you, Sarah. It . . . would be the end for me."

He began to say something else, but Sarah hushed him, placing a finger tenderly to his lips.

"Please, Eric. We are different sorts of people."

"So I have enjoyed noticing," he said with a quick smile. "But if you wish"— he went on seriously— "if you believe it to be too soon?"

"There is so much on my mind, Eric," she said, turning from him to watch the moon-glazed mountains.

"I know. It is inappropriate. Forgive me."

"One does not *forgive* affection, Eric," she said gently, taking his sturdy hand briefly. "But I wished to speak of something else."

"Minna?"

"Yes, Minna."

"I saw her running from your room. My sister," he said, slapping his hands together in frustration, "desperately needs help."

"Did you know she is being drugged?"

"No!" Eric's head snapped up. "You mean it, don't you?"

"I do. She needs to be away from Steinbock, Eric. Home it is to her, yet a prison for her fragile mind as well."

"I know it." Eric stood at the railing, his eyes probing the darkness of the countryside. From below the hum of the string quartet sounded, people were dancing, chatting, planning for tomorrow.

"Who is staying in the dungeon?" Sarah asked quietly. Eric turned to her, his face a mask of puzzlement.

"What do you mean—staying in the dungeon? Is that a riddle? A joke?"

"I saw a cot prepared, a table with a lamp, a tray of food, half-eaten."

"No. It cannot be. The spirits of tortured souls dwell there. No one else." He took her head and lifted it gently. "You are sure, Sarah?"

"I am."

"Will you forgive me?" He hesitated and gestured with embarrassment. "Sarah, you once thought I was your brother. You once saw your brother—or who you thought was Robert—in our very garden. The distraught mind can deceive us."

"Eric . . ."

"Let me go on. I beg you to understand me, Sarah. I would say nothing to hurt you. But what you suggest is quite implausible."

"Eric, I am quite sure."

"All right. I will look into it. For now," he suggested, stroking her hair briefly, "please sleep. I am afraid you are overtired."

"But you will look?"

"Yes. I will," he promised her. "But for now, sleep. In the morning we breakfast with the archduke. I have told him about you. He was disappointed when you did not join us this evening."

He smiled, touched her hair once again and repeated. "Sleep."

She let him go, saying nothing of Helmuth's body, the box, the strange little man in the Ice Castle. Weariness overtook her completely. She was unsure herself what was real and what was not any longer.

Exhausted, her eyes burning, Sarah plopped onto the bed and drew the comforter over her. Morning. Morning would bring clear thought. In the morning there would be time for thinking.

Fourteen

Breakfast was at ten on the terrace. Sarah drew all eyes as she came out, wearing her blue morning dress, a single pearl around her throat. Eric stood and came to greet her, introducing her to the company.

She was seated next to the Countess Sophie Chotek, across from the archduke. The countess smiled dimly and continued to eat with little relish after the introduction, obviously preoccupied. Beside the archduke was a handsome, if harsh-looking man, introduced as the under-minister of defense, Herr Konrad Speidel. He glanced up momentarily and grunted as he buttered his toast.

The Germans, Hermann Glick and Field Marshal Klaus Eisner, were there as well, to Sarah's surprise. Apparently their plans had been changed, or she had misunderstood them. Eisner smiled, perhaps remembering their first meeting when she had mistaken the brutally scarred blond man for an assailant. Glick hardly nodded, his eyes cold as ever, his thick shoulders nearly bursting the seams of his dark coat.

Eric held her chair as she was seated. Her eyes momentarily held those of Eisner, remembering his word: *Mörder.*

"It is refreshing to have youth and beauty at our breakfast," the Archduke Ferdinand said. His mouth smiled faintly as if it were painful. Yet his eyes twinkled as merrily as Kris Kringle's. He seemed a sad man, rotund, weighted by the burden of high office.

"Thank you, sir," Sarah replied.

"Don't thank me," the archduke said, "I have an eye for the beautiful ladies. I appreciate them. As you can tell by looking at my wife," he added graciously.

"I can," Sarah said.

The countess looked away shyly as Sarah said that. Apparently she was still an unpretentious country girl inside. The marriage of the Archduke Ferdinand, heir to the throne, and Sophie Chotek, Countess, Duchess of Hohenberg, by all accounts had been a happy one.

Yet despite her titles, in the complicated order of the nobility, she was deemed unsuitable as the archduke's wife. Their marriage had been declared morganatic, meaning that their children, should there be any, could never lay claim to the throne of Austria.

Perhaps this explained the burden which seemed to rest on the shoulders of Sophie Chotek. Yet there was a quiet pride in her—a pride of self-respect, a pride in being the wife of the Emperor Franz Joseph's nephew. For all of the gold braid, the lace, the titular service, the gold of their rings and accessories, they seemed nothing more than a sturdy peasant couple, like the Huchtings perhaps. And they seemed very much, if quietly, with the reserve demanded by their station, in love.

"I trust," the Archduke Ferdinand said, "that you are enjoying your stay in our country."

"It is a beautiful country," Sarah said.

"But do I detect a note of unhappiness in your response?" Franz Ferdinand asked kindly.

"Miss Chamliss has come to us under less than happy circumstances," Eric explained. "It seems her brother, a scientist, has been lost somewhere in Austria while working."

"Probably butchered by that damned Trentino," Glick said harshly, shoveling omelette into his mouth as he spoke.

"I do not think so," Sarah said.

"No?" Eric's mother said sharply. "What do you know of the problems we have had with this Carlo Bramante and his band? I think what Herr Glick suggests is most likely."

"I still do not believe that is the case," Sarah replied.

"Sarah has met our local Robin Hood," Eric said. "In fact, Bramante seems taken with her. He risked his neck to dance with her."

"And so would I, were I a young man," the archduke said, "and not already happily wed."

"They are a murderous, rebellious lot," Glick insisted, wiping his mouth with a napkin.

"Do you really see them as so dangerous?" the archduke asked seriously. "I had the idea they were simply a band of rabble. Thieves, freebooters."

"They are cutthroats," Eric said, his face set. "Their aim," he went on, "is to disrupt the empire, to stir secessionist fires, to withdraw from the empire. Bramante is a political creature, seeking to encourage the revolt of the Trentinos. He wishes . . . war."

"So?" The archduke glanced at Konrad Speidel. The Austrian under-minister of defense shrugged and answered. "Our present intelligence does not present Bramante in so strong a light, Your Grace."

"I did not think so. But then the Count von Steinbock is closer to the situation than we in Vienna. Perhaps we should reexamine our evidence, Konrad. Nothing so vital should be left to chance."

"Yes, sir," Speidel said, immediately making a notation in a book he produced from inside his coat.

"It is difficult to administer to so many peoples," the archduke reflected, "all with different aspirations. The Serbs are very unhappy; the Croatians restless for self-government; the Trentinos would have their country returned to Italy. Linguistically and geographically this is reasonable. But the empire must be preserved."

"At the risk of war?" Sarah asked.

"What? I do not know," the archduke replied in a strained voice. "I believe that is my uncle's feeling."

"And the emperor is correct," Field Marshal Klaus Eisner said vigorously. "What does this young lady know of the Germanic peoples, or of war?" he scoffed.

"I know that war kills people," Sarah said.

"Such an attitude reveals the American mind explicitly," the Field Marshal said triumphantly. "War does become necessary, young woman. Austria is a German-speaking nation assailed at the present time by fleas and vermin. I am speaking of the various peoples: Poles, Czechs, Slovenians, Trentinos," he said, counting them out on his fingers, "Italians, Serbians. They cannot be assimilated into the Germanic nation."

"Field Marshal Eisner," the archduke said, sipping water from his crystal glass, "may I remind you that there is no 'Germanic nation,' except that envisioned by certain expansionist thinkers."

"No, Your Grace. Forgive me. I spoke only for Germany." Eisner, deflated, sat down.

"I do not know," Franz Ferdinand went on. "Perhaps once one has become the conqueror there is a debt owed. If one regulates, governs, perhaps there is an obligation to serve as well."

"These people! Like Bramante."

"I don't know," the archduke answered heavily. "I have not heard their petitions. But war is a Goliath waiting now to be unleashed upon all of Europe. I would not be the one to unshackle him."

"The decision is the Emperor Franz Joseph's," Glick said haughtily. The archduke did not appreciate the tone of the visiting German.

"Yes, it is his to decide what must be done. Thank goodness. Perhaps he is more fit to make such a choice. His mind is set. Mine gropes for truth and compromise."

"The Germanic peoples . . ." Glick began again.

"I remind you—you speak for Germany, I only as a private man, a single Austrian. For now.

"I am well aware of Germany's political ambitions. The *Drang nach Osten,* drive to the east. Yet I ask you, Herr Minister Glick—exactly how does Germany plan to achieve this drive to the east in its quest for territory without passing through Austria?"

Glick chewed his lip tensely, his ears red.

"This conversation does little to settle a breakfast," the archduke said finally, rising heavily from the table. "I will retire for a time."

"I apologize," Eric said. "My friends have different opinions as do we all. We each wish to serve our individual countries. I assure you we will suppress such chatter. Wednesday we will hunt stag, losing ourselves in the pursuit. Steinbock can be an idyllic retreat."

"I believe my schedule has been restructured, Count von Steinbock." Speidel nodded. "I cannot stay until the middle of the week. Monday we will hunt."

"The day after tomorrow then," Eric replied with a courteous bow.

Sarah went into the garden, her anger still stirred. Yet she had no business spouting off in front of these world figures. Men who would pay no heed anyway.

"I am sorry, Sarah," Eric said, catching her shoulder as she stood in the lath house. "They are political men. It is always on their mind."

"They would start a war!" Sarah said with anguish. "They wish for it, perhaps even pray for war."

"Yes. Unfortunate, but true."

"It is evil."

"Yes. War is evil. But war will come. There are national

movements stirring. Race against race. War will come; these men only wish it to begin on their terms—like all other men."

"There are those who pray war will never come again."

"But they are the dreamers, Sarah. They are soft, frightened. They back away an inch at a time. Sooner or later they are smashed; muddled in their own weakness they are easy prey for the aggressor."

"You sound as if you pity me."

"No, dear Sarah. I do not. I only speak what the lines of history have proven over and again. There will always be war. There will always be struggle. We are built for it; some savage tendency lives in our blood. There has never been a moment in mankind's history when there was not struggle somewhere. Wars go on at this very moment. I pray it does not begin in Austria. Yet I am sure there are others who want it to begin here."

"The Trentinos?"

"I accuse no one," Eric shrugged. "Yet I see it coming, inexorably. Storm clouds gather over the mountains, electricity flashes across all of Europe even as we stand here."

"Miss Chamliss!"

Gertrude came running from the house, waving a piece of paper.

"Yes?"

"Miss Chamliss . . ." Gertrude stopped, panting for breath. "A letter."

"Whatever . . . ?" she tore it open shakily.

Miss Sarah Chamliss, Feldkirch: The man who witnessed your brother's death is in the hospital at Lienz. His name is Boehm.

Fifteen

The hospital at Lienz was small, whitewashed, situated on a small knoll in the shade of linden trees. Sarah's footsteps echoed down the polished, empty corridor. The antiseptic smells of lye and vinegar filled her nostrils. She felt light-headed, nearly free of her body as she was guided through the halls.

"Father Bruno wrote to all of the orders in the Tyrol," the small nun, Sister Bernadette said, "asking about your brother. One of our patients, a woodsman named Boehm, heard me mention the name and came forward. But you may speak to Herr Boehm yourself," she said, swinging open the door to a small room where four men lay in bed.

"That one is Herr Boehm," Sister Bernadette said. He lay near the window, his head swathed in bandages, a ruddy, freckled man of thirty or so, with large hands and the muscles of a man used to hard labor.

Sarah approached him slowly, her heart pounding. She did not wish to know the truth, she decided. She wished to know nothing bad, after all this time. To have searched and hoped . . . to have her hopes crushed.

"Yes?" Boehm had opened his eyes. Large blue eyes which showed some pain behind them, he searched Sarah's face. "Do I know you, Fraulein?"

"No. You don't know me." She drew up a wooden chair

and sat beside the injured man. "What happened to you?"

"In the mountains," he said hoarsely. "A terrible accident."

"I am Robert Chamliss's sister," she said finally.

"Robert! No! . . . I am so sorry," he said, sagging back against the pillow. "It was very bad."

"He is dead?" she asked, fighting back the sob in her voice.

"Yes," he said nodding his head weakly, closing his eyes tightly. "Dead."

"Will you tell me about it." Everything, she wanted to know everything about Robert's death.

"I will," Boehm said, opening his eyes, "if you are quite sure you wish me to."

"Quite sure."

"I met Robert in an inn at Mayrhofen," Boehm recalled, his eyes on Sarah's. "Your brother was asking directions. He wanted to go through the Brenner. A very dangerous journey this time of the year, I told him. Yet I am born of the mountains, and I know them well. As well as any man knows these cold giants. I love them, I am possessed by mountain spirits.

"He was himself possessed," Boehm went on, "with the need to know. Knowledge lured him into the Alps. He told me he had been to Feldkirch to find an Avarian script. There was a tale there only he could read."

Boehm said nothing for a time. Whether recollecting his thoughts or being tormented by spasmodic pain, Sarah could not say. The sun through the window was pleasant, the view of the Alps was stunning, the snowcaps brilliant in the high, clear air.

"The legend told of a place where the Avarian king had hidden much wealth—a place called Hirschfangen. But no one Robert had met could tell him where it is. I know. It is a dangerous, secluded ridge far into the mountains, famous for landslides, deep escarpments, treacherous broken trails. But, as I say, I am a man possessed by mountain spirits. I love to see them beneath my feet despite their vengeance. I told him I would take him."

"When was this?" Sarah wanted to know.

"Three days ago. Yes . . . three days. We climbed well, quickly. Even when we had to use the ropes. Your brother learned the art easily. In eight hours, no more, we had found the Hirschfangen. A towering, weather-splintered mountain standing alone, challenging us.

"I asked Robert—should I go alone?

"'No,' he told me. 'We will go together.'

"I moved up first, driving iron into the clefts. Robert picked his way carefully, wondering all the time at the primitive soldiers who had managed this trail without lines, without iron hooks.

"He told me—'those were men!' I turned to answer him and the world fell in. There was an avalanche, snow and rock—Hirschfangen's fury. I was slapped aside by a falling wall of snow, pounded against the face of the cliff, dangling by my anchor line. Horrible sounds filled the air, snow washing out the blue of the sky, beating past . . . when I looked, Robert was gone. I found him hours later, buried under tons of snow. I dug feverishly.

"I dug until my eyes filled with sweat which froze. My shirt was stiff on my back. Then I touched my scalp. I had not noticed before. It was peeled back nearly to my ears. I sagged to the ground. I could do no more. I could dig . . . no more. I could not carry him . . . back."

Sarah sat immobilized by the man's words. Tears filled his eyes as he finished his tale. Sarah's hands worked against one another.

"Are you . . . sure?" she asked, still needing to disbelieve.

"Yes. Sure. Look there," he said, indicating the drawer in the night stand beside his cot.

Sarah opened the drawer hesitantly. There—it was true.

171

Done with. Tenderly she picked up the ring and held it in her hand.

"His school ring," Sarah said. "The initials. R. D. C."

"I took it from his hand. I'm sorry, Ma'am. Truly." Boehm said. He seemed to have trouble breathing now, his chest rose spasmodically.

"Miss Chamliss?"

It was Sister Bernadette.

"Yes?" she said vacantly.

"Herr Boehm is in some pain. If you have finished with your inquiries . . . ?"

"Yes. Yes, I have finished," Sarah said, rising unsteadily. "I am sorry. Thank you, Herr Boehm."

The mountaineer had fallen off to sleep again. Sarah edged from the room, the nun's steadying hand on her arm.

"I am sorry," Sister Bernadette said.

"Yes . . ." Sarah said absently. "Thank you for your kindness."

Outside the world was bitterly cold, the wind shoving massive white thunderheads before it; the trees quaked in their positions along the road, seeming to anticipate the wrath of the coming storm. Yet Sarah felt none of it, cold nor wind.

Her world had gone empty. She moved without knowing where, why. She seemed absent from the world, apart from her body, yet when she went to climb into the cart her legs trembled so that she could not do it at first.

It was a blurred, watery landscape she surveyed. It was a moment before she realized that it was because her eyes were flooded with tears. She lay her head against her arms. Empty.

To lose someone you love so much is to lose a piece of the world itself. There is a vacant spot from that moment on, which will never again be totally filled. Time may dull the bitterness of memory, but nothing may erase it.

172

It began to snow before she reached Steinbock early in the afternoon. Otto came to take the horse. He spoke, but Sarah hardly heard him and neglected to answer. She went directly to the house. Eric was there waiting and she clung to him briefly, tears staining his shirt front.

"The worst?" he asked.

"Yes. Eric, I . . . please have Gertrude pack my suitcase."

"You can't leave like this," he protested. "Not now. Give it time to heal. You are welcome here. Take a week. There are some things I haven't had the chance to talk to you about."

"No." She pushed back to arm's length, shaking her head. Eric started to speak, but she shushed him. "I want to go, Eric. Back to Paris. I can't stand it here."

"Please."

"No." She was adamant and Eric finally nodded, calling Gertrude. He watched her climb the long stairs, wanting to call her back, knowing it would do no good.

"You are a foolish young man to let her go," the Archduke Franz Ferdinand said. He had come quietly beside Eric. "I admire her. I am sure you do as well."

"Admire?" Eric smiled grimly. "Yes, I admire her. But she is her own woman."

"This is the only kind worth having," Franz Ferdinand ventured. "A woman of will. When such a woman chooses a man of her own volition, with voluntary faithfulness, with considered vows, she stands by him. I know," he winked. "You don't want a girl that can be browbeaten."

"There is nothing more that can be said," Eric said heavily. "She may return—when she wishes. Then she will be welcomed. Welcomed."

It was nearly five in the evening, a cold, gray evening with spotty snow when Sarah reached the depot. The clerk was there, but he refused to sell her a ticket.

"I don't understand," she stammered incredulously.

"No tickets. No tickets," the little man repeated. He gestured toward the end of the depot platform where three policemen stood watching the sunset bleed through the silver and black of the rolling skies. "Ask them," he shrugged, "I don't know."

She left her luggage there and walked to the men, the wind pushing against her. One of them she knew. It was the cobbler, Schmidt, from Feldkirch.

"The stationmaster will not sell me a ticket, Herr Schmidt. Can you tell me why not?"

"*Nein!*" Schmidt said with affected self-importance. "I can tell you nothing. But it is *verboten!* No travelers."

"It is a long way back to Feldkirch," Sarah said angrily. "Yet if I have to take the cart tonight and report this to Herr Captain Flaig, I will."

Schmidt laughed. "Our orders are from Flaig," the shoemaker said grandly. "Go talk to him if you will."

Would nothing go right? Hotly she stalked away, the men's laughter following her. Very well. She would return to Feldkirch. It would be dark in an hour, and she shuddered as she realized she would have to pass through the deep forest in the darkness, but she could see no alternative.

The snow continued steadily. Quietly the ditches and vales were being paved over with white softness. The temperature, which had been mild, had plunged after nightfall.

Herr Flaig was relaxing before the fire at home when Sarah reached Feldkirch, sitting in his undershirt and smoking a pipe. The police captain looked up in surprise as Sarah was shown in.

Upstairs a baby cried. Helga had given birth to a boy the week before.

"Yes?" Herr Flaig asked.

"I wish to leave Austria," Sarah said tautly. "Yet upon reaching the trunk line station, I was told that it was forbidden. I am cold, I am tired, and I wish to return to France. Please tell me why I cannot, Herr Flaig."

Helga had come down, nursing a vigorous, red baby with fine lashes and strong little hands which clenched and unclenched with satisfaction as he ate.

Herr Flaig knocked his pipe bowl out and shook his head. "It is not allowed," he said gruffly.

"I understand that," Sarah said wearily. "But why not?"

"I need not explain," the stocky policeman said, "but I will. The Archduke Ferdinand is staying near Feldkirch . . ."

"At Steinbock," Sarah interrupted. "I know," she went on in response to his curious glance. "I was staying there! I have met the archduke. It is hardly a secret."

"No," Flaig said rising, tugging at his drooping mustache. "That is precisely the problem."

"I don't understand."

"We have heard information—hard facts—that point to an attempt on the archduke's life, Miss Chamliss. We are nearly certain that a segment of the Trentino faction will attempt to assassinate the Archduke Ferdinand."

"But what have I to do with this?" Sarah demanded.

"To maintain security no one is allowed to enter Feldkirch."

"But I want only to leave!"

"I am sorry. The Tyrolian border is closed to traffic. The trains are not running, therefore the trains cannot be used for escape. The trains are not running, therefore no one may arrive on the train. The border, Miss Chamliss, is closed."

"That explains all the extra police," she said. "But still I . . ."

"The trains are not running, Miss Chamliss. If I wanted you to go, you could not go. No trains are running!"

"I see. I am stuck here until the archduke and his party leave."

"Yes. I am sorry. I will not have this murder committed in my parish," Flaig said passionately.

"All right. I understand this. I will simply return to Steinbock."

"Do that," he agreed. "Do just that, Miss Chamliss."

She had a moment to speak alone with Helga. The baby was beautiful, and Helga utterly happy. She went on and on about the baby, her husband, who had returned to the army for his final year, and their plans for the future.

"And the father of the baby?" Sarah asked. "He is quite as happy?"

"The baby's father? Yes," she said smiling deeply, "*Fritz* is quite as happy as I."

She kissed Helga on the cheek before she left, and took one last peek at the baby, a sturdy child who would grow to be a tall, fair-haired man.

The snow washed down in a never-ending curtain of white. It was far to Steinbock, yet she decided to return. Her eyes burned with the need for sleep, her hands gripped the reins woodenly. The trees huddled in isolated stands, their branches bowed by winter's weight. The pony moved along bravely, the wagon wheels leaving deep ruts in the snow.

So tired. She was so tired, yet there was no stopping, no place to stop. The wind had grown again, whipping through the bending trees, flinging snowflakes like great fistfuls of gravel against her stinging cheeks.

"Move on, poor pony," she said to the horse which pricked its ears, hearing the comforting human voice even above the wail of the rushing wind. Sarah drew her scarf more tightly around her face, holding it with one hand as she guided the stumbling, faltering pony.

—Foolish. It was foolish to have left Feldkirch on such a night. She had not seen winter in this high country, these brutal storms, but she had been warned often enough that three feet of snow might fall in an hour with winds of cyclone force twisting through the passes. Foolish.

The pony halted, blowing badly, his wretched head sagging between his front legs. She was sorriest for the horse, innocent, trusting animal.

The snow was heavier, much heavier now. It seemed to fall in clumps, burying everything which lived upon the earth, and the wind positively shrieked with pride in its own strength.

Suddenly Sarah was angry. As angry as she could remember ever having been with herself. A silly ninny. A silly little city girl out on a night which threatened snow, a black, fierce night. She would probably get herself killed. Yet the anger was for another reason.

She realized that she was sitting there. Doing nothing Nothing! And the storm threatened to devour her with its awesome, icy jaws. Get up, girl! Move on. Do something.

Desperately she struggled from the exposed bench and began unharnessing the horse. The steel of the harness was cold, her hands numb, the hooks impossible, yet she somehow got the horse free.

Taking it by the bridle she tugged it off the road toward a stand of trees. There the wind was slowed by the branches and trunks. Something else caught her eye as she searched the white, driving skies. There. Just there—a cleft in a great outcropping of whitish granite.

By main strength she managed to prod the horse toward the wedge in the rocks. Inside it was cold but dry; the wind whistled through the shattered boulders, but the cutting edge was blunted. There was a small alcove where the pony could be kept and another with a bench of rock where a person might sleep. If one were cold, bitterly tired, half frozen . . . and so she slept.

When she awakened, hours later, the snowfall had died to a light, filmy tint in the morning skies. The wind had ceased its constant muttering; and Carlo Bramante was there, watching her.

Sixteen

Bramante was perched on a rock, his cool, dark eyes on Sarah. His cap was pushed back, allowing his dark curls to billow out across his broad forehead. He wore a leather jacket and black pants. Behind the jacket the handle of a Mauser pistol projected.

"You!" Sarah sat up, instantly awake. "What are you doing here!"

"I was simply watching, Sarah—if I may call you Sarah. I feel that I know you so well." He hopped down from his seat on the boulder and stood before her, smiling maddeningly. Sarah wanted to hate the man, but she was no longer sure it was possible. Something about him caused her heart to palpitate wildly. Fear? No, it was not fear of Carlo Bramante which caused her cheeks to grow hot, and she knew it was not.

"I simply wanted shelter from the storm," Sarah said, and she backed away involuntarily as she spoke. Her lips had trouble forming the words.

"I know that, Sarah," Bramante said. "But I thought you were on your way home. I hated to see you go, of course, but I believed that was your intention."

"How did you know that?"

As they spoke Sarah let her eyes search the dark, close confines of the tiny burrow. There was no one else visible. No sound crept in from outside. Bramante seemed to be alone. At that thought her blood again began to race.

"I try to know everything that happens in the Tyrol," Bramante answered casually. He withdrew a step or two, perhaps in response to her discomfort. "And there is little I do not know."

"Then you know the trains are not running," she said.

"No?" He grimaced and shook his head. "Perhaps I underestimated the adversary."

"The adversary." Sarah looked closely at Bramante's boyish, yet world-weary eyes.

"The Austrians," he said plainly. "I view myself as a Trentino, you see. Therefore, the Austrians, at the moment, are the adversary. I am Italian," he continued, touching the tips of his fingers to his heart, "or should have been by birth, by blood, by geography. Yet I am an Austrian by law."

"And so you harass them?"

"Yes," he said proudly.

"Frighten them?"

"I would think so. Yes."

"Kill them!"

"No." Bramante wagged a finger emphatically. "I do not kill the Austrian people. They are my countrymen. They are men. Blood marks any cause with the indelible stain of wrong."

"That is not what they say," Sarah said, her eyes trying to bore into the thoughts of this bandit general.

"No?" Bramante laughed. "Of course not. Why would they credit me with morality?"

"I hear," Sarah said slowly, "that there is a plot afoot to murder someone. A kindly old man whose only crime seems to be the nobility of his birth."

"I have heard the same rumors," Bramante admitted.

"I have heard that Bramante is responsible for this plot," she said cautiously.

"It is absurd. Slander! Illogical!" Carlo said, waving his hands in the air. He stepped nearer once again to Sarah.

"Do not be afraid, little bird. I am not what you think. Nothing is what you perceive it to be. You have been used, tricked, beguiled. You must believe me."

"What do you mean?"

"It is not I who seek to kill the Archduke Ferdinand. What for? He seems to be a man who will listen, and he is the next emperor of Austria. I, who wish to speak, to petition, mean this man no harm. It is those who wish to begin a war who would kill him."

"I don't see . . ."

"But certainly you do. The archduke is killed by a member of a minority group. There must be reprisals, the driving out of the non-Germanic people. War must be declared against Trentino. If Italy should come to Trentino's defense, then perhaps Germany would feel obligated to assist Austria, her sister country.

"It is a game of subterfuge," Bramante said, leaning back as he lit a cigarette, waving out the match wearily. "A game in which war is the goal, death the object. Only an excuse is needed. When nations deem war economically, politically advisable, reasons are not difficult to find, excuses come readily to the mind. One needs only the proper setting, the right scapegoat."

"I see," Sarah said, although she did not see at all. Logically she followed the man; yet if what Bramante said was the truth, or the truth as he saw it, then a plot was being hatched at Steinbock by the Germans to assassinate the heir to the Austro-Hungarian throne in a blatant attempt to begin a far-reaching war on behalf of their homeland.

"You seem little concerned," Bramante said, mistaking her thoughtfulness for apathy.

"Greatly concerned," she corrected, "yet greatly confused. Your reputation hardly lends credence to your

180

word. At any rate—perhaps I do no longer care. About you, about Eric von Steinbock," though that was a lie, and she knew it, "about Europe's petty border clashes . . . all of it."

"But you will. This will not end here. Believe me. In 1913 it is no longer possible to have an isolated war. There are too many alliances, too many formidable weapons and strong-willed men. France will be involved, certainly, and England. Possibly even your own country, Sarah.

"It is fortunate," he concluded, "that not all people feel the way you do about this."

"What?" Sarah's head snapped up. She realized that Bramante was telling her something vital. "What others are involved? A mustached Englishman? My brother Robert!"

"Yes. Since I have told you this much," he said insouciantly, "I may as well admit that. You see, in knowledgeable circles it is agreed that war must come, that certain factions are encouraging it, demanding it, praying for it."

"And those who do not wish for it?"

"They are obligated to work against it."

"Robert . . ."

"Robert Chamliss was working to halt a world war."

"He was simply an . . ."

"He was a great deal you did not know about, Sarah. A great deal," Bramante said seriously. "You could only have been a child when his second career began. A career in which he utilized his scientific journeys to assist certain factions in gaining necessary information."

"A spy!" Sarah said incredulously, gazing in mystification at the tall Italian.

"If you would label it so." Bramante shrugged. "A worker for peace. A man of high principles. A knowledgeable man who knew that war was imminent. All of these."

"But what happened?" she asked. "What did happen?"

"I thought you wanted only to leave," Bramante taunted her.

"You are evil," she said with fire. Her eyes were alight with anger. What right had he to withhold the truth?

"Evil?" Bramante laughed again, that long rolling laugh of his. "Yes. You are not the first woman to tell me that, Sarah Chamliss." Smiling, he stepped toward her.

Suddenly a huge, burly form filled the yellow entrance to the hidden nook—A black-bearded man with fierce eyes and gigantic hands which were clenched around an Enfield rifle.

"They are coming," Ferrara grunted. He darted a disapproving look at Sarah. "Three cars. Twelve men."

"All right, Mirko. Can they find us?" Bramante snatched up his own rifle from beside the rocks. Quickly he moved across the cave like a menacing cat.

"Will they find us, Mirko?"

"I think so if we do not move, Carlo. The lady's cart is still in the road. The snow will have covered our tracks, yet they have only to look for the best cover."

"All right. Quickly then," Bramante ordered.

"And her?" Ferrara asked with a motion of his massively bearded chin. "What shall we do with her? She has seen us here."

"We have no choice," Bramante snapped. "She must go with us now."

"But the plan . . ."

"Damn the plan! We have no choice. Take her horse. Take her!"

With that Bramante was out the door of the small cave, moving silently across the snowfields, weaving among the trees.

"Come on," Ferrara grumped.

"But what of him?"

182

"He is going around them. If they see us, he will open fire. You have been a problem to us, woman," the bandit lieutenant complained.

"I . . ." Sarah sputtered furiously. "I only wanted to be left alone."

Before she could say more, Ferrara took her tightly by the arm and shuffled to where the horse was hidden. He scooped her up in his bearlike arms and sat her in front of him, across the horse's withers.

Riding bareback he walked the horse slowly forward, his rifle firmly in his free hand. She saw nothing at first, but the clang of a piece of iron being dropped on another sounded through the woods, and turning slightly she saw the soldiers in the trees below.

A voice, indistinct, muffled by the wind carried to them. She had only to scream and they would hear. But Bramante would be shooting in return, blood would run. Was she sure she wanted to be found?

An incongruous detail caught her eye as the men clustered around their vehicles, not twenty feet from her abandoned wagon. Their uniforms . . .

Germans. "They're Germans," she whispered in amazement, "not Austrians."

Ferrara grunted disparagingly, his eyes on the soldiers below. He urged the pony on, his legs nearly dragging in the snow. Courageously the small horse drove upward, through the trees and new snow, carrying the unusual burden.

Sarah too watched the soldiers. German soldiers here, deep in the Tyrol. Legally? Or were the Austrian authorities unaware of this? Her thoughts were allowed to run no farther.

From below a shout sounded. A soldier had leaped up and stood pointing his finger at the dark form high on the ridge. At that moment a shot was fired, a bullet, seconds later, it seemed, died dully against the trunk of a tree some twenty feet below them.

There was the sound of cursing and shouting. The soldiers formed a rank, some of them kneeling in their greatcoats, rifles to their shoulders.

Then, from across the valley, another rifle echoed. The soldiers scattered, one of them yelping with pain or surprise. Another shot followed quickly, this one whining off the metal of their truck's hood. Frantically the Germans ran for the cover of their cars.

A horse, stung or frightened, danced across the road, heels kicking high, stirrups flapping free.

In another moment the loud, hectic command to fire was given and the soldiers laid down a volley in the opposite direction, the smoke from their rifles rising in tiny puffs visible before the rolling echoes of their shots reached Sarah's ears.

Again they fired in unison, working frantically at the breeches of their rifles. And again. Sarah felt like shrieking, like holding her ears. "They will kill him!" she said frantically.

"No. Not him," Ferrara said almost without expression. "They didn't even see Bramante."

The horse had climbed well. Already they were at the crest of the ridge, well out of rifle range. There was no sign of pursuit.

"They will not come," Ferrara guessed. "We have the distance. They could not catch us in the timber."

Thoughtfully he nodded to himself, his black eyes small, expressionless. Then he climbed down from the pony's back, leading it as Sarah rode down a winding, nearly invisible trail into the deep, forested glen below.

"Ferrara?"

The man did not glance back. He trudged on through the snow, his huge feet tramping down the snow as they moved through the pine forest. A jay cocked its head in the branches above, called out brazenly once, and followed, hopping from bough to bough before he flew off into the clear sky.

"Ferrara?" she said again.

"What is it?" he replied impatiently. She could see nothing of his face, only the cap on his head, the hulking shoulders, the thick neck with black hairs curling over the coat collar.

"Robert. Robert Chamliss. Is he dead?"

"I did not see it," Ferrara shrugged without hesitating in his rolling gait. He obviously did not want to talk, nor did he want to nursemaid this bold little American girl. "They say so. Yes."

"Why?"

"Why?" he asked. "What do you mean? Why is he dead?"

"Yes." Sarah said. "Could you stop a moment, please?" Ferrara complied and she stepped nimbly from the horse's back. "I'd rather walk awhile."

"Suit yourself," Ferrara shrugged, beginning his ambling, purposeful trek again.

"Why did he die?" Sarah persisted. She had to hoist her skirts and nearly run to keep up with the gigantic Trentino. "For that matter, why were you watching me?"

"I don't know. Orders."

"Which? The death of Robert or the watching."

"Both. Orders," Ferrara said. He whirled suddenly to face her. But the massive ferocious man was no longer so fear-inspiring. She simply stood there, watching him. "Orders," he repeated.

"Who? Someone ordered Robert's death. Who ordered it?"

"You want to know?" he asked, his voice even deeper than usual.

"Of course I do."

They had come around an abrupt, downward curve in the road where it forded a small, gurgling creek. "It was him," Ferrara said nonchalantly, lifting a finger.

"What?" Then she saw him sitting beside the road on a barkless, fallen cedar. Ferrara's finger pointed unwaveringly at a grinning Carlo Bramante.

"But wait!" She grabbed Ferrara's arm impetuously. Bramante was standing now, near the creek. He waved his cap to them. "You can't mean . . . ?"

"Sure," Ferrara replied, jerking his arm away. "It was Carlo's idea. He ordered Robert's death."

Seventeen

She stood in the clearing, tremors of rage washing over her. Like a comet, anger flared in her skull, lighting her eyes with sparking hate.

Bramante took one confident step forward, then stopped, puzzled. Behind him the brook babbled merrily through the deep blue forest, the white of new snow frosting the upper boughs. A lark sang deep in the woods, the sky passed lazily over, smeared with thin clouds. Yet she hardly saw a bit of it.

A curtain had been drawn before the rest of the world, a curtain of fire. Hatred pumped violently in her breast. Her eyes were fixed only on him, flashing razors of contempt which slashed at the bandit. If they could have followed her will, Bramante would have dropped, scored and flayed by their scornful edges.

A light dawned in Bramante's dark eyes. "Of course," he said lightly. "Ferrara has told you our secret."

Smiling, he stepped to her, and without calculation she fell on him, her fists pummeling his shoulders and chest, flailing the air with ineffectual blows, which, if her hatred could have aided them, would have hammered him to dust.

He laughed. An infuriating, amused laugh. His mouth open wide, head thrown back to reveal those perfect white teeth and pink tongue. He laughed!

"I knew you would be upset with us, my little dove," Bramante said, reaching for the thrashing twisting girl, clenching her shoulders, "but not so angry."

"You are an animal. A pig! Viper! Demon out of hell," she puffed, still trying to hit him with her small fists. But he only rolled his head and continued that irreverent laughing.

"She has the blood of a Neapolitan, eh, Mirko?" Carlo asked. Sarah tossed wildly in his arms. Ferrara only grunted from the streambed where he lifted a cupped hand dripping icy water to his bearded mouth.

"So angry . . . I would not have believed it," Carlo Bramante said. "I have apologized for tricking you, have I not?"

"Tricking . . . ?" She stopped, frozen in her motion. Incomprehension dulled her eyes.

"Yes." Bramante looked more deeply into her eyes. "Why are you so angry, Sarah? What was it you told her, Ferrara?"

"That you ordered Robert Chamliss killed," Ferrara growled, plugging his cap back on, his beard dripping water. "That's what she asked."

"But, Mirko! Did you explain no more?"

"She asked no more," Ferrara shrugged. He sat down and began to clean his rifle, slipping out the bolt which he placed beside him on the log.

"Sarah." He put his hands to her hair, and she let him. Her anger was utterly played out, the deep numbness returning. "You did not know . . ."

"Know . . . ?" She looked into his eyes. Then behind him, toward the forest. A man emerged. A tall, slender man. With deep brown eyes, a soft smile, a worried set to his mouth. "It's not . . . no." Too often she had been fooled. Too often her spirits raised, then dashed. Yet he had the walk, the bearing, the expressive hands which he

188

held out to her.

"Sarah."

She stood transfixed. Carlo stepped aside. The man stood there, a rifle slung over his shoulder, an unfamiliar mustache on his lip, slowly reaching to her.

Robert. It was Robert. And she ran to him, her feet slipping, her heart pounding with a storm which found its expression in the tears running down her cheeks. She had come so far. And had had her hope buried.

Then she was in his arms and he was kissing her hair, her cheeks, her forehead. It was he!

"Sarah."

She drew back and studied him again. There was a tiny white scar in his eyebrow where she had hit him with a croquet mallet, a mole between the thumb and finger on the back of his hand. Eyes which knew her, loved her, which had watched her grow, suffering the pangs of first futile love, wrong-colored dresses, hair which would not curl, dolls which would not cry . . . eyes which had watched her, watched over her her life long.

"Robert David Chamliss," she said, and she pressed her head to his chest, holding it there for long minutes, listening to the heart which beat strongly, a living heart, a loving heart.

"Dear, dear Sarah." He patted her hair, his own eyes damp with moisture. "How sorry I am to have put you through this ordeal. But it was necessary. Very necessary."

"Serves her right." The Englishman emerged from the underbrush, also armed. Beside him two Trentinos Sarah had not seen before. "Young lady, it does not always pay to be so persistent. You've played hob with things," he went on, lighting that huge pipe.

"May I present James Dunning," Robert said, still holding his sister tightly by the shoulder. "Pardon his manner, Sarah. Mr. Dunning is a professional who has little patience with us amateurs, I'm afraid."

"They are still very close," one of the Trentinos interrupted, "not half a mile, Carlo."

"All right, Rovato. We should be moving," he decided.

"We'll have a long walk, Sarah," Robert apologized. "Are you up to it?"

"I am. I am up to it. As long as you'll stay with me. Oh, Robert, there is so much I want to know. To say! But mostly I want to be with you, to touch you, to believe that this is no longer a dream."

"Well?"

Sarah's head lifted to the sound of the feminine voice. Katrinka stood there, a rifle in her hands, dark eyes flashing.

"Are we going to chatter all day?" the Avarian girl asked. She wore a dark beret and a khaki shirt, which she filled out extraordinarily, and a man's boots and trousers.

"No," Robert replied. "Not all day. Katrinka, this is my sister."

"Hello again," Katrinka said. Those oriental eyes of hers sparked strangely, her petulant mouth assuming nearly a sulking posture. A look passed between Katrinka and Robert. Robert shook his head very faintly.

They tramped out of the valley, moving at a rapid pace once they had started. They wound through the trees, Carlo leading the way, followed by Dunning, Rovato, then Robert and Sarah. Ferrara lagged some fifty yards behind, watching the back trail.

"I don't expect they'll be coming," Robert told her once as they stopped for a breather atop a windswept, barren crag. "They are a motorized brigade. They'll want to travel fast. After all, they're illegally in the country."

"But why?"

"When the archduke is killed — or the attempt made — these men will rush in to aid in the capture of the perpetrators."

"You?"

190

"Yes," Robert admitted grimly. "But it would hardly pay to capture the malefactors before the crime has been committed."

From where they sat the Alps spread out in a cold, magnificent tableau, toward Italy in the south, and Switzerland in the west. Coldly solemn, appearing stronger, more magnificent with each snowfall, they seemed never-ending, dominating all of the world within view.

"And the Count von Steinbock?" Sarah asked quietly. "The count?"

"If there is a plot to assassinate the archduke and precipitate a war, placing the blame on the Trentinos, and if the act is planned in such a way that it will occur at Steinbock Castle, is the lord of Steinbock involved?"

She stared into the distance, shivering slightly with the cold, not wanting to hear Robert's reply which was short, tense.

"It appears so."

She thought of Glick and Field Marshal Eisner, of the midnight meeting in the castle. Eric had gone into the room. That word: *Mörder.*

Yet it hardly seemed possible. She recalled fondly Eric's pale eyes, the way he laughed, the yellow, wind tousled hair, his kind, weary manner.

"Would he do it in his own house?" Sarah asked suddenly. "It seems foolhardy."

"Anywhere," Dunning snapped. The mustached Englishman was completely unhappy with Sarah's presence, that was obvious. "Let's move on," Dunning suggested.

Another five miles through pine and cedar, over rills and jagged rocks, and they found the base camp of the bandits. Secluded in a thickly wooded glen, it was not a mile from Steinbock Castle. Six additional men were in the camp, all lean, rugged-looking fighters.

Katrinka unslung her rifle and immediately began making tea. When the pot had boiled she served Robert first, a point Sarah did not fail to notice.

"Can you tell me, Robert, will you, what has happened?"

"Certainly," her brother replied, sipping warily at the scalding, black tea. "There is no point in secrecy now." He glanced at Dunning who frowned with disgust and stalked away, speaking momentarily with Ferrara.

"I have been working on special projects for some time for the British government," Robert began tentatively. "My profession gives me access to unusual locations."

"How was it I did not know?"

"Which of us sees everything? Things that go on under our noses evade our attention until they are pointed out. You were busy with your schooling, your own work, Sarah. My sometimes lame excuses were usually accepted."

"In Pakistan!" she said, remembering an odd occurrence.

"Yes," Robert said, smiling. "But this was different. The timetable was revised constantly. The archduke is a busy man. He frequently changed plans. My excuses ran out. It was best to assume silence. Then you, out of love, followed me here.

"We were worried, Sarah, tremendously worried. You were probing tender spots, asking questions you should not have asked, alerting people to the fact that I was here."

"I had no idea . . ."

"Of course not. And so my massive friend there," he said, nodding to indicate Ferrara, "was dispatched to watch you. Then it was decided he should try to frighten you away. But you have too much sand in the craw, Sarah," he said with admiration.

"Too much love, Robert," she corrected.

Carlo wandered over and sat beside them, sitting closer than was necessary to Sarah. Robert lifted an eyebrow but said nothing, a transient smile moving his lips.

"Nothing worked with you, Sarah," Bramante commented. "So strong a woman in such a slight frame," he said with unconcealed admiration. "I conceived the next plan. And the next. I came to speak to you at Oktoberfest . . . that was an abortive episode, if you remember."

"It nearly cost you your life."

"Nothing." Bramante shrugged. "But then came my master stroke. We would simply end your search by pretending that Robert was dead. It is a wonder what fifty English pounds can accomplish. Boehm is a wonderful actor, don't you think?"

"It was cold and cruel," Sarah said.

"Yes." Robert agreed with her. "Yet better you think me dead until I could return to France than to have you embroiled in this and be killed yourself. No, Sarah, I would rather anything than have you hurt."

"It was a good plan," Carlo congratulated himself. "You would have been safely out of the Tyrol now if the order to close the border had not been given."

"That order came from Steinbock?" Robert asked.

"It seems so. Certainly that spineless police captain, Flaig, has not the authority. I believe our velvet-suited friend wished Sarah to remain in his grasp. Perhaps she had said too much, seen too much."

"Perhaps you assume too much about Eric von Steinbock," Sarah said testily.

"Perhaps not," Carlo snapped. "This man! What is he? An arrogant, foppish, petty nobleman!"

Sarah did not reply. Robert, observing the Trentino whom he knew well, thought he detected more than anger in his passion. Was it jealousy!

"I first discovered the proof of this plan," Robert said hastily. "In the Ice Castle there was a small iron box with the details of the plot, the timing of subsequent declarations and accusations."

"So you left a message at the tombs."

"Yes. For Dunning. James and I have worked together

before. But you deciphered it as well. When you began asking, insistently, about the Ice Castle, the word got out, and the box was removed before Dunning could substantiate its contents."

"That is what ruined it," Dunning said, waving a finger. "I could have gotten those papers to London and to Vienna. Proof positive! Yet you fouled the job, young lady."

"It is done, Dunning," Bramante said. "Now we do it my way."

"What is your way, Carlo?" Sarah asked.

"We prevent it by force." He frowned and added, "and pray that we are not accused."

The camp was silent. The men alone or in pairs cleaned their weapons or pondered the past and the future, fraught with risk. The moon slowly pulled itself up over the serrated edges of the tree tops, casting an eerie glow. Katrinka walked impatiently back and forth. Aside from her the camp was still.

"How will it be blamed on you?" Sarah asked. "How can they simply accuse you? Can't you simply withdraw, make your presence known elsewhere, far from Steinbock? Then there would be no attempt on Franz Ferdinand's life. There could not be."

"It is not so simple," Bramante said.

"Why not?"

"Sturzo."

"Sturzo?"

"A man who was once with us," Bramante sighed, "a dark, silent, brooding man who wished to be a patriot. Yet he was not quite right in the head, as we soon discovered. He wished to see his name in the headlines. A little man who wished to be large, to be a hero—in whatever way possible."

"What about this Sturzo?" Sarah asked.

"He was once with us, as I have said. And, he is a

Trentino. Now," he shrugged, "he is with them."

"I saw the master plan," Robert continued, picking up the thread. "I did not dare remove it, of course, since the absence would have immediately been discovered. But the plan was this:

"The archduke is to be escorted on a hunting trip for Steinbock stag. The killer, unnamed in the papers, but certainly Sturzo, is suddenly to burst from the woods, firing, calling out Trentino slogans.

"Of course the remainder of the hunting party—well-armed men all, visiting Germans and loyal Austrians—will immediately turn on this poor halfwit, silencing him forever. With Sturzo's silence the roar of battle will begin."

"It will be put out that the assassination was commissioned by the dissident Bramante. And who in the Tyrol would not believe it?" Carlo asked bitterly.

"Who in all the world?" Dunning said, pointing with his pipestem for emphasis. "The government controls all news releases. The Trentinos will be indelibly branded as criminals. German armies, in concordance with the alliance, will swiftly cross into Austria. The *Drang nach Osten* will begin."

It was colder yet. Sarah sat watching the low flickering fire, the words of the men running through her mind. She had difficulty still accepting the presentation as fact, yet they were all absolutely sure. Her mental block was Eric. What role did he play in this tragedy? Traitor to his own country, glory-seeker, or dupe? All seemed beneath his magnanimous capacity.

She did have a sudden recollection.

"This Sturzo! What does he look like?"

"He is short," Carlo said. "Shorter than average by quite a bit, certainly smaller than you, Sarah. He has glassy black eyes, square shoulders, thick through the chest. A powerful man despite his lack of height . . ."

"With wild, curly hair flying in every direction. A scar just beneath one eye," she continued.

"Yes, but how do you know . . . you have seen him? At Steinbock?"

"Not at Steinbock, but in the Ice Castle. He rushed past me, a frightened look in his eyes."

"And what would he have been doing there?" Bramante asked himself. "If it was him, and I have no doubt it was Sturzo."

"Perhaps," Robert suggested, "there is something else in that frozen pit. A weapons store, something hidden deeply in a secret chamber. I certainly saw but a little of the Ice Castle. Who can guess what else might lie hidden in it."

"Yet we were certain he was at Steinbock," Dunning said. "Perhaps it was not Sturzo. How could he have traveled there without our seeing him?"

"It had to be," Carlo replied. "If not, who?"

It was late, quite late. The moon was dying in the tips of the dark pines along the high ridges. A pale blue, it seemed drawn to the Alps, and it floated toward them, washing the snowfields a soft bluish white. The fire had died to golden embers. The men slept but for those standing watch along the crest and down on the river road.

Yet Sarah could not sleep. She tossed in her blanket, seeing that smiling, lean face before her. A criminal? It was impossible that Eric Mann, the Count von Steinbock, was a criminal.

The moon had paled still more. Rising, she walked up to the low saddle of the ridge, watching the distances. Steinbock's eerie spires, orange in the quickly dying moonlight, as strange and mysterious as the night she had first seen them, jutted skyward.

He was beside her then, and she felt his presence without hearing his advance; she was aware of a chill creeping up her spine. Her cheeks were warm despite the brisk wind off the low valley.

"I wondered where you were," Carlo said. He stood there silently a moment, watching her.

"Here. Just here. There has been so much confusion for me here in the Tyrol. Perceptions sharpened, dimmed, contorted, blackened in turn. My heart torn out of me, miraculously replaced. I am no longer sure I know the real from the imaginary here, Carlo. It has been difficult. So difficult."

"It is not so difficult to find what is real," he said. He stepped nearer to her, his head silhouetted against the moonlight, his hand taking hers. He came nearer yet, so close that his words reached her ears in gentle puffs as he spoke softly. "The Oktoberfest. That was real. This is real—my heart pounding so, my hands trembling. And your heart, Sarah, does it not respond? That is real. Real."

Nervously she turned her face from him, leaving her hand. Her heart was fluttering—fluttering madly. He gave off sparks which leaped across the tiny gap between them. She touched his cheek then, gently, studying those eyes. "I don't . . ."

"Don't speak," he said. "I will speak. You love me, you know it, Sarah. Not this Eric von Steinbock."

"How can you know," she asked.

"If you had loved him you would have stayed with him. No," he said positively. "He is a handsome man. He is nice, polite, a gentleman. Yet he did not thrill you as I do. And he did not feel as I do . . . it would not be possible."

It was then that he kissed her. A slow, deliberate kiss. And it was as if they had kissed that way many times before, as if they came together not for the first time, but for one of many. It was indelible, that kiss in the late moonlight, the wind twisting through the trees, ruffling her dress.

The kiss had been long in coming—an eternity. It was

the right kiss, and one which would last for an eternity. She took his shirt tightly at the sleeves, her fingers tugging at the material.

Drawing back she looked at him. Just looked. A man, a bandit, a pirate, a patriot—none of that, and all. He was her other half. The other fragment of her heart—that missing, longed for fragment which fit the puzzle of her existence perfectly.

He stepped back as well. They looked at each other, imprinting that moment on their memory. *Their memory*—one memory which they shared totally.

He would go. He would fight. Perhaps he would die within a matter of days. That thought bent her neck and she rested her head on his shoulder once more, kissing his shoulder then his neck lightly. She had only just found him. She clung to him like some fragile thing which would blow away if she loosened her grip.

"We will have a few days," he said, not looking at her. He watched the far peaks, he watched beyond them, trying to see his life in the deep reaches of the blue-black sky. Yet the stars told no tales. "Until the hunt."

A sudden panic gripped Sarah. A double-edged fear. She released him and stood back as if slapped. "It's not a few days, Carlo! At Steinbock . . . at breakfast with the archduke. I heard him change his plans once more. It is Monday they will hunt. This morning!" she said in a hollow, desperate tone. All of her life, just now formed, just now infused with hope, purpose, promise, turned to sand, flowing through her clutching fingers. Carlo stiffened, stepped back and studied her, a pained excited expression molding his features.

"Monday . . . this morning! It cannot be. Must not!"

"But it is today they hunt. It is today they will attempt to assassinate the archduke. In a very few hours . . . what will become of us, Carlo?" She clung to him one last time. "Whatever will become of us now?"

"What God wills," he replied, holding her for that last moment in a tight embrace, a clinging embrace of longing, of farewell perhaps. Reluctantly he released her.

"There is hardly time now," he said, delaying the onrushing moment.

"Go then . . . go now."

"But I would . . ."

"Go, Carlo."

She turned from him, her arms clasping one another so tightly that her fingernails bit into her own flesh. When she turned back he was gone, and only the vacant, graying sky, the cold far mountains remained.

Eighteen

The first morning light bled onto the snow beneath the alpine forest, tinting the white of the clearings a delicate pink, illuminating the sparkling, ice-bound pine trees with brilliant reflections, like thousands of tiny mirrors.

The horses, as they moved, blew steam. Steam rose from their flanks and from the mouths and nostrils of their furclad riders.

The Archduke Franz Ferdinand, bundled in otter, mink, and sable furs reclined in the rear seat of the sleigh. When the hunting grounds were reached, he would walk, or ride the magnificent gray gelding which was tied behind the sleigh, but for now he enjoyed the small luxury of warmth.

Morning flitted past in brilliant light and color, playing on the snow, flickering through the deep barrier of stands of trees.

High overhead an eagle soared, stretching broad golden wings to the still red sun. Shadows stuttered past, like a picket fence. A melodic note sounded in the deep glen where the brook rambled through the fern-clotted, rocky slash in the earth.

An automobile, which would be abandoned nearer the hunting preserve, led the way, sliding and spinning its tires. Behind it, three mounted Austrian guards rode, red sashes across their breasts, as fine as if they rode on parade. Then the hunting party itself:

Eric von Steinbock on a white horse, beside him Glick and Field Marshal Eisner. The two Germans rode stiffly, backs ramrod straight, hands rigid, eyes fixed on the narrow, winding road ahead. Following them was the sleigh with the Archduke Ferdinand, then three more Austrian horsemen, two of them carrying the archduke's hunting rifles.

Three miles back, along the shadowed slope of the Eagle's Nest, the small party of snow-shoed Trentinos rushed at breakneck speed toward the preserve, a broad, deeply forested valley beyond the river.

There was no time for talking, for planning, for taking a saving deep breath. Not a word was muttered, but they shared common thoughts. There was no telling from what quarter the attack might occur. Already they were half an hour behind the hunting party; and the hunters were mounted.

Desperation and tense effort drew their expressions. Tendons strained on the throat, the hands, working the snowshoe poles, were clenched like blocks of granite on the shafts. The rifles, cradled on their backs, thumped against them as they swept through the forest, catching mottled light through the rare openings in the deep ranks of pine.

Sarah watched them making their way down the steep flank of Eagle's Nest—seven dark, antlike forms on the vast snow sheet which disappeared into the concealment of the woods.

Robert had extracted a solemn promise from her. She was not to follow. "What good could you do?" he had asked. "You would only be in danger, pointlessly."

Carlo had reinforced the argument strongly, until at length she had promised to remain behind, rendezvousing with them later at the base of Brenner Pass whether they were successful or not.

She watched until they were no longer visible. The two men she loved in all the world, loved above all else, rushing headlong into a common danger from which neither might return.

Slowly she led the horse from its shelter and climbed onto its back, moving slowly in the opposite direction, toward the Brenner. There was no wind, the skies far-reaching, pale blue. The horse moved rapidly, if unsteadily down the slope, zigzagging for better footing. No sound yet filled the empty day. That was good. When the guns began, the day would close around her like a strangling, steel web. She rode on, trying to keep her mind blank; yet her ears waited constantly for that first, violent sound.

She had come through a narrow stand of trees topping a small knoll when she saw them below—the German troops. And they were moving quickly as well—toward the Brenner Pass. Yet they had no reason to be moving southward, toward the border. Unless . . .

Unless they knew of Bramante's plan to escape toward the Brenner! Yet how could they? It was certain from their position that the German forces would engage the Trentinos before they could return to the safety of their homeland, and in such superior numbers that Carlo would have no chance.

Sarah hesitated. The horse, scenting another of his kind below tensed and began to nicker, but Sarah hurriedly put a hand over the animal's muzzle. She watched a second longer. Then, absolutely sure that the Germans would be in a position below the pass, by design or sheer chance, she wheeled the pony around, aiming it down into the pine woods, riding hard toward the ambush site.

The Archduke Franz Ferdinand stepped down from the sleigh, stretching his back and legs, rubbing his hands together in anticipation. They had startled a magnificent stag earlier in the morning, though no one had attempted to shoot it—a great, heavily coated animal with seven points on either side of his antlers. The Count von Steinbock had pointed the creature out.

"That one was nothing, sir," Eric assured him. "A runt. I promise you we shall have bigger game before the day is done."

The archduke signaled for his rifle, and the Austrian soldier handed him first the Mauser Nitro Express .600.

"Lord, man, they won't be that large!" the archduke laughed. "That's an elephant gun. I've seen Italian cannon smaller than that."

The soldier blanched, nodded and returned with the engraved .303, saluting as he presented it. The archduke checked the loads and shouldered the rifle.

"Can you imagine," the archduke said in a low voice to Eric, "what were they planning, a war?"

Eric muttered something noncommittal and moved away with a facile smile. It was only then that Franz Ferdinand, his agile mind now on weapons, noticed that Eric von Steinbock was wearing a sidearm. Casually he let his eyes sweep the rest of the party. The Field Marshal, perhaps from military habit, also wore a handgun. Minister Glick had an unusual bulge under his herringbone coat at the waist. An odd sporting arm . . . the archduke filed the information away in his memory.

From atop a low ridge some half mile off, Carlo Bramante watched the group of men through field glasses. Panting from the exertion, he handed them to Dunning who peered into them, adjusting the binoculars minutely.

"Thank God we're not too late." Robert sighed, sagging against a flat rock, his boot propped up. The sweat drained from his forehead. Katrinka, standing beside him, rubbed his head and smiled. She alone seemed hardly winded. Ferrara's beefy face was utterly red under his coal black beard. The slender Silone was breathing raggedly, his face deathly white from the sprint.

"Not too late . . . yet," Dunning said. Calmly he handed the glasses back to Bramante. "Look there," the Englishman said, "by the oak."

Bramante swung the glasses to the side and cursed softly. A dark man, walking slightly bent forward, moved through the trees, heading toward the trail where the archduke's party would have to pass.

"Sturzo."

Bramante stood quickly, dusting the snow from himself. He motioned to Ferrara and Rovato. Silone struggled to rise to his feet, but Carlo stopped him. "Rest—we may have to run far and fast."

"You wait for me here, Katrinka," Robert said. He kissed the Avarian girl lightly on the forehead.

"And you, Robert," Carlo said, "you wait here as well."

"Never," Robert objected.

"Yes. You must—you and Dunning."

"He's right, Robert," James Dunning said regretfully. "If we are involved in this and something goes wrong, the British nation is also implicated. And America, I might add. It is better we stand aside. At least then, if things go badly, we will be alive to tell the story as impartial witnesses."

"I have hardly come this far to quit now," Robert said, but Bramante would not hear of it.

"I have no time to argue, Robert. We are great friends, but we are soldiers, you and I. You must obey me."

Robert opened his mouth as if to speak, but said nothing, finally shaking his head in assent. "Good luck then."

Bramante nodded, shouldering his rifle. Ferrara was already moving, lumbering down the slope. Rovato was close behind, rifle in his hands. From there they could see that the party of horsemen had begun to file up the narrow valley. Sturzo had disappeared from view.

Katrinka stood by herself to one side, the wind playing in her dark hair, her breasts rising and falling with each breath as if she were greatly excited. A thin smile played on her lips.

"What is it, darling?" Robert asked, moving beside her.

"Only anxiety," she responded. "Soon we will know. Soon."

Robert stepped back, still watching her. She was utterly fixed on the movements of the hunting party, the pursuit of Bramante. Her hands tensed and relaxed alternately, her mouth once forming words, soundless, whispered words.

"She shouldn't be here, Robert," Dunning told him.

"No. But what was I to do? There's no arguing with Katrinka," Robert said proudly. There, he thought, was a woman. Proud, strong, valiant. Dunning stoked his pipe thoughtfully and moved to the far side of a yellowish boulder, trying to watch Bramante's progress.

His breath caught suddenly, and he vigorously cursed the entire feminine race. In the woods below he had caught sight of Sarah Chamliss, rushing toward the axis of the event.

Sarah had been unable to follow the movements of either the hunting party or Carlo's group as she wound through the trees. She rode recklessly onward, certain only that she must warn Robert and Carlo of the trap. She had little time to think about it, but she reasoned that at worst she would arrive to find the archduke murdered. Then, at least, she would be able to speak to Eric and explain things.

If she arrived before Sturzo, perhaps the archduke would listen to her. Surely Speidel, the Austrian under-minister of defense, would be cautious enough to call a halt to the hunt. The man seemed a wary person, utterly devoted to the archduke.

Of her own safety she thought little. She could picture none of them, not even Sturzo, purposely killing a woman. She did not know this demented Trentino, but she remembered the wild, yet almost frightened eyes he had turned on her in the Ice Castle. He was not the sort to kill, she decided, unless convinced that it was necessary, important.

She alone, of all the Trentino force could hope to approach the archduke, to speak without violence. She had begun to hope the entire affair might, with some luck, be finished without shooting.

It was then the woods exploded with a bitter spate of thunder. She heard the staccato hammering of small arms fire from several directions, the shrill, guttural voices of men in extreme, mortal pain.

Nineteen

Only moments earlier Carlo, rushing ahead of the others, had burst onto the perimeter of the clearing where the archduke, having dismounted, prepared to enter the preserve proper. The Austrian guards were sitting off to one side, smoking and talking. Eric von Steinbock paced nervously between his horse and the two Germans.

The archduke had turned to say something to one of his men when Bramante's eye caught the lurking figure across the clearing. Shuffling absently as if on a summer stroll, bent forward at the waist, Sturzo approached the hunting party.

"Are we ready to proceed, Eric?" Franz Ferdinand wanted to know. The archduke looked with disfavor at the sun, now yellow, topping the trees. Already it was late for stag.

"Momentarily, sir."

Bramante eased himself forward, pressing flat against the earth beneath a protective pine. His rifle came to his shoulder. Immediately across from him, yet visible to no one in the party, Sturzo straggled forward, stopping to examine a fallen bird's nest. His pistol dangled from his hand loosely; like a dismal ape he came on.

Sturzo stopped. Recollecting.

His pistol came level. Taking a deep breath he stepped

forward as the archduke's head jerked around.

"Long live . . ." the rest of what he might have said died in his throat. As Sturzo cocked the pistol he carried, Carlo, exhaling evenly, pulled the trigger of his rifle. The sound shattered the silence of morning, smoke filling the clearing.

Instantly they returned the fire.

"There's one of them!" Eisner shouted. He emptied his pistol in Carlo's direction, rushing for the cover of the woods himself.

The archduke stood imperiously in the middle of the clearing, shouting to his men, hands on his hips.

Eric muttered a vile oath and shot toward Carlo's position. But the Trentino was no longer there. A trained guerrilla fighter, he had fired only once—at Sturzo who lay dying on the snow, his blood staining the ground crimson—then he had swiftly rolled to one side, sprinted three strides and dropped to the ground.

"There!" Glick shouted, swinging the muzzle of his hunting rifle around. It was not Bramante he saw, but the unfortunate Rovato who had burst into the clearing, seeking to aid his lieutenant.

The German's muzzle blast flashed with fire, the black smoke rolling skyward. Rovato screamed and rolled into the brush, scrambling away on hands and knees, his face and shoulder bleeding badly.

"Trentinos!" Glick yelled at the archduke who seemed not to hear him above the general uproar. That was the last word he was to speak on this earth. Ferrara, holding the badly wounded Rovato in one massive arm, fired three times in rapid succession, the first bullet taking Glick in the throat.

"Get back! Get back!" Carlo shouted wildly. Ferrara was braced for a final struggle, yet that was not their aim. Their only purpose had been to save the life of the archduke. Bramante had no intention of engaging in a pitched battle.

Ferrara nodded, but it was a second before he moved, and in that second, Eric von Steinbock, finding the massive Trentino in his path, had fired with his pistol, spinning Ferrara around as the bullet took him beneath the collar bone.

Enraged, Ferrara had shot back. Twice he pulled the trigger of his rifle, and both bullets struck Eric. The first was superficial, a narrow furrow burning his neck, spilling blood along his chest and abdomen. The second, more serious wound was in the calf of the leg. Eric felt the bullet bore into his flesh, a searing, violent blow; it took his leg out from under him and he fell, clawing toward his lost weapon as Ferrara backed away, towing Rovato

Sarah crested the small rise among the pine trees as the second flurry of shots began. She rode the pony hard, the animal nearly foundering. Someone was dying in that clearing. Whoever it was—Carlo, Robert, Eric, the arch-duke—she had no heart for witnessing it. Fear and a rising nausea overwhelmed her, a disgust with all of mankind, and its seemingly irrepressible blood lust.

Suddenly she saw them all—Carlo, rolling to one side, the German minister firing, but missing badly, Ferrara dragging someone, presumably Rovato, away as the archduke, staid, noble in his bearing, gestured to his small body of men.

Robert! He was not there, at least not visible to her.

Yet Eric was. His pale hair across his forehead, a stream of blood across his chest. She started forward. Yet at that moment he fired hotly into the trees, emptying the cylinder of his pistol.

Then the other figure caught her eye. Tiny, frail, struggling weakly forward, directly into the line of fire. Minna! She walked in a daze, her feet going frequently from under her. Sick, or drugged, she smiled wanly, unaware, perhaps, of what was happening, or where she was.

Guns erupted on either side of the lost girl, filling the day with sound, with deadly missiles. The archduke, Sarah noticed with a glance, was safe. He had formed his men into a tiny square, rifles at the ready, while the nobleman, arms folded across his expansive chest, watched the woods for further menace.

Instantly Sarah started her pony forward, the exhausted animal obeying reluctantly. Minna traced an erratic course across the snow. With a shock, Sarah noticed that the girl was barefoot and without a coat.

"Minna!" she called out, yet her voice was buried beneath the rage of exploding gunpowder.

Still she wandered forward, eyes blank. A bullet tore at the bark of a tree not five feet from Minna's head. She did not even react to it.

"Minna!"

It seemed hours, yet within seconds Sarah was to the girl. She leaped from the horse's back, grabbing Minna's shoulder with a trembling hand.

"Minna! Come home!"

"Who . . . ? Who is come home . . ." Minna's voice was indistinct, her eyes glassy, her gestures vague. She had been drugged heavily. Her tongue was dry, her arms moved uncertainly, her mouth made sputtering, unintelligent sounds.

"Come Minna! Mitzi will be lost," Sarah said quietly. As she spoke another bullet ripped through the air nearby, tearing a low branch from the trunk of a rough, massive pine.

"Mitzi . . . but Eric!" she said, coming suddenly alert. She scratched at Sarah's face, twisting free, trying to rush to the ambush site. Yet she lost her footing in the snow and fell. Trying to rise she found Sarah on top of her, and in her emaciated state she had no chance of breaking free.

"You must go home!" Sarah said feverishly. The roll of gunfire continued below. Someone yelled frantically. Overhead a crow wheeled and scolded the humans who had disturbed a perfectly peaceful morning.

"Home . . ." Minna nodded and dragged herself to her feet. She stood panting beside the horse. Sarah helped the girl on the animal's back then mounted herself, turning the tired animal toward Steinbock.

Whatever had happened, she could not know nor could she have a hand in it. Minna's appearance had changed her plans. First this sick, tired girl must be gotten under shelter. Then Carlo, if he escaped, must be warned of the trap.

Reluctantly she allowed the pony its slow pace slogging through the slushy snow. It had borne up under fearsome usage, but it would take little more.

The roar of colliding sounds died away as they neared Steinbock. Now and then the low pop-pop of distant fire reached their ears, yet it was only sporadically, nearly an afterthought to the completed clash.

Several Austrian soldiers were in the yard, a much decorated colonel among them. Near the main portico, the grand duchess and the mournful Sophie Chotek waited.

"Too much shooting," the colonel was saying. He turned on his heel at a sign from one of his junior officers and marched up to Sarah. His men were mounted, holding back their finely trapped horses with difficulty. "Young lady!"

"Yes, sir."

"You have been near the game preserve?"

"Yes. But the archduke is fine. Some of the men wished to try out their weapons," she said with only the slightest hesitation. One thing was certain—these Austrian soldiers must not join the chase. Carlo and Robert would certainly be boxed in.

"There was so much firing." The colonel removed his monocle and stared with pale, nearly gray eyes at Sarah and Minna who slipped from the horse's back unsteadily. "Certainly the stags must be frightened away."

"When I last saw the archduke," Sarah said factually, "he was standing with his guards observing the target shooting. Perhaps the day did not lend itself to the stag hunt."

The colonel turned and conferred briefly with his officers. Sophie Chotek had come down onto the grounds. With large, liquid eyes she approached Sarah.

"The archduke is well?" she asked.

"Yes." Sarah took her hand and reassured her. "He is perfectly well, Countess."

"Then there is no need to ride, Colonel," Sophie Chotek said with authority. As the colonel nodded and ordered his men to dismount, she said to Sarah, "I have lately had feelings of . . . doom. Forebodings of great trouble," the round-shouldered, sad-eyed countess confided.

"He is fine, I assure you," Sarah said. On a sudden impulse she kissed the Countess Sophie Chotek on the cheek. Then she released her hand and raced after Minna who had rushed into the house. The grand duchess stood in the doorway, blocking her entry.

"Leave!" Minna's mother said. Her face was utterly tranquil, yet her voice wavered. "I will have no more of this."

"But you will," Sarah said boldly.

"How dare you!" The grand duchess was livid, her mask of composure suddenly falling away. "I'll have you . . ."

"What?" Sarah demanded, her hands on her hips. "Will you have my head on a pike? Will you have me chained in the dungeon! Drugged, like Minna, driven insane?"

"You speak nonsense," the grande dame of Steinbock said, yet there was uncertainty in her words.

"Do I? Did you never notice? Did you blame all of Minna's problems on the curse of the blood? Even fooling yourself? The girl is not crazy! Minna has been drugged, made to belive she was insane. And who, I ask, is close enough to her to do such a thing? Was it you, Grand Duchess? You, who lived in fear of what Minna might become, what she might have seen, was it?"

The grand duchess was too enraged to speak. She did not even move as Sarah brushed past her, breaking into the house. Gertrude was there, standing dumbly, her mouth hung open.

"There, Ma'am," Gertrude said, still awed at Sarah's temerity. She lifted a finger. "She went down there. Into the dungeon."

Sarah hesitated a moment. The grand duchess had turned in the doorway, still unable to speak. Down there—into the nefarious Baron Huebner's torture chamber, that cold pit, the bowels of the diseased Steinbock Castle.

Sarah snatched up a candelabra from the glass-topped table near the portrait of the beast of Steinbock, and lighted it, sweeping from the great hall, passing downward into the crumbling cavity of the dungeon below.

She plunged into the stony abyss, the steps falling away steeply, around the bend in the ancient, decayed footing of the Fortress Steinbock.

Steps sounded distantly. Minna, running blindly through the torture chamber. A filmy, sticky web wiped across Sarah's face. A broken step caused her to turn her ankle. The candles she carried flashed eerily on the walls, painting the gray, water-filmed stone with shifting sepia tones.

Then she was down, onto the water and ice bottom of the seeping dungeon. She passed a splintered, rotting rack and wheel, a rusted ball of chains and wire. Minna's footsteps still retreated into the depths of the place.

Once the girl yelled.

"Helmuth!" her voice a pitiful shriek, a wounded animal's sound taking on a human voice.

Again she passed the furnished cell, cold and savage, where Sturzo had presumably spent his last night. What had the little madman thought of, alone in the rat-infested darkness with running ice-melt chilling all?

Sarah had been this far before, never farther. Yet Minna rushed on, obviously knowing every passage, every dank, musty corridor and cell. Sarah followed, guided by the sounds of Minna's bare feet slapping against the frozen stone.

She turned left. Deadended. Turned right . . . shuddering she confronted a pile of broken, ancient bones. She backed from the low, narrow chamber, feeling still the protesting voices, souls of men butchered seven hundred years earlier, their bones dragged to this depository to remain concealed forever. The rumors of the baron's butchery had been well founded.

Sarah turned back, finding eventually a small, unwalled passageway. Carved out of native earth it led slightly upward. From deep in the tunnel she heard the piercing call once again.

"Helmuth! Dear, dear Helmuth!"

Sarah moved forward, her candles now burning low. Scuttling along the pasageway she found evidence of Minna's passing—splotches of blood where she had torn her hands.

Sarah moved forward, her own hand scraping for purchase against the ragged, icy stone. The wax of the candles dripped onto her wrist, burning her. Her breath came in scratchy, effortful gasps.

The wind began to funnel past her, whistling in the honeycombed stone. The surface underfoot began to be yet more slippery, ice-coated, treacherous. With a start she came to the realization . . . the Ice Castle.

They were into the Ice Castle. They had passed deep into the heart of Eagle's Nest, behind Steinbock, and were emerging into the vault of the Ice Castle on the northern slope of that jagged peak.

Ice began to film the walls, the ceiling. Odd, knifelike projections jutted from the floor, capable of ripping the flesh horribly if the explorer proved incautious.

And there was blood on one such projection, a scrap of material torn from Minna's dress. Sarah moved quickly on. Minna, without a coat or even shoes, in a weakened condition, half aware of what she was doing, was in immediate danger. And, she was injured. How badly, Sarah could not tell.

The Ice Castle. It explained how Sturzo had been able to elude Carlo's surveillance, and why Minna had insisted Helmuth's "grave" was in the dungeon. The iron box containing the assassination plot . . . it was no longer a mystery how or why it had been in a lost location such as the Ice Castle, or how it had disappeared without the Trentino forces having been aware of its removal.

Steinbock and the Ice Castle were connected, by design or nature, she could not guess. Yet they were one. In a sense Steinbock was the Ice Castle. Twin, frigid, sterile freaks of nature, each having outlived its time. The age of feudalism had passed, the Ice Age was a brief paragraph in the history of the earth; yet Steinbock continued, the Ice Castle continued, monstrous anachronisms, intimidating, dominating the world of flesh and blood creatures such as poor Minna.

Minna—she screamed again!

Sarah doggedly crawled forward, finally reaching a nearly level floor in an unfamiliar corridor. Yet Minna's direction was clearly marked by the blood stains on the ice—always the blood. The Ice Castle seemed designed for death, for suffering . . . as did Steinbock.

Minna shrieked again. Much closer, but now there was

a new tone in her pathetic cries—an urgent, panicked horror.

She screamed again and again, her voice producing sympathetic tremors of dread in Sarah's heart. Yet she went on. Now she could make out Minna's confused, trembling words plainly:

"Helmuth! No, you are dead! My God, dear Helmuth, you are from the dead! Go back to your cold death . . ." Minna screamed. Again. "Helmuth, you must go back!"

Sarah rounded the bend in the twisting ice corridor, her candles flaring up then dimming. Minna stood there, her hands to her mouth. And the man was there . . .

Helmuth von Steinbock, blood flowing from his throat and chest. He turned his eyes on Sarah.

Twenty

Helmuth von Steinbock!

The candlelight flickered across his deathly features. Blood trickled from his forehead where pale hair fell. His tunic was soaked badly with blood. Unsteadily he watched her approach. Minna slumped against the icy wall to one side, hands gripping her own throat.

"Helmuth," she moaned, muttering it over and over. Yet as Sarah came nearer her dim light revealed something else.

"Eric!" she gasped.

He stood limply, knees wobbly, a pistol dangled from a bloody hand.

"Eric," Sarah said with relief. She smiled and stepped forward. "In this light . . ." Eric's features were drawn, utterly white. He had bled much.

"You!" Eric put out the palm of a hand as if to push her back.

"It's Eric, Minna! Only Eric, don't be frightened. But you need help, Eric," she said, stepping nearer still until the candlelight cast crooked shadows on the Austrian's pallid face.

"Help!" he laughed, spitting blood. "You help?" He laughed again, a gurgling, mocking laugh issuing from between ghastly, cracked lips. The hand which held the

217

pistol came level. "You cannot help . . . this is partly your fault! Your fault!"

"No," Sarah said sincerely, "surely not." she put the candles on a narrow ledge, head high, and moved toward him. "Let me see to you . . ."

Eric drew back the hammer of his pistol and she froze into position. His eyes were glazed, the hand wavered as it held the gun.

"No," he said quietly. "I would rather die here. What have I to live for anyway? Now."

"You have everything," Sarah replied. Eric's hand had lowered slightly. She relaxed her own position somewhat. "You are a young, handsome man . . ."

"Stop it!" He bent his head wearily against the wall, not moving for a long moment.

"Our plot failed. We will be discovered, I have no doubt of it. The archduke is not such a fool."

"Then you were a part of the plan to kill Franz Ferdinand?"

"A part? I *was* the plot. I lived it, breathed it for years. Years . . ." he sighed. "Now," he said, his head snapping up, "I am simply a traitor."

"Perhaps . . ."

"Perhaps? There is no perhaps. You live in a child's world, dear Sarah." Eric shook his head with some sadness. "I knew immediately who you were. The name Robert Chamliss had been brought to my attention. I asked you to go. I told you about this place—this Ice Castle," he said, waving a hand around the massive chamber which creaked and groaned with its own movements. "Yet you did not have the sense . . . so I brought you to Steinbock to keep you in check. But you had to wander, to pry!"

Minna's soft, pitiable moans resumed. Sarah went to the girl, kneeling beside her, throwing her own coat over Minna's shoulders.

"She is very ill . . . the drugs . . ."

"She will get better. There will be no more of that," Eric said. His eyes closed for a moment and he doubled up with pain.

"You!" Sarah said, aghast at what she had half realized, now that he had admitted it. "You drugged your own sister into this state?"

Eric shrugged, coughed again, and straightened up. The candles were burning low, his features darkening in the feeble light.

"Minna, poor Minna was a person who pried—like you, Sarah. She saw too much. She came time and again to this place to visit . . . Helmuth's grave."

"She was in the way of your plot?"

"Yes!" he said sharply. "It was all-important, Sarah. The great unified Germanic state must rise! These inferior people—Trentinos, Serbs, all—must be driven into the sea."

Sarah watched his ravaged, finely featured, violent face, understanding for the first time the depths of human hatred. Insane . . . she did not speak it, but it was carved onto those once fine lines on Eric von Steinbock's face. Yet how many others in Austria and Germany held similar views just then?

This *Drang nach Osten*—the drive eastward—was a consuming national philosophy, awaiting only the proper moment, a moment such as Eric and his German allies had tried to create with the archduke's assassination.

"I have not seen the world before my eyes," Sarah said somberly. It was true—a schoolgirl in a schoolgirl's world, she had known nothing of German aspirations, nothing of Robert and men like him who fought against war, nothing of princes and handsome noblemen who were adroit at concealing their natures.

"Let us move toward the mouth of the cave," Eric said finally. "This Ice Castle . . . it causes the blood to chill."

He was desperately wounded, that was obvious now. His hands left bloody smears on the wall. Sarah followed, helping Minna.

They moved along through strange blue corridors, passing honeycombs of ice, frozen giants in repose, frozen fire . . . She recognized the chamber they came to next.

In eternal respose the Austrian stood silently, eyes still open accusingly. Helmuth—the knife forever imbedded in his chest, a slight smile of contempt on those lips so like Eric's.

"The Emperor of the Ice Castle," Eric said virulently. "Damn you, Helmuth! Eternal fool. He was a scientist who would be a poet; a poet who would be . . . a fool!

"He wanted to know all of the Ice Castle, to map it, to understand each sink and seep. And," he said in a softer tone, "he wanted to feel the soul of the place. Perhaps understanding our own souls—frozen, magnificent, fearful."

Eric stood before the frozen figure as if it were a museum exhibit. Minna trembled and stretched out a gaunt hand to the icy sheath covering her dead brother. Her eyes suddenly flashed with terrible anxiety; she stared at Eric and backed away into Sarah's protective arms.

"Eric . . . ?" Sarah began. He cut her short with a ferocious, bitter laugh.

"You still have to ask? My poor innocent! Yes, I killed him! He was obstinate, altruistic. I wanted him to join a group we were forming. A military group. We had certain aims in mind . . . he laughed. Then when he was through laughing he scolded. He cajoled, he threatened finally to expose us.

"And so I killed him. Poor Minna was watching. She followed Helmuth here frequently. They spoke the same language. The same insipid, pretty language."

"It drove her insane!" Sarah said, exploding. "Seeing her brother kill another brother. For what, Eric? For what?

Some grandiose plan for world-conquest, some vicious, bloody plan!"

"Yes," he said proudly. "For that. For the Germanic state.

"I must . . ." Eric's voice faltered. He fingered his forehead erratically. "Get out of here. What was I thinking of? I can't hide here!" He backed away from Helmuth's cold, mocking form, creeping up the dark pasageway toward the Satan Room. The candles were very low. Three of them had extinguished.

"Go ahead of me," Eric said. He was feverish, brandishing the pistol dangerously. Sarah agreed, taking Minna by her birdlike arm.

Eric muttered constantly to himself now, struggling to control his weakness. "I can't go to Steinbock . . . they'll be waiting, of course. If Glick got free . . . no. The archduke is no fool. Still," he exclaimed with a loud roar, "it was a grand plan. Foolproof!"

The waning light caught the grotesque forms of the ice gargoyles perched along the walls of the chambers. They seemed to mock as well, hollow eyes flashing with satirical amusement. Great bat-winged creatures of blue ice, toothy, broken-nosed griffins and gnomes.

The wind whistled through the chamber, as always. A sound very much like thousands of small voices chanting obscene, unintelligible canticles. Eric glanced nervously about. There was nothing, no one but the legions of demons, harpies and hobgoblins, ghouls and the twisted, wispy wraiths—all of ice. The chorus continued, singing demonic, condemning hymns.

Eric clapped his hands to his ears and whirled madly in a tight circle. He drew his weapon on one especially realistic, especially grotesque little demon as if he would shoot the ugly thing . . . then, quietly, he lowered the gun.

"They would kill a man," he said solemnly. "Move ahead!" he commanded.

They fumbled onward, gasping for breath now, as the candles dimmed and flickered. The footing was utterly treacherous. They slid back two steps for every step forward.

Minna moaned like some small animal, and no wonder in her condition—cold, frightened, confused. Yet she climbed on valiantly, Sarah scrambling after. Eric drew himself along the low corridor heavily, yet determinedly. His arm seemed to have gone numb, he shifted his pistol to the other hand.

"Eric, we must rest," Sarah insisted.

"No." He shook his head heavily, sweat raining from his forehead, hair in matted confusion. "Out!" he panted. "I must get out of this accursed place. It feels . . . like death."

Sarah said nothing. From time to time, she noticed, Eric did stop and look back, down the long, black tunnel slanting away behind them.

"There!" Eric shouted, his voice echoing down the tube of the crawlway. "Did you hear that? Footsteps. Footsteps," he repeated quietly, crouching down as he peered into the impenetrable darkness of the icy pit.

"It's Helmuth," he said in awe. He wiped back his hair. "But wait . . . it couldn't be." Then again. "It's Helmuth coming for me."

Minna, arms dangling apelike, open mouth dry, tongue extended, nodded her head in agreement, her dark eyes flashing excitedly.

"There's no one there," Sarah said calmly. She did not want the Austrian excited. Not with that gun in his hand. "No one."

"What do you know! He's coming. I tell you he is coming."

They moved ahead another fifty feet over sheet ice and a large group of head-sized boulders, which had tumbled recently from somewhere above.

"He's coming." Eric stood panting heavily, pistol pointed down the gray tunnel. "He wants me to die here. He wants me to be frozen here too . . . isn't that it, Minna!"

Minna smiled mildly, her eyes sunken incredibly, cheeks concave, lips trembling. She seemed unable to speak any longer.

"Quicker. Quicker," Eric repeated.

They became lost only once, in a small cul-de-sac. Minna, obviously knowing that it was a dead end, enjoyed the joke immensely. Eric was soaked with blood and perspiration. His tunic, torn, stiff with frozen blood, was a duplicate of Helmuth's.

At last they saw a speck of yellowish light. The light of day. They had reached the anteroom—the cathedral with its foyers and massive columns, the incredible ice organ which, with the tricks the deep winds played, seemed to intone unearthly, broken hymns.

"I've beaten you," Eric gasped. "He'll never come into the light," he confided to Sarah.

She could only watch sadly. This shattered man, a man born with everything—fortune, power, intelligence. A man Sarah might have loved. Might have—but perhaps she had somehow sensed the deep, bloody flaw in Eric von Steinbock's character. They had never come together in a deep sense.

Yet . . . yet, she had cared for Eric von Steinbock. She cared that he, or any man, would so brutalize himself, destroy himself in vapid quests after vainglorious ideals. Destroyed in his prime, he now gaped at her like some wounded, maddened jungle cat.

He caught her gaze, and just for a moment his own blue eyes softened, a regretful, reaching look filling them. Then again they hardened, some curtain closing over his soul.

The pistol came up suddenly.

"You!" Eric shouted, yet the shout was not directed at Sarah. His eyes, the muzzle of his upraised weapon were on someone standing behind Sarah in the massive, arched entrance to the Ice Castle.

Minna cowered. Sarah turned her head. A quiet, tall, splendidly self-assured man stood there, legs widespread, hands empty, eyes scanning the vault of the cathedral, taking the entire scene in at a glance. Robert nodded reassuringly to his sister.

"Robert," she managed to say hoarsely, "go back."

The pistol wavered in Eric's hand, but neither of them doubted he had the strength to pull the trigger.

"No," Robert said. He shook his head and came calmly forward yet another step. "I will not go. Did you abandon me, Sarah? Would you ever have? I will go," he said, raising an accusing finger, "when this criminal allows you to go with me."

"You speak of criminals," Eric sputtered, "you who intrude in the internal affairs of our nation?"

"Yes. I label you a criminal, Eric von Steinbock. What else may I call a man who wishes to begin a war?" Robert shook his head as if the weight of the world were suspended from his neck. "Internal affairs—you speak of such niceties? You who would smear blood across all of Europe!"

"It cannot be stopped," Eric said, drawing himself to his full height painfully. "There will be war. I only regret that I will miss its glorious conclusion."

"You have missed much in life," Robert said sadly. "Come, Sarah."

"No!" Eric shouted.

Sarah did not, could not move. The pistol was trained on her brother. She had no doubt that Eric, in his present state, would shoot.

"Sarah."

Robert reached out a hand. Minna began to whimper once again. "I can't leave without her," Sarah said.

"Fine. Bring her and be quick. Eric—I do not want to hurt you. I am unarmed. There is no point in hurting me, your sister, Sarah . . . we are leaving now. What is done is done."

"You are wrong!" Eric said, his face a mask of fury. He strode forward a pace or two. "You are enemies of the German people! If I allowed you to leave, what would you do? You would report this incident, discrediting myself, Glick, and Field Marshal Eisner."

"Glick is dead."

"But Eisner is not!"

"No." Robert admitted. "You are dying, man," Robert said softly, nearly compassionately. "Would you take me down with you? Your sister? Sarah?"

"Yes!" Eric assured him. "For the cause."

"For the cause? That is like saying you would kill for the sake of killing. Killing is the aim of your *cause*."

"You could not understand," Eric said.

"No, my friend. I could not understand," Robert said, bitterly. "I cannot understand you at all."

The Austrian said no more for a long moment. He held the pistol at arm's length until it began to waver, moving in small circles. He closed an eye to aim, then lowered the gun to wipe the perspiration from his eyes.

"I am sorry," Eric said, "you seem a gentleman."

"Yet *I* am not!" Carlo Bramante said, announcing himself roughly. And he was not unarmed. He carried a carbine in his hands, and he focused it on Eric. "I am not a killer, however. Do not make me kill you, sir."

Eric laughed briefly, harshly. "The Trentino bandit! How fitting. Now I may kill you both."

"You may try," Carlo said roughly. "First let the women walk out."

"No!" Eric's eyes flickered dully. He was near to death—so near—yet hatred kept him on his feet, alert. "You may shoot me—what does it matter!" he laughed. "But you! I have the opportunity to do the Germanic state a last, great service by killing you, Bramante."

"You have the opportunity to do a greater service for all of humanity," Carlo said coldly. "Lay down your weapon and die, Count von Steinbock."

Sarah had begun to edge slowly toward the mouth of the cavern, leading an unprotesting, quite bewildered Minna.

"Halt!" Eric ordered her, catching the movement from the corner of his eye. His gun hopscotched from Bramante to Robert, to Sarah. His eyes lighted brilliantly.

"I'll kill her first, Bramante." Carlo clenched his teeth tightly, having no move left to make. Eric was no longer afraid of death, being on its doorstep now. He could not be threatened with it.

"Von Steinbock . . ." Robert said, but Eric cut him off with a sharp gesture.

"No! I will have to kill her . . . yet, Sarah . . . I did . . ." his voice wavered violently. His hands trembled, and his legs seemed hardly capable of supporting him. "I did . . . if only you could have been taught . . ."

His eyes closed briefly in thought, and before he could open them again, Sarah burst toward the archway, dragging Minna behind her. At that moment Eric fired. And fired again.

Twenty-one

The world trembled, shivered. It stood motionless a brief second, then came angrily to life. Some savage, sleeping behemoth, struck by Eric's wildly fired shots stirred beneath the floor of the Ice Castle, roaring angrily with incredible, animal fury.

The pillars, massive, brittle, fragile for all their size, swayed slightly. A block of ice the size of a cart ripped free of the ceiling, shattering against the floor not ten feet from Sarah. Robert shouted something she could not hear above the deafening, incredible sound.

Ice moved against ice, delicate balances inside the icy bowels of the cavern, disturbed by Eric's shots, released their tenuous grips on the building blocks of the massive ice cathedral.

The world groaned again, heavily. Carlo went to her and he took her roughly by the shoulder, dragging her toward the archway, the world outside which seemed desperately far now.

Eric lay there still, blood staining the ice. His eyes looked up at the collapsing world. The Ice Castle swayed, dropping frozen barrages. It shuddered deep within its throat and finally detonated with the screeching, booming unearthly sounds of a powerful avalanche.

Sarah slipped, was jerked to her feet by Carlo. She

looked across her shoulder to see Robert rushing after them, Minna across his shoulder. Nothing could be heard above the rolling thunder of the collapse of the planet. She tried to warn them, but her mouth made no sound . . . a tremendous arch collapsed on top of Robert and Minna. Yet he somehow came through, dragging the limp Minna now, blood streaking his forehead.

The mouth of the cavern was barricaded with great chunks of ice. Still the place moved, crawled with moving ice. Pillars fell like shattered mirrors, broke, tumbled, splintered. The ice . . . Eric was still there, his hand twitching near the revolver.

Carlo glanced up quickly. The archway, heavy with eons of ice, was near to collapse. Forcefully he pushed Sarah ahead of him, driving her from the pandemonium.

She stumbled across the last barrier into the cold, bitter air. Carlo had already turned back. Moments later he emerged, helping Robert with Minna. Then it went. The archway sagged and swayed, coming apart at every fragile seam. The gaping mouth of the terrible Ice Castle slammed shut with vengeful icy teeth, swallowing Eric von Steinbock.

For a moment still there seemed to be an open passage. Robert looked hesitantly at it, and Sarah rushed back. Carlo took her arm in a viselike grip.

"He may still be alive," she protested.

"Stay out! I love you! You stay out," Carlo said sharply. He held her arm still, so tightly that it hurt. Their eyes met for a brief moment before the final sound called their attention to the archway where the Ice Castle, groaning in its final demise, creaked and collapsed in a settling sigh.

Then there was nothing but a cold mountain, the biting wind, the arms of a man who loved her. Whom she loved.

She loved him and she clung to him as she clung to life. She trembled, but not with fear, there had been no time for fear in the violent moments following the triggering shots. She looked up at this dark Trentino. His eyes were on the vanished Ice Castle. He held her even more tightly, then turned those soft, dark eyes on her.

"There will be a time for us, Sarah," he said quietly. "I know it." His lips brushed her hair and they turned to where Robert waited.

Minna was sitting on a snow-covered rock while Robert worked feverishly at her half-frozen feet. He rubbed them gently, then wrapped them in strips torn from his own clothing.

"We must go," Carlo said regretfully.

"Yes . . . the girl is badly off," Robert said.

"They will kill us," Carlo reminded him, "if they catch up."

"You can't go through the Brenner," Sarah said quickly. "They know about it—somehow. I saw them traveling that direction. That's why I came back."

"They couldn't know. How could the Germans know, Robert?"

Robert shrugged, standing from his task. "They couldn't—unless there is a traitor among us, Carlo."

The two men's eyes met and Carlo nodded. It was true. There was no other possibility. Someone in the organization . . . it seemed incredible. Perhaps it was only a good calculation by the German officers.

"You are sure you saw them, Sarah?"

"Absolutely sure," she replied.

"What other options do we have?" Robert asked, his methodical mind approaching the problem directly.

"Very few," Carlo said worriedly. "Back to the base camp, I suppose. The Emperor's Nose."

"But if we have an informant among us, they will probably go there as well," Robert conjectured.

"There is no other choice."

"Doesn't that mean going through Feldkirch?" Sarah asked.

"Not necessarily."

"But I must go through the town. Minna," she said, nodding toward the thin, pathetic girl. "She must be helped. I want to take her to Father Bruno, and see that she is."

"It would not be easy," Carlo said cautiously, eyes alert to the suggestion. "There are many special police, but mostly farmers with badges."

"I agree the girl must be cared for," Robert said. "I will escort Sarah. Take your own way, Carlo."

"No, my friend," Carlo laughed. "I will go as well. These people—they want us all dead. It will do their cause no good to have word of this episode reach the outside world."

"You don't think they would . . ." Robert glanced at Sarah.

"I know it, Robert. Any of us. All of us who know what has transpired here."

At a grove of oak trees along a frozen creek bed they rendezvoused with the rest of the team: Katrinka, Dunning, Ferrara, Rovato who still bled, but superficially, and the slender Silone who seemed nearly as exhausted as Minna.

Katrinka rushed to them, her dark hair streaming, and she clung to Robert, her head on his chest, murmuring something Sarah could not hear. Words which were not meant for other ears.

Ferrara stood angrily, hands on hips, his black beard wildly tangled, black eyes hard. "What is the delay?" he demanded. "They will be upon us, Carlo."

Carlo explained briefly about the Ice Castle. "Von Steinbock is dead."

"So? Good," Ferrara snarled. "Now let us go. If it snows tonight," he said, nodding toward the angry skies to the north, "the Brenner Pass will be deep."

"Not the Brenner," Carlo said. Ferrara stiffened.

"Not the Brenner? Where then?"

"The Emperor's Nose. Feldkirch first, then the base camp at the Emperor's Nose."

"We can't!" Ferrara was virulent. "You know what that means! The only pass is over Hirschfangen. In the summer it is passable. Now, it is treacherous. Why, Carlo?"

"I have my reasons, Mirko," Carlo responded. "Will we go, now?"

"The girl." Ferrara muttered suspiciously, looking at Sarah. "She has changed your mind."

"Yes. But not Sarah. The other woman must go to Feldkirch."

Ferrara looked uncomprehendingly at Minna von Steinbock. "Isn't that . . ."

"Yes. Come. We will go now."

Carlo swung his pack onto his back and Ferrara, mumbling deep, Italian oaths into his beard, followed.

Dunning, puffing a dead pipe, let his disapproving eyes sweep over Sarah, Minna, and Bramante. "Hell of an operation," he said rigidly. The Englishman snatched up his pack and followed Ferrara. Katrinka and Robert walked together, arms around each other's waists.

By sundown the wind was cutting off the north, the trees bending in unison before it. Lights were already appearing in the windows of Feldkirch as they approached the tiny hamlet from the low knolls beyond the barley fields.

They skirted the main portion of the town, finding their way to the church with little difficulty. Only twice had they seen the special village police. Once the man was sleeping peacefully under a bare apple tree. On the other occasion, the guard, a shy, serious-appearing man, seemed uncertain what the proper option might be, and he simply waved, gawking after the wretched crew of strangers.

Father Bruno opened the door to their light rapping, his thin red hair tousled as if he had been awakened. Yet his

231

breviary stood open on his desk beside the low, cheery fire. He smiled at Sarah, hesitantly shook hands with Robert then, with a gasp, noticed Minna standing with them, emaciated, hollow-eyed, feverish.

"Lord! Get the girl in here."

Father Bruno put her on a cot near the fire, pouring a cup of tea which Minna seemed barely strong enough to lift.

"What happened, Sarah?"

Sarah explained briefly, finishing with her conviction that Minna must be taken away. "It's not only the drugs, Father. It's the Castle Steinbock itself, cluttered with brooding memories. The girl needs sunshine, sleep, fresh air."

"Yes," Father Bruno agreed, nervously pushing up his glasses. "I think you are right. Something must be done. I believe we can find her a place to recover, to find herself. She has lived in the shadows of Steinbock, Baron Huebner, Helmuth far too long. Still," he said with a short shake of his head, "I find it difficult to believe of the Count von Steinbock." With a sigh he let his own gaze study the evidence of Eric's crimes.

"We cannot delay, Sarah," Robert reminded her.

"Don't worry," Father Bruno said. "I'll see she's taken care of. The doctor will look at her. When he sees the condition she's fallen into, the grand duchess will have no choice but to bow to our decision. A sin," he muttered, sitting beside Minna, petting her straggly black hair compassionately, "a sin."

Carlo waited in the cold dark shadows. Rovato had positioned himself where he could watch the road from town in case of pursuit.

"Well?" Carlo asked, lifting his head.

"We can go," Sarah said.

"None too soon," Ferrara grumped.

"Does it look like snow to you?" Dunning asked,

gesturing at the gathering skies with his pipe. There was a bitter edge to the wind which had not been there before. There was not a single star in the heavens. The sky itself seemed massing to pursue them.

"By midnight," Katrinka said, and no one disputed her words.

"Quickly then," Bramante said. The crew strung out ahead of him, finding the winding trail toward the Emperor's Nose in the highlands.

They wound along the narrow path, creeping higher into the foothills. The higher they climbed, the colder grew the wind. By the time they had crested Geier Watch, with the Emperor's Nose still two miles ahead, a mile higher, it had begun to snow. A cold, wet snow, it clung to all, frosting the men's hair, sticking to the shoulders of their coats, forming sudden drifts in the low spots along the rocky path.

"We must make the camp," Carlo said, breathing heavily. Ferrara, nodding his agreement without speaking, panted and looked to the northern skies. All was black as sin, inky, cold. Twice they nearly had an accident on the slick trail. Rovato fell once, clinging by his fingertips to a knob of granite until they could pull him up to the shelf. The other time, Dunning, unused to the exertion, stopped to rest, sitting on a nearly square boulder which immediately tore loose from its feeble moorings, toppling into the gorge five hundred feet below, leaving Dunning shaken, eager to continue to the base camp.

Shortly after midnight they reached the Emperor's Nose camp. The snow, heavier with each passing hour, covered all.

Carlo clambered up a slick, vertical cliff face to recover the tents and tins of food left when they had broken camp. The main party had returned to Trentino as Carlo's guerrilla group had rushed to halt the attempted assassination. They had intended to take the Brenner Pass

233

escape route; now Carlo thanked whatever cautious impulse it was which had caused him to stow these emergency supplies in the crevice.

Cold as it was, not one of them was willing to take the shelter of the tents before they had eaten. A row of tin cans, tops carved open with a knife, boiled and gurgled over the wind-whipped campfire.

It was not until they had eaten from the cherry-red cans which produced only cold mouthfuls of hash by the time the wind-chilled fork reached the mouth, that anyone noticed someone was missing.

Carlo had to speak above the howl of the wind. The fire lapped over the ring of stone, dipping and snapping at their feet and legs.

"Rovato? Where is Mirko!"

Rovato, in utter disbelief, could only shrug. "I have not seen Ferrara," he shouted back.

The rest of the party could only look at one another. No suggestion was made to go looking for the massive Trentino. The elements protested against any such argument. The snow, piled by the wind in the passes, continued to fall; the winds tearing at their clothing, once felling a tree sixty feet from the camp.

Bramante's features were grooved with concern, but he said nothing, only shaking his head slightly, looking around the perimeter of the camp, tented now by complete darkness.

"What can it mean—Ferrara's disappearance?" Sarah whispered as she and Robert settled into the tent they shared with the Trentino, Silone.

"Nothing," Robert said sleepily. "Or any number of things."

The fabric of the tent whipped and snapped. The poles buckled. Outside the raging storm continued, and Sarah slept, her dreams a jumble of snow and fire, blood and ice.

Twenty-two

A hand touched Sarah's shoulder and she jerked suddenly awake. There was no light in the sky showing through the open tent flap.

"Quickly," Robert said. "Don't worry about anything but your warmest clothing."

"There's trouble, Robert?"

"They're coming. The German Army contingent. Looks like Eisner is on our trail."

"How close?" she asked worriedly, drawing on her boots.

"Half an hour," he said tensely. She nodded, understanding the need for speed. She grabbed her coat and rushed outside, still buttoning it.

The wind in the pre-dawn hour stretched out an icy hand and slapped her as she raced for the small, huddled group. They strode from the camp, the snow still swirling, the dark hour still upon them, the abandoned tents slapping against themselves in the stiff wind.

They climbed higher. Long, jagged arrows of red from the coming dawn pierced the heavy cover of the snow-laden clouds, lighting the mountain peaks as they labored along the gray, ice-cracked shoulders of supporting mountains of the great Hirschfangen.

Boehm had been a great, quite convincing liar as he

related the tale of Robert's death on the Hirschfangen. Yet his description of the great, jagged, weather-scored peak was brutally accurate. She asked Robert about it.

"Yes. Boehm was injured here. Seriously. The only inaccuracy was his description of my death. No one, no one but a madman or a fool would attempt to scale the north peak."

"Yet he did," Sarah said. Her eyes swept up the pyramidal form of the weather-beaten pinnacle. If Boehm had tried that, he was indeed "haunted by mountain spirits" as the mountaineer had told her.

The way they were trying was little better, Sarah learned. They went along treacherous escarpments, over deep crevasses bridged delicately with concealing snow. None of them but the Trentinos were experienced climbers. They carried no ropes, no cleats or iron.

And the weather continued to trumpet the arrival of winter. Swirling clouds, sometimes above, often below them twisted and unleashed barrages of hard, crystalline snow. And constantly—the wind.

Finally, short of breath from the crushing altitude, they reached the ridge called *Unwetter:* the tempest. Carlo crept to the very edge of the gray mass of frozen granite and shook his head heavily.

"They are there," he said. Slowly he sagged back, eyes closing briefly.

Sarah peered over the edge of the ragged precipice, and she too saw them. A long, snaking line of gray uniformed soldiers, well outfitted, well trained in mountain techniques. Surely, equipped as they were, they would overtake them before the border could be reached.

"What now?" Dunning demanded, settling beside Bramante.

"Drive on!" Rovato said excitedly.

"No," Carlo argued, "we must rest. We must! An hour. Only an hour."

236

"They'll be in rifle range in an hour," the Englishman complained.

"Yes," Carlo responded, his breath coming heavily. "And if we do not rest, they'll have no need to use their rifles. We'll be found facedown in the snow. Their work already done."

"No!" Rovato said heatedly. "I want to live. There are many women, many evenings on the terrace in Naples— the light in the olive trees. I will not wait to die in this frozen wilderness!"

"We have been together five years," Carlo said. Gently he took Rovato by the back of the neck, bending the Neapolitan's head to his until their brows touched. "Trust me."

"We must go!" Rovato insisted.

"Then go on."

Bramante turned his head away. Slowly Rovato rose and wandered off, his footprints deep in the new snow.

"Rest!" Carlo ordered the others. "He will never make it."

"Carlo!" Silone pleaded. His hands were outstretched. The thin man's eyes flickered down the long whitened slope to the file of German soldiers.

"Go if you will," Bramante said in a steely voice. Already Silone was exhausted, his limbs unsteady, his flesh unnaturally pale. He stood stock-still a moment longer, his palms up in a gesture he never continued. Slowly, with a heavy sigh, Silone sat down.

"Anyone who wishes to . . . go on!" Carlo Bramante said sharply, but none of the others moved.

"I'm sure you know what you're doing," Dunning said placidly. He squatted on his heels, attempting to light his pipe which would not catch fire in the wavering wind; angrily he stuffed it into his coat pocket.

Silone sat miserably to one side, head buried in his hands; the German soldiers, so near they could distinguish the features of their faces, weaved up the broken, snowbound slope of Hirschfangen.

Sarah stood near to Robert, their eyes meshing in mutual faith, apprehension, love.

"What would you have voted for?" Sarah asked.

"Carlo is our general," her brother answered. "One follows one's generals."

"Yes." Sarah rested her head against her brother's shoulders, watching affectionately, yet with pangs of anxiety, as Carlo watched the climbing German force.

"Yes," Bramante muttered. "I see you, you pirate." He squinted through the field glasses, the glare of white snow coloring the lenses with brilliant prisms. There he was, the scoundrel—Field Marshal Klaus Eisner. The brutally scarred face set stonily as he labored ahead of his troops. "You will be the first, my friend," Carlo promised, fingering the rifle beside him.

"How near will he let them come?"

"Who can say."

"And if they take us?"

"They will butcher us," Robert said quietly.

They waited, Sarah clinging to Robert as Carlo, measuring their reserves, the speed of the expedition below, calculated to the final, split second, the odds.

"We will be all right," Sarah said. She lifted her face to Robert. He smiled and drew her nearer yet.

"Yes," Robert said with a confidence he could not feel. Yet he regretted nothing. Nothing but the risk of the life beside him, and Katrinka's life. To see these young existences threatened in the hour of their sweet budding was intolerable. Yet Robert had learned to believe—to believe in the capabilities of Carlo Bramante. If Bramante had decided that they must wait, then it was a valid assessment of their chances which had decided it.

He rested his head against Sarah's, gripping her shoulder tightly, hoping that she would understand the depths of his gesture, the love which provoked it.

Katrinka walked steadily backward and forward along a path she had beaten in the snow, worry furrowing her features. She glanced once at Robert, emotion coloring her black, open eyes.

"She is beautiful," Sarah said, watching the straight spine, the full bust and perfect, wide hips of the girl.

"Yes," Robert admitted hopelessly. "And she loves me." He studied her full lips, remembering their touch, the vital energy in her eyes, the rich figure of Katrinka.

"She must be entirely alluring to a man," Sarah suggested. "I thought that when first I saw her, with her old mother."

"Her mother?"

"Senta—the old Avarian queen. She was the one who first translated the inscription for me. The one you underlined."

"The inscription?"

"In the tombs. The inscription which read Ice Castle. It was Senta's translation which led me to the Ice Castle." Sarah looked at Robert closely. Her brother shook his head oddly.

"What is it, Robert? Surely you have met the Avarian queen."

"Senta? Yes, I have met her, Sarah. But Senta is no Avarian. That limb of mankind has long since died out. Senta is no Avarian queen, nor is Katrinka an Avarian. Their people are Romanian gypsies. Senta could not have read that ancient inscription."

"But she did, Robert."

"No. It would be impossible. Only I read it. I am probably one of a handful in all the world who could," he assured her. "And our knowledge of the language, even the pronunciation of certain phonemes is flawed."

Yet Senta had read it . . . or so it had seemed. Sarah watched Katrinka as the wind spilled over the mountain-tops, bringing still more snow—thin gusting sheets like waving battle flags above the mottled gray peaks.

She revived the scene in her mind. Katrinka had given the paper to her old mother. Katrinka had translated her mother's words. Senta might have said anything—but Katrinka had said Ice Castle, sending Sarah there. To the place Robert, Dunning, and Carlo had done everything to keep hidden from her.

"Robert!" Sarah clutched her brother's arm tightly. She spoke in a low voice. "Katrinka is the one who told me to go to Steinbock. She told me you had gone there."

"That makes no sense," Robert said. "She knew we wanted you out of Feldkirch."

It made no sense—Sarah pondered it as she watched Robert's troubled eyes. It made no sense if Katrinka were a patriot as she claimed.

Go there—that was what Katrinka had said—*that is where your brother went.* Yet Robert had certainly never visited Steinbock Castle. Eric alone wished Sarah kept near Steinbock, under his watchful eye. Eric alone . . . and Katrinka.

"We go!" Carlo said, standing suddenly. "Quickly. Our lives depend on it. With luck we will be through the pass ahead of them."

And without it . . . ?

They rushed pell-mell up the steeply sloped, snow-washed peak. Barren of tree or shrub, there was no cover of any sort along the expanse of Hirschfangen mountain. Thin streaks of gauzy cloud marked the blue sky above them. Below the storm still dropped tons of snow from its twisted, frozen fingers.

If Carlo had miscalculated . . . each of them plodded on, not daring to turn their heads, to peer over their shoulders at what might be behind them.

Bramante was banking on the exhaustion of the pursuers. He was hopeful that even if they were spotted, the Germans would not have the strength left for a final push. The pass, if it could be negotiated at all, was three miles from a village called Imst where a cadre of resisters might be contacted, and with luck . . . again luck . . . they might be swept out of the countryside before the troops could cross into Italy. They might be welcome in Austria, if begrudgingly so, but the presence of German soldiers in Italy would not be tolerated.

A still form lay in the snow. Stiff, colorless. Rovato had not made it. They walked by quickly, with no time to help the dead, the specter of such a death brought suddenly closer.

Sarah's heart thumped heavily in her ribcage, her breath, at this terrific altitude, was a stream of burning, ragged inhalations, frosted exhalations steaming into the high sky.

The wind shoved into their faces, gusting violently at times. Sarah's feet went from under her and she felt Carlo's hands on her arms, pulling her desperately up.

As she rose she turned and saw, half a mile below them, on the white flanks of Hirschfangen, the file of German soldiers. She struggled on. They had achieved nothing.

They halted briefly, every one gasping for breath, doubled over, at the corridor of escape. The pass: a ragged, snow-clotted tunnel through which the wind thundered, the mountain rising precipitously on either side. Tumbled boulders and snowslides blocked the easier access.

Carlo looked upward, sighed, and pointed.

"That way!"

Sarah followed his pointing finger and her breath caught, her knees went shaky, her face, cold as it was, flushed hot.

Carlo was indicating a mere hairline of a trail winding steeply upward for fifty yards or so before bending toward the south, waving along an irregular, frozen cliff face partially blocked with sliding snow and rock.

"God!" Dunning moaned. "We'll never make it! The wind will slap us off like insects."

"Do you wish to surrender?" Bramante shouted above the shriek of the wind.

"No, not that," Dunning decided, his eyes flickering to the line of gray-coated soldiers below them.

"Then come on," Carlo said, slinging his rifle across his shoulder.

They lunged after him, moving dreamlike up the jagged mountain. The wind, never ceasing in its protesting, furious howl, snatched at their clothing and hair. The cold numbed their fingers as they reached for the tiniest toeholds, outcroppings, any tenuous grip to hold them to the rock.

Below the Germans plodded on—or some of them did. Three men lay facedown in the snow, others faltered badly, the pace quickened constantly by the maniacal Field Marshal Eisner.

They rounded a bend in the trail, Sarah pressing to the face of the cliff. The path beneath her feet was a mere eighteen inches wide. There was snow on the trail, with ice under that. She could not see Carlo, who led the way, picking the trail, probing ahead of his feet with the stock of his rifle. Robert crept ahead beside her. His hands, she noticed, were cracked with the weather, his lips nearly blue. The wind whipped his dark hair; the concentration in his eyes was absolute . . . there was no room for error.

Below the spines of mountain ridges ran for miles in every direction. Primordial chaos thrown up when the world was in its infancy, the great, hulking peaks scorned man and his small endeavors.

Ranges thrust up and broke off without apparent design or reason. Crooked gorges fell thousands of feet to knife-edged rocks below. Treacherous crevasses were deceptively frosted over with a fragile thatching of snow.

These rugged, eternal things!—how lovely they had seemed below in the valley, beautiful and aloof, placid and cold. Here their menacing bulk threatened to tear the heart from an interloper. The wind snarled and sneered, objecting with all of its elemental strength to these feeble, two-footed fragments of blood and flesh.

Just behind her Silone suddenly screamed. She turned to see both of his feet slide over the edge of the precipice. His mouth open, he stretched out a hand, pleading.

Sarah edged back hurriedly, her own foot nearly slipping. She crouched as low as possible, her hand reaching to him. His eyes open in anguished dread, he clawed at her . . . their hands never quite meeting.

Silone's eyes opened even wider. He roared with utter horror and then was gone. A bit of snow followed his cartwheeling body into the empty space at their feet.

Sarah buried her face against her arm, pressing to the cliff face. No more! She could endure no more. Let it end, let them take her. She stood shuddering, her legs trembling crazily with fear and exhaustion.

"Sarah!"

She glanced up to see Robert waiting, his hand outstretched. "No more," she murmured.

"A little more. Just a little more. Come on now!" he said severely. "You've never been a quitter. Don't quit now!"

Somewhere she found the strength. From some reserve deep within her resolve fountained forth. She moved on woodenly, frightened half out of her wits, but onward. Hardly aware of the cold now, or of the time, she followed Robert, dipping into a deep hollow, scampering up the other side.

The path was somewhat wider now, still icy underfoot. Rounding a bend they found Bramante and Dunning leaning against a rock. Katrinka, her own face a mask of exhaustion, rubbed her shoulders, trying to keep the circulation going.

Above them the snake-ridged, broken Hirschfangen loomed massively. Carlo watched them one by one, rising to hold Sarah tightly for one long, blessed moment.

"Silone?"

"He fell," Robert reported.

"I think we've gained time on them," Carlo said, "unless Eisner is using a whip on them. We'd better rest here. At least there's some shelter from the wind."

They readily agreed. Sarah sagged to the cold earth. Dunning's tongue lolled out of his chapped, weather-cut mouth.

They were at the bottom of a long chute which ran to the very pinnacle of Hirschfangen. An icy, incredibly quick freshet wound through the bare rock, carving the chute it flowed in. Sarah dipped a drink from the stream. It bit at her mouth with its coldness. She looked up then to see them.

Not a hundred yards back six men in German uniforms rounded the last dangerous bend in the trail, a bloody, wild-eyed Eisner leading them forward, a handgun brandished.

The wind cut off his words, but they saw his mouth open in sudden triumph as he spotted them.

"Run for it," Carlo said, pushing Dunning ahead of him.

"Run?" Dunning laughed, sagging to his hands and knees in sheer prostration. "Run where?" he laughed madly, rolling onto his back in the deep snow.

Eisner's men were nearer, hurrying as fast as the dangerous trail and their own exhaustion would allow. Carlo himself seemed to have quit. He stood watching them.

The trail ahead was straight for nearly a quarter of a mile. The Germans could pick them off the rocks like clay ducks. Run where indeed?

Eisner shouted something else which did not carry. Then bloodily he began to laugh until his ears caught the strange rumbling sound overhead.

They froze as one—Germans, Trentinos, all, their ears seduced by the odd, crackling whoosh overhead. Then as one they bolted, frantically scrambling away from the mighty avalanche.

Two thousand feet above, near the pinnacle of Hirshfangen a magnificent, yet deadly cornice of blue snow had broken free. A thousand tons of frozen death now raced down the mountainside, and they ran, every person, as if they had never felt fresher. Weariness had no meaning, only a second electric impulse—the will to live.

Caught on the narrow ledge the Germans never had a chance. To hurry was to fall, to travel slowly to be crushed by the avalanche. They were swept away, nearly to the man, brushed off the mountainside by a brutal winter fist.

Perhaps one or two escaped. Eisner, perhaps?

Sarah's party was more fortunate. They had the long, wider trail ahead of them, and although the mountain of snow swept by with the bellowing thrust of a hundred locomotives, standing their hair on end, striking cold fear in their hearts, there was no real threat.

"Dead. Gone. Uselessly." Sarah watched the empty, bleak slope. Not a sign of life wriggled in the snow mass. There was not a candle of hope for the nameless, faceless German soldiers. She turned to find Carlo there and he held her. The snow had begun to fall again. Ahead of them the long pass opened onto a broad high mountain meadow. Yet the other men . . . "uselessly," she repeated.

Carlo swept the hair back from her forehead, his lips lingering there a brief eternity. "There will be more," he said thoughtfully. "Many thousands more. All . . . uselessly."

It was nearly dark when they reached the high meadow, a cirque scoured by an ancient, moving glacier. Carlo halted the team near a pair of shattered, lightning-scorched pine trees of incredible age, wind-twisted, nearly free of foliage.

"What are we stopping for?" Dunning demanded. "It's damnably cold yet. And no shelter for miles."

"We will wait."

"I'm nearly tired of your whimsical leadership, Bramante," Dunning said testily. "If it hadn't been for that stroke of chance or fate with the avalanche . . ."

"Chance? Fate?" Bramante said, shaking his head. "I would not trust to such things."

"What are you going on about?" Dunning wanted to know. He had to wait only another few minutes for his answer.

He came down the deep snowy shoulders of Hirschfangen, hip deep at times in the snow, his rolling, massive shoulders fighting forward. His broad face, bearded and scarred, was split wide with an expansive, toothy smile.

"Ferrara!" Robert said.

"Come on, Mirko!" Carlo laughed, waving a hand. "How long must we wait!"

"But I thought . . ."

"That Mirko was a traitor? Ridiculous," Carlo said.

"Then where was he?"

"Where?" Carlo lifted his head. "There. Hirschfangen."

"He climbed it! Alone! Impossible!" Dunning said scornfully. Then his eyes lightened. "The avalanche! The bloody avalanche!"

"Yes," Carlo said. "He was our fate, our chance happening."

Mirko Ferrara ambled to them, his face still beaming he slapped a fist against his bloody palm, shouted and clapped Carlo on the shoulder. "I did it!" he shouted again.

"Yes. But you cut it too fine," Carlo chided him.

"Wait until I see Boehm!" Ferrara roared, throwing back his head to allow a booming, glorious laugh to escape from his throat. "Wait until I see that Boehm . . . never again, Carlo," he added, completely subdued. "Never!" He stood watching the distant, thrusting peak of Hirschfangen, wagging his head in astonishment.

Sarah bandaged up Ferrara's hands, and his feet as well. Incredibly lacerated, they were swollen, bloodless. The great man's legs were quivering. Yet he continued to smile.

Magnificently the dying sun bled out across the snow-crowned peaks, tinting all with a brilliant pink, then a quickly passing deep violet. Only the last peak held a lingering touch of golden yellow—Hirschfangen, looming over them, beaten, yet glorious in its eternal presence.

"What now?" Robert asked.

"We will make Imst in three hours," Carlo guessed, watching the full yellow moon rising through the broken clouds. "Then a train to Venice. It is the nearest seaport. From there you will have no worries. Paris or London . . ."

Sarah felt her heart stutter and fall. "But you, Carlo. You can't stay in this area. You are a marked man. In time . . ."

"In time," he said confidently, "it will be over. But I must be here through that time. I must be here to stop the advance of these men who love war."

"But I . . ." Sarah gave no thought to proprieties, to the presence of others, to anything. She threw herself against him and he clenched her so tightly that her breath went from her. He kissed her and her tears were salt-tasting on their mouths. They stood together, saying nothing, wanting nothing but that moment. That final moment.

"It is a cold world in which we find ourselves," Carlo said. He stepped back, smiling that tantalizingly rich, deep smile, putting a finger under her chin to lift her eyes to his. "Yet you make it warm for me. Let me make it warmer for others. Others who might live in some safety because of our small effort. It is a cold world. But for you."

He took her and they walked off a ways together,

studying the massive mountain chains, seeing in their moonlit beauty nature, being, their own love.

"I would not have it any other way," Carlo began.

"Say no more." She kissed him again, her throat pulsing, a long kiss until they dared hold it no more. They drew apart, shaking with the moment of knowing.

Slowly they walked back. Mirko had started a small fire. Robert stood stiffly to one side. Dunning was attempting again to light his tobacco which had been soaked in the escape.

"And you, Katrinka?" Carlo Bramante said suddenly. He still held Sarah, firmly, desperately.

"And I?" she said innocently.

"You. Who else could it have been? Who else was there to have betrayed us to Eisner, to have caused Rovato and Silone to die, to have nearly cost us . . . all? Who else would have directed Sarah to Steinbock when we had agreed we wanted her out of danger? Who could have translated a poor old Romanian's words to the term Ice Castle? Only you. Only you, dear beautiful, deceitful Katrinka."

"Robert . . ." Katrinka turned to him, but he would not look at her.

"No one else," Robert said. "I thought . . . "

"I . . ." Katrinka shrugged. Ferrara's gaze was merciless. "Yes!" she exploded, her eyes flashing with hatred. "So— kill me! I do not care."

"Why, Katrinka?" Sarah asked. "Why?"

"Why?" the girl repeated, with a scoffing, terrible laugh. "Do you think you are the only ones who love? I did it," she said, touching her fingertips to her heart, "for love!"

"Eisner?" Robert asked, astounded.

"Eisner?" Katrinka laughed, mockingly. "No, poor fool, Robert. It was Eric," she said softly. "He knew I was in the Trentino movement. He came to me. Perhaps," she went on quietly, her eyes beginning to stream with tears, "he was using me. I don't know . . . I didn't care! I would have thrown myself off a cliff for him. A god—he was a god on earth. You think I am insane? I was only . . . in love."

They stood staring at her. But for Robert who had turned away, walking from the dull light of the low fire into the deep shadows of the cold night.

"What will we do with her?" Dunning asked, his pipe finally catching fire. He did not ask vengefully.

"Go."

Carlo said it so softly that at first they did not understand him.

"Go, woman!" Carlo repeated. "Live with it if you can. Go. Into what, I imagine, will be a very lonely, cold world."

Carlo turned his back as well. Sarah alone was left to watch the girl wander off into the bitterly cold night, her tracks uncertain meanderings against the background of new snow.

Twenty-three

Paris thrived in the short, mild winter of 1913-1914. Nothing could dampen the spirits of this colorful cosmopolitan center of western civilization — not the early snow or late rain, the coal shortages, or the constant whisperings of coming war.

Sarah Chamliss studied with desultory weariness, alone in her winter, alone in her thoughts. Lines sketched in charcoal on linen paper now seemed pointless, a foolish luxury in these times when men across the world struggled with impending doom.

Dr. Lacroix, desperately disappointed with her, constantly scolded Sarah, examining her work with complete bafflement.

"It's lost! That delicate feeling. Your lines are stronger, much stronger, Sarah. But the softness . . . What did you leave behind you in Austria!"

She tried to think as little as possible. With Philippe and Susi she frequented the coffee shops on the rue aux Ours, as in earlier times. Yet it was pointless. The conversation seemed empty, contrived, the people children living on the fringes of reality.

Robert stayed on for a while, but his restlessness took him to England. From his letters she judged that he wished to return to the field, but having had his identity compromised, he chafed under the burdens of a desk job. His letters were tinged with black apprehensions despite his forced cheerfulness.

On the morning of June 28, 1914, the Archduke Franz Ferdinand was assassinated, along with Sophie Chotek, by a deranged Serbian national in Sarajevo, Bosnia, Austria-Hungary.

The winds of war stirred across Europe. In France people laughed it off, yet there was a tautness in their voices as they discussed the event.

Austria declared war on Serbia on July 28, 1914.

On August 1, 1914, Germany, citing Russian mobilization in defense of Serbia, declared war on Russia. Two days later France was invaded.

Through the summer the delicate house of cards collapsed before the heated breath of warfire. Nation by nation, some charging gloriously into battle, some dragged protestingly into the bloody conflict, signed pacts of warfare.

Belgium was invaded August 3, 1914, precipitating England's declaration of war on Germany and Austria. In the following weeks the Allies were joined by Japan, Montenegro, and Serbia, while the Ottoman Empire sided with the Central Powers. In a crazy chain-reaction nation upon nation attacked with bitter invective, and finally with artillery and men until civilized countries from China to Siam, Haiti to Liberia, San Marino to Bulgaria—and finally the United States—entered the bloody, worldwide conflict.

The world had gone cold. The lights were out across Europe. All of the civilized world was a great, frozen Ice Castle.

There was little dependable word from the far flung fronts. Now and then Sarah read of Trentino in the papers.

The Germans made deep incursions into northern Italy during the summer months, inflicting heavy casualties.

Yet the winters drove them from the Alps, the local forces gaining the upper hand.

A touching letter, printed in shaky letters, arrived from Berne.

I pray daily for your safety, it read in part, *and for those near to you. It is a mad world, Sarah. One clings fondly to the memory of people like you.*

Last night a shower of stars in the northern sky. A sign? A fiery protest by an angry nature? Bless you. Minna.

Another battered letter, marked and overmarked, arrived during 1916. The censor's hand was heavy, yet the unhappy news had not been blacked out.

. . . and so Rudi was inducted into the army. They take them so young, fodder for the pride of old men. Be well, Renate Huchting

She could not picture the flaxen-haired, happy boy with a rifle in his hands, nor did she want to. She put the letter away in her desk, gazing at the gray clouds over Paris.

Robert managed to visit briefly in the early fall of 1918. He had grown older, limping heavily from a wound he had gotten in some distant place.

"They tried chaining me to a desk," he said cheerfully, "but it was no good. I'm not cut out for that."

She asked about Dunning, but was sorry she had.

"The old man was killed in White Russia. He was with a party of Americans. Massacred near Minsk. So it goes . . . we all rush to our fates."

All but Sarah who could do nothing but wait, wonder, and make futile inquiries. Robert, despite his connections, could tell her nothing.

"All I do know," he said in a low voice, "is that Field Marshal Klaus Eisner is in charge of the expeditionary forces in Italy. Even that is classified information."

It left little doubt what Carlo's fate would be if he were captured.

She could only wait and hope, working distractedly. Dr. Lacroix continued his visits, although the university had ceased to function.

"Bad," he said, shaking his head with consternation as he studied her latest work. "Very bad—what can we do?"

The answer was nothing. Nothing could be done.

The weeks dragged on. One heard reports of settlements, treaties, cease-fires, yet nothing came of them. Bread was in demand, milk impossible to obtain, eggs unheard of. Only one thing was constant. Dr. Lacroix's criticism.

"Bad," he said worriedly again. "Such promise you held, Sarah. But this—it is bad."

Days turned into months. War raged against itself, a consuming beast limited only by the resources of nations. Steel, oil, men. It would not wane, this fire, until all had been consumed.

Agonizingly Sarah sketched a portrait of a dark-haired, laughing man. A soldier, a lover. Carlo Bramante's amiable, sturdy features gazed out of the oil rendition, strikingly realistic.

"Bad," was Dr. Lacroix's decision.

It did not matter, this memory. A flat, dead caricature of a warm, living man. Yet it was all she had. All . . .

The war years, having bled Europe of its vitality, its young men, its sanity, passed. In November the armistice was finally signed. The mobs of Parisians danced in the street, singing, starting bonfires which sparked into the cool fall skies. Yet there was no joy in it. Sarah turned from her window, sagging onto the bench. Carlo's portrait still stood in the center of the room, half-finished.

"Bad. Very bad. I do not see the vigor of the man. The heart."

"I . . . " her eyes came up suddenly, the blood rushing to her head. Carlo, grinning, eyes laughing, stood there, hat in hand.

She leaped to her feet and was across to him. They met, kissed, clung together, kissed again, and stood, eyes closed tightly, the world outside in celebration. The world, which had been ice and bitter winds, warmed to a gentle, flowering season of eternal spring.

Make the Most of Your Leisure Time
with
LEISURE BOOKS

Please send me the following titles:

Quantity	Book Number	Price
_____	_____	_____
_____	_____	_____
_____	_____	_____
_____	_____	_____
_____	_____	_____

If out of stock on any of the above titles, please send me the alternate title(s) listed below.

_____	_____	_____
_____	_____	_____
_____	_____	_____
_____	_____	_____

Postage & Handling _____

Total Enclosed $_____

☐ Please send me a free catalog.

NAME _____
(please print)

ADDRESS _____

CITY _____ STATE _____ ZIP_____

Please include $1.00 shipping and handling for the first book ordered and 25¢ for each book thereafter in the same order. All orders are shipped within approximately 4 weeks via postal service book rate. PAYMENT MUST ACCOMPANY ALL ORDERS.*

*Canadian orders must be paid in US dollars payable through a New York banking facility.

Mail coupon to: **Dorchester Publishing Co., Inc.**
6 East 39 Street, Suite 900
New York, NY 10016
Att: ORDER DEPT.

MORE BLOOD-CHILLERS
FROM LEISURE BOOKS